FORBIDDEN GARDENS

FORBIDDEN GARDENS

CLARE CASTLEBERRY

NEW YORK   LOS ANGELES

Jacket design by Rejenne Pavon
Jacket Copyright 2023 by Winding Road Stories
Interior book design by A Raven Design
ISBN#: 978-1-960724-14-4 (pbk)
ISBN#: 978-1-960724-15-1 (ebook)

Published by Winding Road Stories
www.windingroadstories.com

"Am I one or two? If I cannot live with myself, there must be two of me: the 'I' and the 'self' that 'I' cannot live with. Maybe," I thought, "only one of them is real."
—Eckhart Tolle

My brother Marcus and I were settling into our new place in Key West when I found out that Chloe and her baby were killed in a car accident.

It should have been freeing, with trauma in the distant past, and nothing but the future and a vast teal sea to look upon and fuel the mind with possibilities. Free, with a future stretched wide as the sea before us, with nothing but lingering memories behind us.

But death's cold hands have a way of reaching out, pulling a person back no matter where they were in life, forcing them to confront old ghosts.

I never imagined I would return. The draping curtains of oak limbs and the looming towers of grave stones were so suffocating, reminding me of losing my parents. My knees nearly buckled as reality crashed back through my body once again: This was a funeral. A double funeral: my best friend, a soul who had drifted away when she got pregnant in high school, as well as her baby, Elle.

Chloe was my closest friend all through school. She protected me when I couldn't speak up for myself, and she stood up for

Marcus, too. When Blake, one of the most popular guys in school and our most troublesome tormentor, asked me out, I said no. He turned his attention to Chloe. She got knocked up right before graduation.

I couldn't help but wonder what would have happened if I'd said yes. Would I be pregnant? Would I be dead, too?

"A mother and child, who will forever rest peacefully together in the hands of God," the preacher said.

Chloe's mother wailed. The only other sound was the squeaking of the casket lowering device.

Chloe was two weeks away from her nineteenth birthday when she crashed her car into a tree. I had to force myself to listen to the funeral service instead of thinking about her, her forehead split open, glass glittering red and lodged into her pale skin, her blonde hair tangled and littered with gore, and her child, Elle, still clutched in her arms. She had been holding the baby while she was driving. I knew that much to be true from what Marcus told me. He winced as I forced him to tell me the details. But I had become fascinated with death, as if finding out all I could about it would somehow keep it far away. But it only seemed to be drawing me closer.

Now, I'd never have a chance to mend things with Chloe.

Damn the deadly curves of those swamp roads with their non-existent shoulders and slick surfaces. My parents died on that same road. I received the call from Marcus, who had wandered back to Louisiana to pick through the smoldering remains of the old family estate I had burned down in haste—a desperate attempt to set fire to my tumultuous past. Now Marcus stood next to me, his face as gray and washed out as the graves, his blue eyes darkened with grief. There were so many terrible secrets shadowed in those eyes, wise beyond his years, eyes that had seen so much pain and suffering.

I took his hand. It was hot and clammy as the September bayou air. I squeezed, trying to convey some sense of comfort. He didn't squeeze back. Dark clouds twisted above us, rumbling with thunder, the air thick with the prospect of storms. It was hurricane season, and it seemed to reflect our moods, or more so, Marcus's.

Now nearly sixteen, he had finished his G.E.D. We were making enough on his website designs and my writing to afford rent in our little apartment down in the Keys, but it was difficult to get by. We were both shades of our former selves, pale and malnourished. But stubbornness kept us there, away from the horrific memories of Azalea House.

Only a moment of peace. Only a flash of time finding reprieve in the sugary beaches and warmth of Key West. Now, we were back, the pain and trauma from those times bubbling over, a forgotten black kettle. So much sorrow radiated from the graveside, a young mother and a child who died too early.

Chloe's mother threw herself onto Elle's tiny casket, displacing the pink roses from the surface. Chloe's father and Blake, her fiancé, whispered comforting words, trying to pull her off.

"Don't you touch me!" she screamed. She twisted her body to face Blake as she clutched the casket. Down she went into the ground with her granddaughter.

"I'll take care of it," the preacher said with a hand on Blake's shoulder.

I felt eyes on me from across the grave, and a strange sense washed over me. When I looked up, it was Blake, looking at Marcus and me with such a strange expression, I could not read it. Marcus let go of my hand, unraveling from it like it was full of venom. When I glanced his way, he blinked back tears.

Marcus had retained some semblance of friendship with Chloe since he left. He had been to visit her several times, doting on her like a waiting uncle. I had to admit, I resented him somewhat for it. How could he remain friends with someone who had a child with *Blake* of all people?

Marcus was as close to Chloe as I was. It was as much a shock to him as it was to me that she got with Blake and had his baby. Blake, the jock who tormented Marcus about being gay so much that Marcus brought brass knuckles to school and broke his nose. When Marcus got suspended, my aunt wanted to send him away to conversion camp, but he wisely ran away before she could have her way.

I guess he never wanted to let go of his friendship with Chloe.

But Blake had been such a jerk in our high school days. Maybe Marcus could forget more easily than me?

Marcus stepped back and massaged his neck. "I can't take this anymore."

"I know," I said. "It's—"

"You don't know," he said, exhaling with puffed out cheeks. "You don't." He looked out across the graves at something.

I followed his line of vision until I saw Blake. Blake. Dressed in his expensive suit, most likely chosen by his shopaholic mother who only worked at the mall in town to fund her extensive wardrobe. Not that she needed to work. Blake's father was a real estate agent with tentacles reaching as far as New Orleans. Chloe and her baby were going to be set for life, yet here Blake was, his eyes dry, his face handsome, the nose Marcus had once broken now set straight by the miracles of plastic surgery. Another problem solved by money.

The service came to a close. The preacher finally led Chloe's sobbing mother away. I let the yellow rose I held in my hand fall to Chloe's grave, the last whispering of our friendship soon to be buried deep in the soil.

"Marianne," a voice said. I turned to see Blake standing close to Marcus. "I'm so glad you could make it. I know being back here must be difficult for you."

I said nothing, my gaze bouncing back and forth between Marcus and Blake. Marcus had made no move to leave, as if he was waiting for Blake.

"Chloe appreciated your friendship very much. You know she named Elle after your mother because she adored you all."

"Janelle was no saint, Blake." I smoothed my velvet dress out, wanting to break from this speech of his. I was beginning to sweat. Velvet was a terrible choice for a sweltering September funeral. "I hadn't spoken to her since before graduation," I said, hoping to ward him off with sarcasm and negativity. "We kind of fell out because *you* came into the picture." I made no effort to hide the poison in my voice.

"I know she missed you, though," he said, his eyes barely misting over with grief. "And I would like to show my appreciation to you for being such a good friend."

"What is your point?"

He hesitated, his hazel eyes drinking me in and swallowing me whole. "My father would like to purchase your land," he said. "I believe he could offer you a high price, much more than what someone would normally ask."

My stomach churned in disgust. I stared at him, at his expensive suit, his sickeningly handsome face. The thought of Blake's family acquiring the land that had been in my family for generations, where my twin brothers slept eternally. The thought was revolting to me. Would they turn it into a shopping mall? Build a cookie cutter house there?

"No thank you," I said, jutting my chin at him. "Marcus, I'll meet you in the car."

I stared at Blake before turning away. He put his fingers between his shirt collar and neck and pulled the fabric away from his skin. "Let me know if you change your mind," he said. "I promise my father will be more than fair with you and Marcus."

Marcus's shoulders heaved. He and Blake exchanged a brief glance before Marcus broke away to catch up to me. Blake turned to walk back to the line of black limos.

"How did Chloe just…run off the road like that?" I asked with more edge than I'd intended in my tone.

Marcus sighed and lifted one shoulder in a shrug. "You know how those roads are."

He glanced at me, sharing that mutual sorrow of losing our parents on that same road.

"I'll be right back," I told Marcus once I was sure Blake was gone.

I stalked back through the cemetery gazing at the tombstones until the names became familiar. My parents, my cousin, and now Chloe were all buried here. I visited each of their graves for a brief moment, reflecting on the past that still felt present.

I was nineteen now, still coming into my own. In another year, it would be 2000, the beginning of a new century. The Internet was changing so much, and scandal draped the world. Breathless accounts of the President's sex life with an intern flooded the news, and the impending doom of Y2K lurked around every corner. The tragedy of Azalea House, the horrible things my aunt did, and the details of my parents' lives, peeled back layer by layer like an onion, all fell to the wayside as our family's news was eclipsed by scandals much more bingeworthy.

Leaving the cemetery, it felt as if something pushed me aside, invading my space. I looked over each shoulder. The cemetery was empty.

Maybe my exhaustion was keeping me company.

I took another step. That feeling came back. I swallowed hard, the uncomfortable sensation still lingering—someone trying to shove me out of the way to make room. I literally felt like two different people within one body, and the invader was trying to gain control.

Off in the distance, a black figure silhouetted against the tree line. I blinked, and it was gone.

I shook it off as best I could, walking faster towards the car. I was sick of feeling crazy. If I lost my mind again, the media would love it. They had backed off a bit over the summer, but every tragedy brought them new opportunities.

Marcus was leaning against the car, arms crossed over his chest. Paparazzi loomed on the edge of the cemetery, snapping pictures of us, wanting to capture our grief. I slipped on a large pair of sunglasses, and Marcus and I stepped into the Lincoln Town Car we'd hired for the day.

Our parents were in Spellbound Hearts, an indie band that had a few moments in the sunshine. Even though the drama of my twin brothers' murders had died down, there were still tabloid leeches hanging onto our family history, trying to profit off it.

"I know you don't want to talk about it," Marcus said, "but we need to discuss the land."

"St. Charles and Walnut," I told the driver.

"Marianne," Marcus said again through clenched teeth.

"You're right, I don't want to talk about it." I looked out the window instead, focusing on the gray pillars disappearing off in the distance.

"Marianne," Marcus said through his teeth. "We need the money."

"We'll be fine," I said, wiping the tears threatening to fall again. I despised talking about the property. Getting money from the sale of the land meant thinking about all the awful things that happened in that house, and I had left it behind for a reason. "We'll have the insurance money from the fire soon. It will get us by."

"Not for long. Grand'Mere Lily will think of something—"

I shook my head. He was right, though. Lily had been sending us threatening letters, ranting that she knew there was more to the story.

We had something to do with the death of her children, as well as my cousin Vivienne, she insisted. They were in a world of pain the moment they stepped into that place. It was our fault. We must pay.

And I know Marianne had something to do with the fire, she had written. Reading that sentence made my head roar with worry and guilt.

Once I discovered the truth about my aunt, how she had drowned my half-brothers in the pond on the property, I set fire to Azalea House, burning it to the ground, desperate to be done with the secrets the house held, the tentacles of the past. I had nightmares that someone would find something—a witness to my crimes, evidence of something, or would be able to read my mind in some way. If they found out it was arson, I would be doomed. My mind still whirled with guilt and worry, even though months had passed since the fire.

Azalea House could only hold those terrible secrets for so long.

"That land is ours to do as we please," I said, nodding my head as if that finalized it. "Lily can't do anything about it. It was all in the will."

"But we haven't received the payout from the fire yet. Blake's father knows the ins and outs of all this. And he knows people in high places, if you know what I mean. If we sell the land, we'll really be free—"

"Marcus, I don't want to talk about it right now."

We rode in silence to our hotel. I didn't dare look at Marcus, avoiding his blazing eyes. He wanted to be done with it all, to move forward. Part of me did, too. But I was much more sentimental, always hanging on to the past for fear I would forget the things most dear to me.

And I certainly didn't want to sell the land to *Blake's* family.

"You won't let it go, will you?" Marcus persisted.

"The twins are still buried there."

"You're right. Our mother wasn't a saint. But who is? Who cares about her affair? Who cares about the twins? And most of all, why give a fuck about Aunt Julia?" He looked me up and down as if reading my energy. "You're looking for revenge, aren't you?"

"Julia didn't just drown the twins, Marcus. She did awful things to you, too. She blamed you for murdering Uncle Joseph. Never forget that."

I glanced at his profile. He nodded once, as if confirming what I said with reticence. "It's true," he said, "but you can't let go unless you forgive or forget."

"You and Blake are so high and mighty, aren't you?" I spat. I couldn't help myself. How could Marcus just push the past away? "And he sure is forgiving of you, considering you rearranged his face with brass knuckles."

"I didn't hit him that hard."

"You shattered his nose."

"I could have killed him. That's what brass knuckles are for.

He knows that. He knows I held back. He says he respects me for that."

"*Respects* you?" I scoffed.

I was not pleased that Marcus and Blake had some in-depth conversation about forgiveness and woo woo shit. Maybe men were transactional like that, willing to sacrifice their beliefs for their desires. They fought it out, broke bones and drew blood, so physical. The women in my life, my aunt and cousin especially, fought with words. Some days, I would have preferred they just beat me. At least the wounds would have healed. In my mind, words cut deeper.

Deep down, I knew he was right. But so many people hurt us and our family. And I knew Momma was partially to blame for everything that happened at Azalea House. But Julia seeking revenge on her by killing the twins—the physical result of my mother's affair with Julia's husband—wasn't the way to go about it. And even though Julia poisoned her own brother, Joseph, to ensure all my parents' wealth went to her, there were fates much worse than death. Joseph never, ever paid for what he did to me and Vivienne, the way he touched us when we were only kids. The way our parents looked away from it all. He was simply excused until he became inconvenient, and then he was exiled into the peaceful arms of death without justice.

I crossed my arms over my chest and tensed. I wanted control. I wanted things to go my way, to sell the land to people *I* deemed worthy. And I wanted people like Blake to stay out of my way.

2

I had time to distract myself on the ride from the cemetery in Metairie. I pulled out a briefcase with some notes and photographs.

"What is all that?"

"Work," I said, not looking up.

"You and that damn book. And on a day like today, too." Marcus shook his head.

I shot him a side-eye glance and flipped through notes and photographs. I had been working on a book about my parents, a band biography that would do them justice, but I was mostly using it as a way to purge old memories and keep myself from ruminating too much.

"I just need something to take my mind off everything," I said.

I paused at a picture of Azalea House.

This all started with that damn house.

Azalea House was built back in the 1800s on land that was tainted from the very beginning. A Portuguese slave trader cleared land originally settled by indigenous people and built a sprawling estate. When his slaves revolted, he was said to have responded by setting fire to their quarters. Azalea bushes were planted in their places, and thus, the name Azalea House was born. Despite trying to cover up the tragedy with beauty, the spirits who dwelled there made sure they would never be forgotten.

It was like the land down to its very roots was angry and out for revenge.

"I hated that place," Marcus said, leaning in to look. "I'm glad you burned it down, but the land could be of good use."

"It's cursed."

"I can't believe you still are into all that superstitious stuff."

Someone bought the house as a gift to my great aunt, and she ran it as a boarding house. Since it was in a river town, it attracted myriad of travelers, from wealthy uppity New Orleans types to criminals desperate to postpone their fates.

With that as the backdrop, it was easy to see why the house was haunted. I had first-hand experience with the ghosts, too.

I flipped over to a photograph of Aunt Bessie sitting on the front porch of Azalea House.

"I thought for sure there was nothing left after the fire," Marcus said, suddenly intrigued by what I was doing. He still had his little brother moments, always being nosy, despite his attempts to be mature.

"I grabbed a few things before I left," I said. "A few photo albums, some letters..."

When Aunt Bessie died, my grandfather, Ed, sold Azalea House, but deeply regretted his decision. After my parents started up a synth band, Spellbound Hearts, and made some decent money from it, they were able to buy it back and restore it. Momma tirelessly worked to keep up the beautiful gardens.

Their careers settled down.

They had a family.

But not us. Not me and Marcus. Not yet.

Momma had two twin boys who were adored by everyone in the Easton family. It was like those two children and their winning Easton grins chased away all the bad things that happened at that house. At least, until they drowned.

For years, I didn't even know I had twin brothers. When Chloe got me a Ouija Board for my birthday, I could feel them trying to communicate with me. Chloe thought I was crazy. They told me where they were buried, in the woods near Azalea House. My own family wanted to have me committed with such talk.

When Momma found me digging near their graves, she screamed and went into shocked silence for days.

That's right. Easton secrets run deep.

I flipped over to a photograph of the twins.

"Funny how we never met them," Marcus said. He snatched the picture out of my hands and studied it. "They don't look anything like us."

"You're right," I said. "They look like Uncle Theo."

Aunt Julia was married to a tall handsome man named Theo during the time the twins were alive. Theo had an affair with my mother. Everyone assumed the twins belonged to my father.

"That must have been very obvious to Julia," Marcus said. He ran his hands along the photograph as if trying to commit it to memory. "Maybe that's how she found out Theo cheated."

"Who knows," I said. "I'm not going to focus too much on that in the book. It's mostly about the band."

"But why not make it juicier? You have a better chance of selling the story if it's *scandalous*," Marcus said with a bit of flair.

"I don't think Momma and Daddy would like that."

"They're dead."

"And so are the twins," I said. "The story's pretty much over."

"No, it's not," Marcus said. "Julia's sitting in prison still. What are you going to do if she blabs her story to the press?"

I sighed and took the photo back from Marcus. Of course I had been thinking about Julia this whole time. How couldn't I?

Everyone said the twins drowned. A gardener who worked at Azalea House, Carter Leblanc, was convicted and sent to prison for murdering them.

But it wasn't Carter.

It was Julia.

On my sixteenth birthday, my parents died in a car accident right down the road from Azalea House. Aunt, Julia, her young husband, Troy, and Julia's daughter, Vivienne, all came to live with us at Azalea House.

I will never forget that day. When she walked in, Julia began evaluating everything in that house, all the antiques my parents had restored in their last years, all the memories, all the good things about that place. There weren't many good things, but I wanted to cling to them tightly.

I don't know what prompted the spirits of the twins to visit me again. Perhaps since my parents died, I was their last hope for the truth.

"You managed to grab all these pictures, but you forgot Momma's ruby ring, though," Marcus said. I glared at him, hoping to shut down his accusatory tone.

"Believe me," I said, diving back into my notes, "I regret it after we had such a hard time getting it back."

I was surprised Marcus remembered that. That was what set off the whole chain of events in finding out the truth behind the twins' death.

The Ouija Board, the thing that made people think I was crazy, kept telling truths. After our parents died, the twins used the board to tell us about Momma's ring. Vivienne had gotten it somehow, and by following the Board's instructions, Marcus and I found it in her room.

That's how I knew what was happening was real. It really *was* the twins coming through on the board.

"Crazy."

"Hysterical."

"It was just a dream."

I heard things like this over and over until I couldn't take it anymore.

Carter Leblanc had been set to be released from prison right after my parents died. Maybe that's why the twins were haunting me.

If only it were that simple.

I went to visit Carter after his release. He told me truths about Azalea House I always intuitively knew: it was cursed. Haunted. It held secrets. And eventually, I was convinced of Carter's innocence.

The spirts of the twins wanted me to know the truth: that Julia had drowned them because they were a result of Theo's affair with Momma.

The next photograph was difficult to look at. It was a modeling photo of my cousin, Julia's daughter, Vivienne.

"You two look a lot alike," Marcus said.

"Shut up, Marcus. We don't."

"You do," he said. "Same eyes."

It was a black and white photograph of Vivienne in a black tank top, her sleek hair gathered over one shoulder, her eyes penetrating and dark. I recognized that look. We all had it. The Easton Stare. A look that could freeze someone in their tracks, a look Marcus often wore when he was angry or about to emotionally check out.

What was she thinking in that photograph? Was she thinking about Uncle Joseph and his perverted ways? On that fateful sixteenth birthday, Joseph gave me a white bra and panties set, in front of my mother and aunt, because "I was becoming a woman now." In my room, he asked me to try them on. Then he touched me, asking me to promise to keep our little secret. So many secrets.

Vivienne would later tell me that he molested her too. Maybe she was trying to escape her own ghosts that followed her to Azalea House?

"What?" Marcus asked. "You're making a face."

"I was thinking about Joseph."

"God, why? Forget him. You don't have any pictures of him, do you?"

"I tore them all up."

"Good."

Joseph died, probably as a result of some toxic Thanksgiving combination Aunt Julia had given him. Of course, she took the opportunity to blame everything on Marcus. That's one of the reasons he took off.

I should have gone with him then.

There were no photos of Troy, Julia's second husband and Vivienne's stepfather. Troy was much younger, only in his mid-twenties, tall and handsome, much like my Uncle Theo. I could never understand how my aunt could captivate these men, making them her dutiful servants.

One night, I discovered a hidden staircase in Azalea House that led to the closet of my parents' old bedroom where Troy and Julia stayed. The staircase was likely the lost remnant of a house where guests had to exit quickly and discretely to stay one step ahead of the law.

The first time I peeked through the closet door, there was my mousy Aunt Julia, with her hair released from its bun, flowing beneath her shoulders. She wore a black latex catsuit that accentuated a body she kept well hidden in designer clothing. She pinned her much younger husband to the bed by burying her stiletto heel into his chest, making him wince. It was the first time I ever saw a man aroused. Their secrets became my secrets, as I would spy on them again and again.

The memory of spying on him all those times at Azalea House came to mind, and like every time I thought of it, it spurred strange, sexual feelings laced with guilt that I swallowed back down.

As I got close to my eighteenth birthday, Troy began spending more time with me, taking me on long drives, listening to my favorite music. Sometimes he would wink as he added vodka into my orange juice. Occasionally he would protect me from my bullying aunt and cousin. As my body developed rapidly in high school, so did his interest in me, as did the interest of other men.

Troy's flirting became more daring, and the forbidden nature of it, along with my growing sexual curiosity made it both exhilarating and terrifying.

On my eighteenth birthday, Troy snuck into my bedroom and spooned with me. His hands brought me pleasure, guilt and shame. It would be the first time I would ever have sex with a man, and to this day, I still grapple with how much I enjoyed it and how wrong it was.

There was no use spending time thinking about Troy. His letters and attempts to contact me ceased. He was probably back in New Orleans, drinking his life away as he did at Azalea House.

The thought of running into him again while we were staying for the funeral crept across my mind, the temptation to look him up steeped in curiosity.

But no.

We were due to stay another night or two, then it was back home to Key West again, to the brighter future I'd always hoped for.

3

Marcus and I had chosen to stay at an inn on St. Charles Avenue in New Orleans, twenty minutes from Chloe's burial site. It was a splurge. The Azalea House grounds were only an hour away, but its hold on me squeezed my heart with a tight grip, reminding me that it would never quite die. As we turned onto Carrollton Avenue, with its arched, oak-lined gateway and lumbering green streetcars, I felt an unusual pang of sorrow.

Marcus exited the car without a word and stalked up to his room. I lingered in the bar area and ordered a coffee, hoping it would bring me out of the exhaustion from the day's events. I scribbled in my journal, hoping to shed the horrible feelings of loss and guilt. Oh, if only I'd done what Marcus had done and forgiven Chloe for going out with Blake. But I truly felt that by dating the person who bullied both Marcus and me, she was betraying us.

I sensed a presence in a black suit hovering behind me.

"You," I snapped. "Please leave."

"Please, just give me a moment," Blake said.

I shut out the twisted look of grief on his face. Feeling sorry for him would only dampen my emotions.

I stood up, knocking over my coffee and spilling it on my beloved leatherbound journal. Blake retrieved some napkins nearby and helped me clean up the mess.

"I don't want your help," I said.

Once finished, he locked eyes with me.

"You know that immature boys do stupid things when they like a girl, right?"

I recoiled, fury coursing through me. How dare he say something like that on the day of his fiancée's funeral.

"That's inappropriate, Blake."

He slipped his hand inside his blazer and retrieved something white and rectangular.

"My father's real estate card," he said, placing it on top of my journal. "If you change your mind, he can offer you quite the sum. Please reconsider."

"I believe we're done here," I said, gathering up my things and pushing past him. He smelled of sandalwood and clean linens, that hungry gaze following me as I retreated up the old stairs. I had to hold tight onto the banister to steady myself, for I was sure his gaze was on my back.

How dare he insist on business on a day like this. I threw myself onto the bed and wept, remembering all the comfort Chloe had offered after my parents died, the way she protected me.

But, I reminded myself, Blake had seduced her. Somehow, he managed to come between me and my closest friend.

There was something in those hazel eyes, something quite cold and wicked, something that didn't care so much for convention. Yet he was popular in school, a bully. That sort of toxic masculinity was celebrated in the South. It was rewarded with high-powered jobs, arm candy, and respect.

But hadn't Marcus taught him a lesson? If Marcus could forgive him after all that, why couldn't I? Maybe when Marcus broke Blake's nose, it was a way of evening the score. He put Blake in his place. I needed to do the same.

The late afternoon coffee left me quite restless. I tossed and turned in bed, jumping at every creak and rustle in that old inn before I decided to get up and soothe my insomnia. I dressed and went outside to nearby Audubon Park.

I always found comfort in the dark. The quiet, unknown world felt like a warm blanket to me. As I stepped out into the humid night, I was reminded of many nights at Azalea House, wandering the moonlit paths, pouring out my grief over my parents upon the twins' graves. In death, they brought me comfort, like they were sharing my sorrows.

Even in that moment, I felt they were with me as the trees danced in the wind, their brittle, tired limbs chattering like weary bones, siphoned dry from the intense summer heat. Most of the trees' limbs and leaves had fallen to the ground in quilt-like autumnal patterns already.

In some ways, parts of Audubon Park reminded me of the grounds near Azalea House, with its carefully sculpted gardens and ancient oak trees. Perhaps, I thought, in a new house on similar grounds, I could capture the best aspects of it, while leaving behind the worst of it.

I continued my walk along the path. Magazine Street, usually illuminated by street lights, was completely dark.

I was too deep in thought, worrying about the future of the property. I didn't notice the figure behind me until he laid his cold hands on me and pulled me to his chest. The fetid smells of decay and alcohol made me squirm, and even worse, he clasped a hand over my mouth to contain my shrieks as he began to pull me off the path.

"Stop it!" a male voice said. "I have a gun!"

The grip tightened, then relaxed, and then I was pushed towards my savior. My savior! He wrapped his arms around me in a protective embrace as the attacker fled into the interior of the trail system, a golf course during the day, a haven for criminals at night.

I looked up to meet the man's face.

Blake.

I shoved him away.

"You again. Are you determined to follow me everywhere?"

I gathered up my blouse. The attacker had torn it, and I tried my best to cover myself and escape Blake.

"Wait," he said, touching my elbow. "I did follow you out here. It's not safe out here at night, and I just wanted to——"

"Protect me?"

He shoved his hands in his pockets and nodded.

Damn him. He was doing everything he could to be likable. And he had found the perfect opportunity by rescuing me.

I stormed back to the inn.

Marcus was in his suite, a blue light filtering from the crack under the door. He had insisted on bringing all of his equipment from Florida, packing it all into suitcases and checking it at the airport. I had no idea how he was able to get online, but he had his ways. I went back to my room and threw myself on the bed.

I had not eaten in days. My stomach burned with emptiness, but there was a certain comfort in it. I had control over something in my life. If I was going to suffer, it should at least be by my own choice. But the weakness that accompanied my hunger didn't help.

The attack still tingled my nerves with apprehension. What if Blake hadn't followed me to the park? Was my life that fragile, so easy to disappear in the night? New Orleans wasn't exactly the safest place, and I had been foolish to venture out after dark.

The parts of my body the man had touched burned with a strange sensation, as if I had been touched by fire. I went into the bathroom, stripped off all my clothes, stood in a scalding hot shower, and scrubbed myself until my flesh was raw and red.

I tossed and turned in bed. In the few moments I did fall asleep, I dreamed of phantom hands grabbing me, my flesh yielding until the stranger was inside me, taking over my body and doing insane things. Wild things. Sex with strange men. Drugs of every color. I was soon reaching out and taking hold of people I'd never seen before, pulling them into the shadows and draining their energy, this stranger inside me taking over.

Soon, the full moon's light filtered in through the window and

I could no longer take it. I sat up, my heart galloping. Then, that familiar feeling of being shoved aside swept over me. The room went cold.

Laughter from across the street.

Familiar laughter.

I got up and looked out the window. The streetcar rumbled by. I saw faces there, twisted and maniacal, some clawing their eyes out, some covered in blood and slamming their fists against the windows.

I squeezed my eyes closed, jammed my knuckles into them until I saw patterns. The streetcar's bell sounded. When I looked back, everyone was seated normally.

The laughter tittered over by the park this time, then sounded closer.

The next thing I knew, I was in the streetcar, heading downtown.

When I looked down, I was wearing a tank top, no bra, jeans, sneakers.

I pulled my shirt away from my skin, horrified at seeing my nipples poking through the thin material. This was a shirt I'd normally wear to bed, something I wore for comfort. It suddenly felt like an invitation I didn't intend. I looked up to see several college-aged boys grinning at me.

I got off the streetcar, hoping another would arrive from the opposite direction to rescue me back to the inn.

I walked along the road, trying to shorten the distance back, navigating the seedy area where the bars always seemed open and tattoo parlors advertised their wares with still-aglow fluorescent signs.

Decadence flowed from everywhere. Seductive music from jazz clubs filtered out through the doors. Laughter reverberated off the streets. When I looked inside the bars, there were liquor bottles of every color, a tempting kaleidoscope of danger.

I went inside one of the tattoo parlors and looked around, lost.

Phosphorous, neon lights glowed in alluring hues of hot pink and purple, and the air-conditioning was a welcome reprieve from the evening's humid air. The parlor's smell reminded me of the deep, potent fragrance of Azalea House's gardens, and a nostalgic pang gripped my heart. I followed the scent to a stick of incense, its smoke curling and dancing under the influence of the air conditioner.

A tattooed woman with grey hair looked me up and down.

"Look at you!" she said staring at my shirt. "Have you ever had one of your nipples pierced before?"

I shook my head no.

"I think you'd really like it. The look… the sensation…"

I found myself nodding.

When she led me back into the depths of the parlor, it was like walking inside some hidden part of myself. In the back room, on the table, it was like opening up to myself. I watched the needle impale me. The concentrated pain pulled me back to reality, made me want more.

"It's in," she said. "Good job. You didn't even flinch. How do you feel?"

I looked at her and said, "Hungry."

4

I returned before Marcus woke up. I saw Blake in passing as he checked out, while Marcus and I had breakfast in the lounge. I made sure to shoot him a nasty glance. He flashed a quick smile.

After such a long hiatus from food, I actually enjoyed eating. The piercing burned, a reminder of the shock I'd encountered in the park, the pain distracting me from the horrifying experience.

People at the breakfast nook stood up and looked out the window at some commotion on the street. The receptionist got up and closed the curtains.

"Really, folks, just try to enjoy your time here! It's New Orleans. There's always something going on," she said, wringing her hands.

"What is it?" I asked, hoping they caught the guy who had grabbed me. But New Orleans was fraught with crime. It seeped through every corner of the city. Behind every laughing parader was a mugger or someone ready to take your money and your life. Behind every mansion was someone lurking in the shadows, ready to break glass.

"Some guy who lives across the street," said an older woman.

"He hired a girl and things went south fast." She looked me up and down, probably trying to decide if I was worthy of the gossip.

"And then what?" someone asked.

"You shouldn't go out at night like that," she said, her face drawn into a scorn. "I heard you coming and going. This isn't the sort of place for that." She drew herself up taller, gave me another look up and down, and turned on her heel, leaving me gaping. How dare she! I opened my mouth to explain, but Blake came up behind me and put a hand on my shoulder.

"This fat cat lawyer hired a hooker. Sounds like he was into some weird stuff. Hung himself with a belt while his pants were down. Who hires a lady to do that?" he said in a low voice. "People were talking about it as they brought the body out."

"He died?"

"Afraid so," Blake said, looking out the window and shaking his head. "It was some sort of uh, auto organic, or auto something fixation, I think. At least, that's what people are saying."

Auto erotic asphyxiation. I had snuck into Marcus's room one day and read about it on some online forum, under the headline, "YOU HAVE TO TRY THIS!!!"

Ever since I saw Julia and Troy through the closet in our old house, I became fascinated with BDSM and what it would be like to be a dominatrix, even before I knew what it was called. It was as if when Julia put that latex suit on, she had superpowers. She could make men do what she wanted. And the more she ordered Troy, the more aroused he became. I thought about that night ever since.

After that night, I went to the mall and bought a bodice that hugged my body. Sometimes, I'd wear it out underneath my clothes like a superhero, waiting to show off my powers. My senior year of high school, as unpopular as I was, Vivienne took me to a party where the cheerleaders were. The head cheerleader whose house it was invited me to her bedroom and I showed it to her. It was the first time I ever had sex with anyone.

More than the sex, it was the power that came with it that fascinated me. As I would watch Julia and Troy, I would think about the constricting sensation of the tight latex, the way it must have felt caressing her most intimate places, the way it made Troy swoon with desire. I wanted that power, any power.

Still, dominatrixes were like unicorns to me. Did they really exist? Or was that just a figment of a man's imagination?

A rich lawyer in a mansion in a ritzy area of New Orleans. He was likely married to someone who fit his bill, some arm candy in her heyday. And now, he was dead because of his darkest desires. What kind of man snuck around and hired someone like that? And why did it have to be kept so secret, anyway? If he was honest with his wife and told her, would he still be alive?

In this uppity part of New Orleans, people were expected to behave and act a certain way. They weren't allowed to cut loose and laugh and stumble all over the street in the middle of the night. This part of New Orleans was all linen suits and hair that defied humidity, expensive cars and holding it together with toothpaste-commercial grins during the worst divorces and scandals. Part of me understood why it had to be that way. Part of me felt it was sad to be that way.

And who was she? Did she stalk through the night in a black catsuit like my aunt? It was hard to imagine seeing someone like that in real life. I longed to slip into the shadows again, to find a way to protect myself from all the demons lurking in the dark, to overcome all my fears and blend in seamlessly like a black thread on black clothing. I wanted to be a voyeur and learn about that hidden world, to blend in so I could observe.

I didn't bring up either event to Marcus. He sat down next to me at breakfast and barely made eye contact.

"I know you don't want to talk about it, but we need money, Marianne," he said. "Haven't you thought about college? I have. We need some way to pay for it, right?"

"We'll get scholarships," I said, not looking up. I focused on buttering my bread.

"How am I supposed to get a scholarship with a GED?"

"And whose fault is that?" I snapped, meeting his eyes. "You know, you didn't have to leave."

He set his coffee cup down on the table with a loud clattering noise. People paused their conversations and looked over at our table.

"I ran away because I'm gay, Marianne. Do you remember where we lived? Smack dab in the middle of the bible belt? And Julia was trying to find any excuse to send me off to some conversion therapy camp. And school? Don't you remember?"

"I do," I said, my teeth clenched. "And I especially remember Blake being nasty to you. How can you be buddies with him?" I asked, keeping my voice low. I pierced the bread with my punctuated movements and set it aside, irritated. "After what he did to us in school? And aren't you suspicious that he's not showing much emotion after Chloe and Elle died?"

"You don't have to forgive everyone, Marianne. But some people change, and some people do want to help. You can give and take things from people, and it can end at that."

I stared at my bread.

"Chloe wanted me to forgive him, and I did. And he was upset when they died. I saw. I was hanging out with her a lot, helping her. You forget how much she helped me. And you. She wanted you there," he said, staring at me. "Blake got payback in life by losing Chloe and the baby. Trust me on that. But you could stand to let a few things go."

"Don't turn this around on me," I said. I got up to clear my plate.

Oh, how I yearned for someone to tell me it was going to be okay. Part of me missed having someone to lend me strength. Marcus had his moments, but he was still so young, with so much life before him. My chest clenched as I thought of Troy and his warm hands on my shoulder, telling me it would be all right. There was no one around to tell me it would be okay. I desperately wanted it again, some sort of validation that things would continue to be easy for us in Florida.

Troy. Aunt Julia's young husband, who turned his attention on me after things went south at Azalea House. He was always the one person who tried to protect me, but after our relationship turned sexual, forbidden, I began to wonder if he was just another man who was there to take what he wanted—sex, the house, the inheritance. It got to the point where I couldn't trust anyone, even myself. So I burned it all down and escaped.

I started back up to my room, but not before casting one more glance back at Marcus. His eyes went dark, full of suspicion.

We were still waiting on the insurance money from the fire, but the inheritance from my parents came through, and it was sizable enough to send Marcus to college, but not enough for me. It would cover living expenses for a couple of years for me, but if I didn't land some enormous book deal or get a scholarship, I was afraid I'd be doomed to taking on some boring job I didn't really want, getting sucked into the dull round way of life that so many people subjected themselves to. I couldn't do that, not after everything my parents accomplished with their band.

Most people who had graduated high school were doing something, like going to trade school, community college, or university. It was common for people to get married right out of high school, too; hell, most girls in school I knew lived for the idea. I was taking care of my younger brother and struggling to write a book about my parents. But I'd have to do something soon.

While Julia was living with us at Azalea House, she had drained a good portion of the money on lavish things, like new clothes for herself and a shiny new BMW for Vivienne. It still made me seethe. She must have known she had to live it up while she could. I wanted to visit her in prison just so I could tell her off. Every night, I dreamed of ways I could take revenge on her.

"Miss Easton?" the lady at the desk said as I was halfway up the stairs. She had her hand over the mouthpiece of the front desk's telephone. "There's a call for you."

I glanced at Marcus. He shrugged.

"Who is it?" I asked. The receptionist smiled and said it was a lady, but she would not give her name.

A lady? Thoughts of Julia calling from prison to torture me came to mind, but how would she know where I was?

"Hello?" I said into the phone, my throat constricting.

"Marianne, dear," Grand'Mere Lily said. "We need to have a chat."

MAPLE STREET BUSTLED with Tulane students studying for finals, coming back and forth with books tucked under their arms, carrying coffee or chatting with study buddies. Oh, to have such manageable problems such as studying. I'd take that any day over property disputes and death.

Lily sat before me, her plain coffee still steaming, a red lipstick stain on the edge of the white cup. She was dressed to the nines in a white linen shirt, black velvet slacks, and shiny loafers. And pearls. Always pearls, in her ears (clip-ons, of course, because no civilized person got piercings, only "natives" as she said, whatever the hell that meant), and on her neck.

"I believe that after all our mental suffering, Ed and I should be taking over the sale of the land, dear," she said, her cold blue eyes piercing me. The ache in my throat bloomed and festered. I tried to swallow it back down so I could say something, anything to defend myself, but the words wouldn't come.

"You and your brother received inheritance, which should tide you over for many years. Not to mention, the insurance payout and everything *else* you've received throughout your privileged lives."

"It…it…" I managed to say.

"What, girl? Spit it out." Several people looked our way at her loud, raucous voice that was so similar to Julia's.

"Marcus and I would both like to go to college," I said as fast as I could. I wiped my palms on my skirt, hoping it wouldn't leave sweaty streaks behind.

She threw back her head and laughed. "You and your *gay* brother wouldn't be able to get into any sort of school even if you tried. I've told you all your life, you're destined to be a spinster, at best, and your brother is better off doing whatever it is he's doing.

Leave him be if you know what's best. He'll waste away from AIDS in no time."

I began to sob, my body shuddering, desperately trying to exorcise the sadness.

"Ah, yes. Of course." She folded her neatly manicured hands in front of her coffee cup. "Of *course* that's your reaction. This just proves to me that you're too immature to handle the property transaction. I am filing a plea that states that you and your brother are both mentally challenged, and that all transactions are to be handled by *me* from now on."

All I could do was stand up and start walking out the door. Several people were staring at the scene we had created. My face burned like it was on fire, just like that last day at Azalea House. She knew I did something. She knew I wished them all dead. And this was her revenge. Even if I won, a lawsuit would surely drain us of everything we had. I walked back to the inn, hugging myself for some semblance of comfort. Oh, the things she said about Marcus and me! My heart ached and throbbed.

Marcus and I checked out, but I wouldn't tell him anything about my tear-stained face until we got back in the car on the way to lunch.

"Well," he said, blank-faced, "we'll just have to take on more work. Finish your book and start querying. Someone is bound to pick it up after everything that happened. And I'll just start hustling for more web design work."

"Lily will probably sell it to some developer and make it into a strip mall or suburbia," I said.

Marcus shrugged. "What difference does it make?"

I glared at him.

"Oh, fine. Yes, the twins. They're such spoiled brats they'll come to Florida to haunt us. Look," he said, turning in the seat to face me. "Blake's father wouldn't do that. They were talking about building another house there, a family home sort of reminiscent of Azalea House."

I thought about that for a moment. Hadn't that been the very thing that set off all the wicked events in the first place? I looked at him gravely and said, "I don't know if I like that any better, Marcus."

"You like the alternative better?"

As we pulled up to the restaurant in the French Quarter, the last stop before heading back to the airport, I thought about why Lily hated us so much. Were we so tainted that she regarded us as mere weeds, and not the lovely blooming flower of a person she somehow saw in Vivienne? Vivienne could charm and talk her way out of anything, which Lily valued. Vivienne was, at one point, doing well in her career as a model, that plastered on smile of hers the perfect false façade for the world to see. Lily hated me for shining a light on the past, but Vivienne was the perfect liar, the ideal model for maintaining the perfect Easton myth. And now that Vivienne was dead and Julia was locked away, Lily was set, I supposed, to seek out her revenge on us.

As we stepped out of the car, I heard someone calling my name. It wasn't incredibly unusual in the city; fans of our parents' band, Spellbound Hearts, often recognized us.

"Marianne!" called the voice again.

"Ignore him. It's Troy," Marcus muttered in my ear, taking me by the elbow and pulling me into the safety of the restaurant.

Troy!

I couldn't help but look. I hadn't seen him in months, and it felt like years since he helped me have Julia locked up. I didn't read the letters he constantly sent professing his love. I let Marcus handle it.

"He's a desperate stalker," Marcus would say, shielding me from seeing the letters. "He's only after you for your money. What kind of man would prey on a teenage girl like that?"

I couldn't help but freeze, turn, and look.

He was thinner than I'd remembered, his clothes loose, his arms sticking out of his sleeves like chicken bones, his jaw much more pronounced. But as he approached, his eyes were clearer. Something about the cadence of his steps was much different. Confident. Alert.

I went so numb that Marcus's urging, the noise on the street, the stench of the French Quarter fell to the wayside.

"I heard," he said, placing his hands on my shoulders. They felt warm there. He smelled the same, so comforting I swooned until I was back in reality. "I heard about Chloe and the baby. I saw it in the paper. I'm so sorry."

He wasn't wearing his wedding ring. When I really looked at him now, he was dressed in a white button shirt and black slacks, something a waiter would wear at an upscale restaurant.

"How are you two doing? I tried to call and write—"

"She knows," Marcus said. "Marianne, come on. We have a reservation."

I motioned for him to go on, reassuring him with my eyes. He shot Troy a death glare before going inside.

"He really never liked me," Troy said, stuffing his hands in his pockets.

"He's protective of me." I stepped back. His cologne was suffocating. "What are you doing down here?"

"Bought a restaurant with Julia's money. Got a place." He shrugged. "It's been okay." He cocked his head to the side. "But I miss you."

I stared at my shoes.

"I'll let you get back to your brother," he said. "But come by some time." He produced a card and handed it to me. "I just wanted to see how you were doing. It was good to see you again, Marianne."

And then he turned and walked away.

I was expecting more push from him, like when we lived together under the same roof. But he had merely made his presence known, said hello and then retreated on his own. He didn't look back.

Something squeezed my chest as I remembered all those times we had gone off in the car together, just the two of us, listening to music and just talking. How I yearned for someone like that in my life again, someone older and wiser in some ways, someone to look out for me. It was great living with Marcus, but there were many times I had to take over and be the responsible one. Not that Troy was very responsible...or was he? He had managed to buy a restaurant and live down here after everything that had happened, and he seemed to be doing fine.

Then, of course, there was that sexual tension between us, almost tangible, like I could reach out and touch it. I know he felt it too. He had looked at me the same way he always did, and I felt almost a magnetic pull to fall into his arms like I always had in times of stress.

But as I recalled how thin he looked, did I really think that was the truth? What else was going on in his life? Did he miss me? Did he have a girlfriend? Did he quit drinking?

The last time he'd tried to call was a month ago, and the letters ceased mid-summer. So, he had given up on me that easily. It was no wonder. Troy was a very attractive guy, with that whole mysterious quality girls swooned over. Dark hair and eyes that could magnetize. I was sure he did well dancing for bachelorette parties here in the Quarter back in his college days.

But he was Troy. However nice he was to me, he had still tried to manipulate me into being with him so he could freeload off of me, and he'd snuck into my room on my eighteenth birthday to have sex with me. Part of me wanted it to happen, but part of me regretted not pushing him off.

I still had the black bustier I'd exchanged at the mall, the one that got Troy's attention, the cheerleader's attention, and even though I wasn't seeing anyone, I'd still put it on and look at myself in the mirror, noticing how different it made me look. With my shoulders pulled back and my chest out, the bustier always seemed to make me taller, sleeker, meaner…not anything like the old Marianne, the quiet Marianne that stared at her shoes or hid behind her mother.

That time with Troy was unfulfilling, quick and secret in the shadows and privacy of my bedroom. I wanted to see how things played out. I wanted to be the one in control of my own pleasure, not just some sex doll someone was using to get off.

Troy had taken me to the mall to swap out Uncle Joseph's

ridiculous bra and panties birthday set for that black bustier. I couldn't help but think that part of Troy was just like Uncle Joseph, just looking for something visually appealing, like a Barbie doll to dress up.

But that wasn't me. I wanted to do things my way, to wear things that made *me* feel good. I didn't want to play dress up for some man.

There was a sex shop down the street. I had looked it up in the phone book one day, curious about the kinds of secrets New Orleans held. As many times as I had walked past, I never had the courage to pursue my curiosity in front of the judgmental stares of passersby. Seeing Troy brought back a flood of memories and reawakened my yearning to learn more.

Surely, Marcus wouldn't mind waiting a few more minutes.

It took me a moment to find the shop, as the lettering that read "Adult Store" was small and neatly tucked away under an awning. There it was, hiding in broad daylight, sandwiched between one of the fanciest restaurants in New Orleans and a high-end shoe store. I walked up a flight of stairs and opened a blacked-out glass door.

I had never seen anything quite like it. There were rows and rows of magazines with scantily clad women on the covers, and wall to wall vibrators and dildos of every color imaginable. And clothing! There were several versions of the black latex looking catsuit that my Aunt Julia wore. The racks were full of any sort of variation on that outfit a person could think of.

I had glimpsed into this world of forbidden pleasures the other night when I got the piercing. The barbell pressed against my shirt, daring me to take in as much as I could. The thrill of looking around and touching the fabrics had my head spinning.

"Help you find anything?"

I jumped and turned around. The cashier, a tall, lanky brunette with a shiny bob, towered over me. She looked me up and down and grinned, her red mouth spreading wide like a Cheshire cat.

Thank goodness it wasn't a man. That would have sent me running and screaming from the store.

"I think I'm into this," I said, running my hands along the latex rack. "But I'm not sure." It was the most I'd probably ever said to a complete stranger.

"Do you want to try something on?" She looked me up and down, taking in my conservative clothing. I looked down at the floor, embarrassment coursing through me. My face felt hot. When I looked down at my shoes, my hair hung in my face, limp and plain and unkempt in comparison to hers.

"What do you like about it?" she asked softly. When I looked up, she was still smiling, but there was something more to it than just a customer service smile, like she was used to newbies coming in here.

"I don't know. I had something like this once," I said, pulling out a latex halter top from the rack. "It was more…plain. But I liked the way it felt. It was like…I dunno…"

"Comforting? Like a hug?"

"That," I said, "and I made a certain guy all stupid."

She laughed.

"Is he your…boyfriend?"

"Not exactly."

"A sub?"

I looked up at her, searched her curious eyes for meaning. "I'm not exactly sure what that is."

"I know just what you need. Follow me."

She disappeared behind the register and came back with a glossy magazine. On the cover was a leather-clad woman, her hair similar to the cashier's, standing behind a shirtless, collared man. I stared at it for a moment, mouth hanging open.

"There are a lot of how-to articles and stories in here," she said, flipping through it. "And in the back, there are personal ads. Take it. It's a freebie. And when you know what you want, come back any time."

I stuffed it in my purse, thanked her and scurried over to the restaurant, hoping no one else would see me. I felt the same mix of arousal and shame I felt when I was with Troy.

I spoke briefly about the meeting with Lily to Marcus, who still pressed on about letting Blake handle everything.

"Everything was stipulated clearly in the will, Marianne," he said in between sips of prosecco. The owner knew us and was one of the few people who really seemed to feel sorry for us, so he slipped us a bottle of it. Marcus kept polishing off glass after glass of it like it was water. "If Blake's father buys it directly from us, he'll give us over market value. Trust me. Plus, Lily will fuck off, right? She can't exactly say we're insane if we get over market value for the house, can she?"

He had a point. I sighed.

"Come on. He wants to make up for what a dick he was in high school. Sometimes you just have to take an apology and run with it."

"Would you care for another bottle?" a waiter asked.

"Yes," Marcus said.

I put up a hand. "No."

"God, Marianne. Seriously? I just want to pass out on the plane back to Florida."

"Oh?" the waiter said, a strange expression crossing his face. "Where in Florida?"

"The Keys," I said, shooting Marcus a look. "May we just have the check, please?"

"Certainly, Miss. But you may want to check on your flight. A big storm is passing through."

Marcus and I exchanged glances.

"Storm?"

"Hurricane Floyd. Worst one in years."

Great, I thought.

Marcus grinned. "We'll take another bottle."

Back at the inn, where I'd booked us another night, I watched news coverage as winds whipped through the state, covering beaches with debris and flooding the roads. It didn't look like we'd be flying back to Florida anytime soon. Thoughts of our little apartment ravaged by winds and flooding were etching deeply into my mind.

This was a curse. The universe was conspiring to keep me here. Seducing me, even. The nipple piercing tingled like it was already healed, and I felt a shiver of odd pleasure begin at the apex of my thighs.

I sighed and fished around in my purse to look at the magazine, and Troy's business card slipped out and landed on the coverlet. I picked it up and ran my fingers over the print, committing it to memory.

Guidry's. 529 Bienville Street. Troy Guidry, Owner.

It listed the business number and his personal number.

Guidry. I had forgotten that was his last name. Aunt Julia was always so insistent on keeping her last name as Easton and dominating every aspect of her life that I had a hard time remembering little things about Troy.

And now he had a nice little Italian restaurant in the Quarter.

We took the car out to the Azalea House grounds the next day as the hurricane ravaged the Keys. In Louisiana, the weather was humid, overcast, the late summer air suffocating, with fat grey clouds blotting out the sun.

The plan was to meet Blake there and come up with a plan we could all agree on. I tried not to think about our small apartment complex and all the newly acquired things I'd worked so hard to get. Ghost, our cat, was with a friend of Marcus's, who had evacuated to the Gulf side of the state.

I thought about his soft fur, the lull of the ocean, the sun…

And then I thought of Chloe's car. It would be in the same junk yard as my parents'.

And then I felt it hit me like a punch. The voices. The ghosts of Azalea House. All of them.

Marcus shook me and said, "We're back in the village."

"Yes," I said. "We certainly are."

5

The wreck yard, full of twisted hunks of metal warped into strange monsters, was a maze. I remembered coming here with Troy after my parents died, just to make it real, just to tell myself they were really gone. I had to do the same with Chloe's car.

"I'm staying here," Marcus said. He sat in the backseat and fidgeted. The Town Car's driver stepped out and lit a cigarette, probably wondering when this job driving two teenagers around would finally end.

My veins froze over when I saw her familiar Firebird. She'd gotten it soon after she'd gotten pregnant. The whole front end was smushed up into a V-shape from the tree she'd hit. I walked around to the driver's side. Dried blood. I turned away and caught my breath, then forced myself to look again.

Why was there so much clothing in the back seat? It must have been her clothing, hers and the baby's. Where was she going?

Something twisted in my stomach, anxiety and unease. I ran away, back towards the safety and newness of the Lincoln.

We drove to Azalea House, the familiar twisting roads bringing back a flood of memories. First, thoughts of my parents riding in the car came to mind, and how they slipped off the road due to the sleet storm that came on my birthday. We took another curve too fast, and I was reminded of the way Troy used to drive on these roads, uncaring, drunk on screwdrivers, wanting to escape the confines of that house and life as much as I did.

Azalea House was down to its foundation. Even after many days of rain, the surroundings still reeked of fire.

There were a few items still clinging to existence, like the frame of the hideous couch Julia had purchased, that were reduced to skeletons. Everything else was an unrecognizable heap of black tar, diminished to nothing but jumbled black masses.

The azalea bushes were just skeletal fingers, but in some places, they persevered, the flowers opening up into succulent, fragrant flowers.

The pond was covered in a slick, electric green algae, stinking and reaching the shore. New weeds had sprung up, making the path to the twins' grave difficult to find.

"I'm not going back there," Marcus called out. He was standing by the car, arms crossed over his chest, watching me. He had not wanted to come, had not really seen the point of it unless we were to meet with Blake's father about discussing the sale. But he had not wanted me to come out here alone, probably for fear I would do something stupid or hold my ground about not selling it.

I went anyway. How hard would it be to find the twins' graves? I knew the way, had it committed to heart. But as I pushed bramble and limbs out of the way along the old path, I realized the Louisiana heat and soil propagated lush green life after only a short period of time.

Kudzu. The vines were everywhere. Strangling, invading so fast I could see it move, as if in time lapse. A freezing breeze rolled through. I pulled my sweater down past my knuckles, the chill passing through my body. I shivered and searched for ghosts.

It was quiet, save for the trees dancing in the wind. Nothing but bones, soon to turn to dust, a skeleton of a house, and what was left of the sumptuous gardens.

But the kudzu grew right before my eyes, snaking around the

trees' trunks, crawling through branches and leaves, and soon burying everything in a sea of writhing green tentacles.

I ran.

That wasn't kudzu. Maybe some kind of super kudzu, something stronger. It seemed to hunt for something to invade, some orifice, because its behavior told me it looked, searched, like it had a goal.

My mother used to delight in telling me spooky stories about plants.

"You know," she'd say, her voice all sing-songy as she gardened, "there's this variant of a plant, something that tunnels down into a grave and wraps around bodies as they decompose. Someone found this plant inside the white dome of a skull, and a large bud cracked it open, then bloomed. It was after a hurricane in New Orleans, when the bodies all washed up from their coffins. They say the flower smelled strange. Like rotten meat. And it looked like there was an eye inside."

I hated that story. Maybe she told it to me to teach that there was always beauty to be found, even in death. Maybe she told it to me to appreciate the foliage she loved so much, as if it were my sibling. Maybe she told it to me just to keep me out of the garden, to obscure the past and keep me from discovering where the twins were buried.

I finally reached their graves.

Alone. I really felt it at once as I sat down where they were buried, listening in the quiet for any sign of them.

We had taken the grave markers to the cemetery to place them next to our parents. If anyone found out they were buried here, they would mob the place. I thought of a story my mother told me about Oscar Wilde's grave in Paris, how it was full of lipstick kisses. I couldn't imagine what strange things rabid fans of Spellbound Hearts would do after the media frenzy of this past spring, but I wasn't ready to find out. It was better to lie to any real estate agent and say the land was, as far as we knew, free from any buried secrets.

I knelt before their graves and pulled weeds out of the way before settling in and closing my eyes.

Nothing. Not a word. But this was what they wanted. They wanted peace, they wanted their murder solved, and now I had no one to confide in, no one to pray to.

I was almost in a trance, being back in such a familiar, comfortable place, that I did not notice what was creeping up my ankle. I kept my eyes closed and brushed it away.

But it was back. I opened my eyes, agitated, ready to kill the creature that kept pestering me.

It was a kudzu vine. I brushed it away again, ready to resume my meditation.

But I could feel the vine circling my ankle. I unraveled it and pushed it away. How was it possible? I scooted back, my nerves searing from the weird energy. Before I could stand, several strands of it curled around my body like little green snakes, grasping, constricting, squeezing.

I gasped and stumbled onto my back. The vines entered my mouth, my ears, and traveled through my hair. I tried to scream, but it came out muffled. I flailed and yanked with my one free hand, pulling at the stuff until I could see skin again.

When I stood, I heard laughter.

A woman laughing. Hysterical. A muffled, choked sound.

Wicked. Evil.

"Only you," the voice said. "I'll kill anyone else, Marianne. Don't let them come here."

I ran towards the car, towards the sane safety of Marcus.

He stood up straight as soon as he saw me. "What the hell happened to you?"

A voice threatened me, I almost said. It said we can't sell the land.

Instead, I said, "I fell." I straightened my clothing and looked around, listening for the voice again.

I had imagined it. It was just the horror of being back here again, that was all. I needed to get rid of this place, to let it go so it wouldn't terrorize me again. Now, the land was essentially a blank canvas. But what would happen to it?

I had to let that thought go. The twins were at peace, as were all the other people who had suffered here. I had followed through with their requests and delivered what they asked for. There was no reason to keep it.

But what did "only you" mean? And who said it?

"Let's walk it off," Marcus said, taking my arm. "Look, some of the roses and azaleas are still back here. And look! Some curcuma ginger, too. It'll be really pretty in the spring."

"Carter Leblanc gave me that," I said, a little glimmer of hope back in my voice.

"I still cannot believe you went to see him," Marcus said, shaking his head. "He could have killed you."

"He didn't kill anyone."

"But he *could* have. People do all kinds of crazy shit when they're wrongfully imprisoned."

We walked through the garden, back to where our bedrooms used to be. Something stuck out of the black rubble at an odd angle, noticeable because it was the only fully intact object in the fire-ridden pile.

"Marianne," Marcus said, his voice thin and whiney, like he had regressed back to a child.

"I'm just going to see what it is," I said. It was like the object called out to me. I stepped into the charred pile and pulled it out.

YES. It was the first word I saw before I began brushing it off, finally remembering what it was. An old Ouija board Chloe gave me on my birthday several years ago.

"Of course that thing didn't burn," Marcus said, backing away. His walk was similar to when he was a child, almost like he needed his crutches for his cerebral palsy again.

"It's just a board," I said, more to myself. "Chloe gave it to me."

"That thing brought on a lot of fucked up shit. Let's try to burn it again," Marcus said, his eyes wide with ideas. "I want to see it for myself." He staggered further away.

"That fucked up shit let us talk to our brothers and find out Julia killed them, Marcus."

"You're not *keeping* that, are you?"

I glared at him. "Of course I am. Chloe gave it to me."

He shook his head. We continued to walk, but Marcus kept side-eyeing the board. Finally, I walked back to the car and tossed the board in the trunk.

When I turned around, Marcus was back to his adult-like self, standing up straight and confident.

"A house wouldn't be bad here, Marianne," he said, his arms behind his back. "It's a pretty piece of property. We could build on it again."

"No."

"Then let's sell it."

"Marcus," I said, clenching my fists, "I'm thinking."

"It's just a plot of land. Nothing's going to hurt you."

I sighed. "Alright. I'm willing to discuss things with Blake."

He beamed. "Good. I don't think you'll regret it."

❧

"My FATHER SAYS people get too attached to places," Blake said. "He says that memories are made with people, not places."

We were all three walking around the property, Blake commenting on all the positive things about it. Marcus had convinced me to go into the village and call Blake immediately, probably for fear that I would change my mind.

I was already regretting it.

"Look at the way the land slopes up to the foundation," Blake said.

"It creates a slough in front of the property," I said.

Marcus frowned.

"But it means any new house you build up here will be safe from flooding," Blake said with a grin worthy of a toothpaste commercial. "And I love all the landscaping."

"It's being overtaken by kudzu," I argued.

"That can be easily remedied. And back here," he said, leading us to where the back gardens used to be before Vivienne tore them up, "you could put in a pool."

"Oooh," Marcus said, starry-eyed.

I rolled my eyes.

"Marianne," Blake said, wagging his finger at me in jest, "don't focus on the bad things in the past. Remember, someone can make a lot of wonderful new memories back here. It's a wonderful piece of property."

"Your father didn't have a family rooted in the same place for generations," I said. "You all came here from Mississippi, remember?"

He looked at me with a little glimmer in his eye. "I just say that because I don't want you to be upset."

"What are you going to do with it?" I asked.

"Marianne," Marcus warned. He wanted us to be on our best behavior with Blake. No whining. No getting emotional. Just sell.

"Build a family home. Something beautiful. Happy."

I sighed.

"Why don't you come with me back to the office? We can go over numbers. That's all. You don't have to sign anything today."

I looked at Marcus, who had a cold, calculating look in his eyes.

"Just numbers?" I said.

Blake smiled and nodded.

We drove back to his office. His father had drafted up an offer. There were mountains of paperwork, things I didn't understand. I flipped through it all and kept quiet. The amount was well over the actual value. It would definitely help ease the burden of not being able to stay in the Keys. And I would be able to go to college, too.

But why was he doing this? Did he feel guilty for being such a pain in the ass? Was he going to ask for some favor?

I wrung my hands. Maybe it *was* best to have Lily handle everything.

"If your family already lives here," I said, my palms

dampening the paperwork, "then why would you want to build another house?"

"It's really for me," he said with an uneasy grin. "You know, Chloe would have loved it if I did this. She always loved it so much back here. It was like a reprieve for her, you know? When I think of restoring it, I can swear I feel her presence, telling me to do it. I mean it when I say she all adored you so, especially your mother. She always talked about how admirable it was that your parents put a hold on their careers so they could restore the property," he said, his eyes misty.

I bit my tongue to avoid saying something sarcastic.

"She never stopped being your friend, you know," he said, sniffing back tears. "Anyway, I can get my father out here to explain everything. He's out showing houses, but——"

"So your parents are buying this for *you*? Damn. Aren't you lucky," Marcus cut in. "And basically, you get to build any house you want?"

I shot him a look. He responded with a sassy shake of his head.

"That's right," Blake said. "I am very lucky. One of these days, I'll have a happy family to live there, too." He looked at me and smiled.

"You're nineteen and already thinking about this?" I asked.

He shrugged. "I don't really need to go to college to get a real estate license. I know what I want. Why wait? I wanted that with Chloe. But I don't want to put my life on hold for too long. I'm young. I want a family. What's wrong with that?"

Typical Southern mindset, I thought, my mind shifting over to college. They all wanted to get married before age twenty-one and pop out kids. I wanted a future. I wanted to be independent.

"Where are you two going to live now that the Keys are a mess?" Blake asked. I was relieved for the change in topic.

"I don't really know," I said, focusing on the birds fluttering about outside the window. "We've been racking up fees at the inn on St. Charles Avenue. Marcus loves it."

"I have a better idea," Blake said.

I looked over at him. "Of course you do."

Marcus shot me a look.

"My family has a condo on the far end of the Quarter that's furnished. Stay there until you figure things out."

Marcus's eyes glimmered. "Does it have a pool?"

"Yes, it does." Blake rummaged around in the drawer and produced a set of keys. I crossed my arms. He jingled the keys. "Come on. I'm not using it. You can stay there for a little while. If you like it, I'll give you a reduced rate on rent. Really, you'd just be paying condo fees and the electricity bill. It's paid off and we never use it."

Marcus reached around and snatched the keys out of his hands before I could refuse. I grit my teeth and gave him a side-eye glance.

"Thank you, Blake. This is very kind of you," Marcus said, annunciating every word as if teaching manners to a child. "Don't you agree, Marianne?"

I nodded.

"I'm going to wait in the car," he said, bouncing the keys from palm to palm. "You two should exchange niceties. Okay? Okay." The bell rang as he pushed his way outside.

"Look, I know things have been trying after this hurricane," Blake said. "I'm sure you're struggling trying to decide what to do. Would you like to have dinner and talk? We don't have to talk about the house if you don't want to." He picked up the paperwork, straightened it out, and filed it away. "You can sign when you're ready."

"What will we talk about?"

He laughed. "Chloe mentioned you were working on a book. My father knows a good agent."

I kept watching the birds. "I'm always suspicious of people trying to help me, Blake."

"I can see that. But Chloe chose you as a friend for a reason."

"I bailed on Chloe after she got pregnant."

He nodded like some sage. "I know. I understand."

"You do?"

"I'm sure she demonstrated how jealous she was of you. But she didn't hate you. You're the dark and mysterious type. People always wondered what you were thinking, what you were up to. Chloe wore her heart on her sleeve more than you ever have."

"People are going to wonder if they see us together," I said. "I already created enough scandal by getting involved with my aunt's ex-husband."

He shrugged. "It'll help sell a book, that's for sure."

The bustier underneath my shirt seemed to hug me in reassurance. I had a sudden urge to rip it off and throw it in the trash. What was it doing to me?

"Just dinner," I said.

MARCUS and I rode back to New Orleans to a condo out of a French Quarter dream. We entered a lush courtyard with fountains, plenty of shade, iron latticework and a glistening pool. I could easily see myself sitting there, jotting down notes for books. And we wouldn't need a car. Everything was within walking distance, and we could take the streetcar to cross town.

"Uh huh," Marcus said, studying me. "You like it, too. Admit it."

"It's nice."

"Nice? Come on. It's a condo in a historic city and it has a swimming pool. We didn't even have that at Azalea House, just a murky, nasty pond. Come on, let's go inside."

I sighed and followed him upstairs.

Inside was tastefully decorated with bright whites and neutral colors. Two bedrooms, two bathrooms. Not as much space as Azalea House, but it was much bigger than our Keys apartment, a cramped one-bedroom which, with a cat, felt like I was suffocating all the time.

"Think we can bring Ghost here?"

I didn't answer. Instead, I chose a bedroom and flopped down on the bed, wondering what on earth we would do next. We would sell the land to Blake. It sounded ideal. So why was my mind grappling with it?

Only you.

I remembered how Carter, the man accused of killing my brothers, had said that the land around there did things to people. You could cover it up with beautiful flowers and a gorgeous house, but it didn't fix what happened there.

Then, there was the upcoming dinner with Blake. I was dreading it.

What did he want?

6

Once we were settled into the condo, the scratching sounds began.

Rats. It had to be. New Orleans was full of them.

I put off dinner with Blake until it became chilly enough to wear a jacket. I dressed carefully, not too sexy, not too dressy.

I flopped down on the bed and studied the business card Troy gave me. I had walked past the restaurant he owned several times, never quite working up the nerve to say hello. I stared at blank pages for hours, wondering how I would get something down that resembled a band biography, something that would do my parents justice.

I also obsessively flipped through the magazine I'd acquired at the sex shop until the pages were worn. All those powerful women, standing up tall in their beautiful outfits, exuding the confidence I so wished I had. Their world felt so far away. The bustier I got in high school had begun to fray around the edges. The piercing healed, and I played with the ring while I thumbed through the magazine, thinking about a different life, one much more grown up. One where I would have control over men instead of them having control over me. A life where I was in charge, wore what I wanted, and didn't have to look out for my little brother.

I listened to Marcus chat away with his Florida friends, who were visiting to drop off Ghost. "It even has a pool!" one of them said. "Man, you really did alright by yourself."

I stood up and locked my door, wishing I had broken away from Azalea House sooner. At least Marcus had friends.

I took a cab to the restaurant to meet Blake. The French Quarter was draped in lights and tinsel, the shop windows full of quirky Christmas decorations and trendy tourist trinkets.

I had never been out on an actual date, or whatever it was we were doing together. It certainly felt like a date with the cloth napkins and dim lighting. A pink rose was poised perfectly in a slender little vase, and piano music drifted from across the restaurant. We even got away with drinking wine.

"I'm sure my dad's friend would love it," he said after I pitched the book about Spellbound Hearts. "It's dramatic, traumatic—"

I lowered my gaze.

"Are you finished with it?"

I shook my head.

"Well, you could pitch it first. If you get a bite, it might be worth finishing. A published book may help solve some of your troubles."

"And so would selling the property. I get it." I met his eyes for a brief second. He gave me a polite smile.

"Will you return to Florida?"

"I don't know. I thought it would be an escape, and so did Marcus. But with the hurricane and all, I just don't know."

"Stay at the condo as long as you like," he said. "We'll get you in touch with that agent."

"Why are you doing all this?"

He set his drink down. "Is the condo not to your liking?"

"It is," I said, flustered. "Everything is. It's just that I don't understand why you're doing all this. You could be making a lot more money by renting it to someone. All we're doing is paying electricity and the association fees."

"It's hard to find good people to rent. It saves my father money because we don't have to pay for all that. He'd rather have someone there who won't trash it."

"Blake," I said, trying to make my tone even and serious, "why do all this? I mean, Marcus could have killed you with those brass knuckles. Why do you want to help us?"

He picked up his drink again and smiled at me. "Do you always push away people who like you?"

Yes, I thought, but he probably already knew the answer to that.

"The truth is, I've always had a thing for you. I'm sure you know that. It's just that I've decided to be more mature about it. I'm not ready to date again. But I'd like us to be friends."

I stared at my drink, watching the bubbles rise to the surface and pop. Maybe if I stared long enough, I could float to the surface, too. Because at that moment, I felt like I was drowning, or an expanding bubble, ready to pop.

"It still feels like she died yesterday," I finally managed to say. "It's too much for me."

"I know. It's been three months. I do want to move forward one day, though. I hope it's with you."

I couldn't believe he was saying all this. So he wanted *me* to move in with him in this new house on the Azalea House property? How could I possibly do something like that?

Still, I kept hearing that voice inside my head. *Only you.*

What could I possibly do to protect Blake? He knew about the affair, the murders, Vivienne… But did he know I heard voices there?

Maybe he was attracted to me because of his own grief. It radiated off of me still; my parents' deaths seemed like they happened yesterday, and I was still coping with the fact that even though I hated her, I found Vivienne after she'd committed suicide. On top of all of this, my best friend was dead.

The thing was, I didn't know if I wanted to wait, or date

anyone at all. An iron ball formed in the pit of my stomach. What would people say if they knew I was dating the widower of my best friend? More scandal. More unwanted attention.

"I still need time," I said. "And I feel like I'm using you for the condo."

"Like I said, it really does help us, too. Dad doesn't want it to be empty all the time."

We finished up dinner by talking more about the book, but the property weighed on my mind, heavy as a cinderblock. If I said no to Blake, would he back out of the deal?

I took a cab back to the condo, my head back against the cool leather headrest as I watched the twinkling Christmas cheer outside. Another Christmas without my parents. Marcus was now the age I was when they died. My parents, my best friend…who else would I lose?

Blake could take care of me, that was for sure. He demonstrated that many times. But did I want that? I thought I wanted to be independent, free from having to worry about a man of all things to lean on. So many girls from my hometown said they wanted to go to college just to find a husband. I wanted to go to college for me, not to find someone to settle down with. It was the last thing I wanted. I wanted to follow musicians, to write about them, to understand their process and be creative myself. How could I do that if I was bonded to someone like Blake, who wanted to have a family, a normal life, a well-kept trophy housewife?

Marcus was in his room, laughter drifting from under the door, the bass from Mindless Self Indulgence thumping away. I went in my room and dug around for a little white card in my purse. When I found it, it was frayed at the edges, a dusting of makeup coating it, but I could still see Troy's number.

I locked myself in my room and called the number.

It took a few minutes of holding. Dishes clanked together in the background, voices called out. This was ridiculous. He was busy, this was ridiculous—

"Jesus," I muttered.

I was about to hang up when I heard, "Marianne?"

"How did you know it was me?"

"Uh, well…I guessed, honestly. What are you doing? Are you in town?"

"Marcus and I are renting a place on Esplanade until we figure things out. That hurricane wiped out Florida."

A pause. "I heard."

Did he hear I was living in New Orleans? Or about the hurricane? I decided not to ask.

"I'm done here in about an hour. I could pick you up and we could go somewhere quiet to talk."

What would Marcus say? I'd have to tell him I was going out again after my date with Blake. But riding around in the car with Troy again sounded so good. I gave him my address and told him I'd meet him outside.

I dressed carefully, pulling on new clothing I bought on the sly. I had been slowly adding to my wardrobe since we moved into the condo, things I had picked up in the French Quarter. Scandalous things, skin-tight and black as three a.m. Things that made me look and feel like those women in the magazines. I bought black halter tops and skin tight jeans, silk camisoles that showed the outline of my piercing. I'd even invested in a few good pieces of lingerie, not just the cotton, plain stuff I'd had as a teenager. Black, lacy things, and even a corset that I hadn't yet dared to put on. I had shirts with plunging necklines, and even a few short skirts, too. Things that Momma would have hated. Things that made me feel like I owned my body. At least while I was wearing them in the safe confines of my room.

I decided to see if I'd feel the same way out in the real world.

"I'm going out," I called out to Marcus on my way down the stairs. I hoped I would be out the door before he caught me, but he snatched the door open. His jaw dropped when he saw me, which was the very thing I dreaded. His friends drifted out and looked me up and down, too. I flushed.

"Where?" Marcus asked.

"Goth *queen*," one of the guests said with a finger snap.

"Just out," I said.

"Are you going to see Blake again?"

"Marcus," I said, trying to slip into the living room shadows.

"You're wearing makeup. And that outfit—"

"I made a friend. Okay? She works late and wants to grab a coffee." My mind shifted to the girl who worked at the sex shop.

"A coffee, huh? Wearing that?"

I looked down at my very adult suede boots, form-fitting black jeans and crop halter. I grabbed my jacket and threw it on.

"Yes, Marcus. I'm tired of looking like a dweeb all the time. I'm nineteen."

"Whatever, fibber."

Before I could say anything else, they all retreated back to his bedroom and slammed the door.

Troy stood outside, watching me as I descended the stairs. Nerves came over me again, fresh memories still picking at my brain. I hated the way he made me feel. I should be feeling this way about someone else, not Troy.

I met his eyes. They devoured me like I was completely unsampled flesh, a truly visceral look that nearly sent me to my knees. Blake didn't look at me this way. But Blake hadn't seen me dressed like this.

I steadied myself and walked towards the car. Julia's Mercedes.

"I kinda missed this thing," I said.

"I missed you," he said. I met his eyes again. They glimmered with emotion. Too much. It was overwhelming. I just wanted to get in the car at that point and have the shadows obscure me. I regretted what I was wearing.

"I've *really* missed you," he said.

I let him open the car door. He played something slow and sludgy, which I recognized as Leather Strip.

"So," he said, punching in the lighter, "why'd you call me?"

"I don't know," I said honestly. "I needed a familiar face."

"Ah." The lighter popped and he wedged a smoke in between his lips, lit it and rolled down the window to let the cool humidity in.

"When did you start smoking?"

"They're cloves."

I rolled down my window. "It's still smoking."

"Oh, relax. You could stand to loosen up a little. Don't be so nervous."

I straightened up and faced forward. The nipple ring shifted against my top.

"It's me, Troy," he said, teasing me. "You going to tell me what you want to talk about?"

"Blake is acting like he's interested in me."

He took a drag and laughed, letting out rings of smoke. "That's because he is."

"Troy. I'm serious."

"Guys like Blake want to get married early to a trophy wife, take lots of pictures, have lots of babies. You'd be wealthy. Is that what you want to hear?"

"No." I sighed. "Yes. I don't know."

"I don't know what to tell you. Is that what you want?"

Was it?

"He was my best friend's fiancé. I can't help but feel a certain kind of camaraderie with him. And he's always so nice to Marcus."

Troy chuckled, smoke coming out of his mouth and nose in curling puffs.

"Shut up. Give me one of those."

I expected him to scold me, but instead, he shook one out of the pack. I took it, punched in the lighter, and sniffed it. It was pleasant, like the incense smoke always pouring out of the head shops over on Decatur.

"Let's go get a drink."

"I'm not twenty-one yet."

"You never let that stop you before."

Down There With You was playing. "Where are we going?"

"You'll see."

It was a quiet, dimly lit place with low music and a courtyard that served wine. The interior was decorated with velvet couches, antique Persian rugs, and old cemetery statues. There were rows of old hardcover books on oak shelves, and I longed to browse them. It was illuminated by red and pink lights, giving it the effect of a Bordeaux. We ordered and Troy let me out into the brick-walled courtyard, which was densely covered with tropical plants. A large fountain in the center filtered out any street noise, yet it was close enough to Bourbon Street to hear the revelry that was too much for me. Troy had chosen wisely, but he knew it.

It wasn't until we sat down that I noticed he was drinking water.

"You're not having anything?" I asked, looking at my wine glass.

He shook his head and smiled. "I'm happy to get you anything you want."

I shook off the uneasiness. He was just trying to be cool by buying me a drink. That was all.

"Are you staying?" he asked, a little glint in his eyes that told me he hoped so.

"For now. I suppose I could do some interviews and some writing for the book I'm working on."

"About your parents?"

I nodded.

"Marianne Easton! All grown up and writing and talking to people!"

"Stop it. I hate when people talk about that."

He laughed and lit another clove. Even though I'd be asking questions and getting people to talk about the band, and they'd be doing most of the talking, the idea of interviewing people unnerved me. What if they suddenly focused their attention on me? That's not what the book was supposed to be about.

"I'm just proud of you for challenging yourself. Anyway. Are you seeing someone?"

"I don't have time," I said. I took one of Troy's cloves again and lit it.

"How about we make meeting up a weekly thing while you're here?"

I blew out the smoke and looked down at the clove, enjoying the cauterizing effect it had on my throat. What exactly did he want to do? I knew it wouldn't be just wine and cloves and industrial music every night. He had a plan. I could see it in his eyes, the way they were twinkling with mischief. But how bad could it be? Troy pretty much just wanted sex. They all did. But he had a way of making me feel important. Wanted. And he was part of the reason I was interested in all that stuff at the sex shop, too.

The further we got away from the experience, the more I didn't care for the secret sex we'd had in my bedroom on my eighteenth birthday. But there were times I got the impression Troy wanted something taboo, and after remembering the hold I'd had on him just by wearing something sexy, a light began to flicker in my mind.

I still could not get the image of Troy and Julia I'd seen through the peephole out of my mind. Ever since I saw Julia dressed in that powerful looking latex catsuit, the dim light reflecting off the planes and curves of her normally conservatively dressed body, I wanted something that like that. Something I could wear that would transform me from dowdy to powerful.

When I saw the way she dug her heel into his chest, the way his lips parted in wonder, the way he looked at her, I wanted that, too.

I wanted that thrill. I had glimpsed it through the peephole that night, had gotten that rush of looking into the forbidden world of adult activities, but I wanted to step into it.

He had planted some sort of seed, if only just a notion.

"Fine," I said.

I only caught a flash of a grin, like he didn't want to be too proud of our agreement and overeager.

We finished our drinks, talked about college, and he brought me home. I was hoping to see where he lived, how he lived, if he had a girlfriend. But it never came up. And I didn't ask.

7

I walked through the courtyard, my grown-up high heels clicking on the pavement, smiling to myself and enjoying the lingering nostalgia of being with Troy.

Damn him for being so charming. Damn *me* for being—

What the hell was that in the window up in my bedroom? It flashed by so fast, I couldn't tell if it was Marcus or—

Was that a *woman?*

No, it had to be Marcus, but what would he be doing in *my* room? He had his own room with a window that faced the courtyard. He could just spy on me from his own room if he wanted to.

Fucking nosy little brat.

I stormed upstairs and flung the door open, ready to tear into him. The condo was quiet.

No blue light under the door. I shoved it open.

He snorted awake from his blanket mountain. "What?"

"Were you in my room?"

"No. Fuck off. I'm sleeping. Unlike you, Vampira."

I shut the door.

No. This couldn't be happening. I *did* see something. Or someone.

I opened the door to my room and flicked on the light.

Nothing.

Scratch, scratch.

The presence in the cemetery…the vines…and now, this.

Familiar feelings came back, feelings of dread. My heart dropped into my stomach.

Did I hear sounds like that right around the time I started talking to the twins on the Ouija Board? I couldn't remember.

A strong scent hit me full on. I dry heaved, the wine and the cloves combined to create a toxic burn in the back of my throat. I ran to the bathroom.

I heaved again, and when I came up for air, her scent was still there. That flowery stuff she wore all through high school.

Wait, did Chloe and Vivienne wear the same perfume?

Then it was gone in a trail, followed by a cold sensation—like something left the room.

The feeling of being watched felt violating. My skin prickled. Was that the same person at the window?

I remembered. They had long hair. I wasn't sure if it was a man then, but they had long hair. I remembered it then, parts of it hanging in limp strands, hunched over…

Dead.

Was it Chloe? Vivienne? Both possibilities sent my mind reeling.

Then I guess I passed out. I don't remember what happened, but I woke up to Marcus screaming his head off—and when my eyes focused, I saw why. The bathroom was splattered in blood.

Most of it was on my legs and stomach. I backed away from it, away from Marcus's screaming. The tile was slick with it, the coppery smell fresh, the blood thin and bright red.

"Calm down."

"But—" Marcus sputtered. He held onto the door frame for support.

"It's just my period."

"Marianne," he said, white as a worm, "look at your feet."

They were covered in grime. I had tracked it from outside. There were footsteps out of the bathroom and down the stairs, out our front door. They stopped at the courtyard.

"It rained last night. Where did you go?"

I stared out at the courtyard, the puddles, remembering the figure I saw at the window.

"I don't know."

That was the truth. I didn't know how or what I'd done that night, or if I wanted to know. Marcus wanted to call the police, to see if anyone witnessed me being hurt in some way.

"Please," he kept saying.

It had to be Vivienne. Chloe wouldn't do something like this. Would she?

But she was the one who gave me that goddamned Ouija Board in the first place. That was how all this started. The twins came through on it. This was all her fault. The way she'd chided me about playing on it. She knew living in the shadow of my dead twin brothers was a stain on my life, and she exploited that, didn't she? She probably loved to see me go crazy, so she could push me out of the way. And get Blake. That's what this was all about. Maybe it was her. And now I was thinking about dating her fiancé. Why wouldn't she want revenge?

Then again, Vivienne was such a fucked up person. She hated living in my shadow, I guessed. Her father chose my mother, and even though that wasn't my fault she sure as hell took it out on me. But she had other problems too. Joseph groped her, or who knows what else. And I got paid for it, as she said.

I had read something once about how once you play on a Ouija Board alone, you open yourself up as a channel. Sometimes, the weak can be possessed, it said.

Was I possessed?

Was I that weak?

I opened my closet several times and stared at the board. It didn't have a single burn mark on it.

I stared at blank white pages for days, until they became

entangled with my red typewriter, the black keys, the white letters, the red blood from my period, the black clothing, the bones from the twins, the blood I imagined from Chloe's crash site, the blackness of death. It all became a weird kaleidoscope.

Scratch, scratch. I banged on the wall, hoping to scare the offending creatures away.

Pounding on my door.

"Marianne," Marcus said, flinging the door open. "You're wearing black all the time, you're thin as a rail, and staying out all night. Did you go on a binge or something last night? You know some nosy freak is going to come by and take me away if you don't get your shit together."

Did I go out again? All I remembered was staring at the blank pages.

I wandered back into reality. "Okay. It's just stress from the book. That's all. I'll start working on it tonight. After a nap."

It was the first time in a while that I'd slept for more than two hours. By sunset, I was somewhat rested. I called around and made interview plans.

"I'm going to go out and interview a dive that hosted the band back when they got their start. You should come," I said, throwing on a leather jacket.

"No."

"Marcus."

He pushed his glasses up. "I can drink here. I don't have to go out all the time."

He looked at me, that dark suspicion back in his eyes.

"I'll be back at a reasonable hour. Don't get too fucked up."

He produced a fake grin.

I had questions prepped and things went smoothly, but the whole time, my mind drifted back to that night I saw the face in the mirror. Where had I gone?

I read that stress was a contributor and that sleepwalking can happen, but what was the perfume? I couldn't get it out of my head.

Troy materialized by my side just as I was thanking the owner.

"We have a date."

The owner frowned and left.

"I don't know if I feel up to it tonight."

"Oh no, you promised."

I didn't, actually, but Troy got me drinks. My brain awash with alcohol, I half listened to Troy talk about music, but most of my mind was still fixed on what happened. Was I traumatized from childhood? Or was something possessing me? I still felt that uncanny sense of being watched. I cleared my throat, flustered.

"You're not listening," he said. "You really should check out that new Godflesh album. You'd like it."

"My mind is still stuck on Chloe. And things back at the house," I said, fidgeting with my necklace.

"You still have that," he said, pointing to my neck at the evil eye he'd given me for Christmas.

I couldn't help but laugh at the lesson. I knew what he meant before he said it.

"Don't let negativity get you down."

"You're right. As usual. I need to look out for my brother."

We locked eyes for a beat. He parted his lips like he wanted to say something, and his eyes twinkled with that familiar devious glint.

A thrilling jolt of anxious longing coursed through me, starting at the apex of my thighs and ending at Momma's voice in my head, warning me of the dangers of men.

I broke eye contact and looked down at my feet, the old, goody-two-shoes Marianne rearing her head.

"Can we call it a night? I want to write some of this stuff down before it gets away from me."

He hugged me and said, "Next week."

Proud of myself, I walked the three blocks back home, confident and sure I'd write it all down. But getting a good night's sleep was a different story. It was going to be a long night.

It was around two a.m. when the banging started. I froze, unsure if I should call out to Marcus or go see what the hell it was, banging against the window like that.

Damn that window. What was it with that location? Was it a portal or some shit?

I had been writing on the bed, and scooted forward to look.

It was a crow, hurling itself against the window repeatedly. It saw me and flew away.

I tip-toed out the room. Marcus's light was off.

I went to the bathroom to splash water on my face. When I turned on the light, there she was, right over my shoulder in the mirror. Just a flash.

It wasn't enough time for me to gather any semblance of who it was.

It was a woman, though. Just a silhouette.

"Momma. Daddy. Protect us."

I couldn't think of what else to say.

I went back to my room, wrote down the rest of my notes from the tape recorder, and fell asleep with the light on.

Something was trying to take hold of me. Of that, I was sure. I knew that when I woke up. Was it a ghost, or was it guilt? Both could be demons.

8

I flipped through the magazine again and thought about Troy. I had thumbed through the magazine so many times now, I had it memorized.

There was one image that had burned into my mind, one of a brunette woman in a tight black leather zip-up top. Her hair was cropped short, and she wore deep, red lipstick. She had one arm in a loose chokehold around a shirtless, muscly man with a collar around his neck. She looked at the camera, but he looked up at her.

I knew it was probably intentional for the camera, but it was so well emotionally staged, I could not stop looking at it and wondering what he was thinking. Was he mesmerized by what she was wearing? Or did she say or do something in particular to get him to look at her in that way? What would it feel like to hold that kind of power over someone?

I again thought about the time I'd spied through the hole in the wall and seen Julia. At the time, it almost felt like she was wearing a costume. It fascinated me, the way she had power in that room, but outside of it, she was barely keeping it together.

In the back of the magazine, there were personal ads that I

practically memorized. I liked to imagine what the person on the other end would look like. Were they like they said in the ad? Tall, dark and brutal and looking for a sissy maid? Or small and lithe and looking for a cruel Mommy type? I read them so often I began making up stories about them in my head.

Banging out those imagined scenarios on my typewriter was exhilarating, leaving me feeling like I could explore that world safely without fear of judgment. I'd reread them and experience that riveting, cerebral feeling all over again. Then, I'd stuff them in a folder and hide them in the back of my closet.

Marcus blared music from his room, interrupting my stream of consciousness as I typed out another story about the brunette woman in the leather top.

"Marcus," I yelled. "Turn that down. I can barely think."

I heard a door open and he appeared in the hallway, his eyebrows drawn into a scorn. "It's not like you're doing anything."

"I'm…I'm thinking," I said. But he and I both knew that wasn't true. I was flailing, trying to figure out what to do, embarrassed that he was making more money than I was.

"We're running out of money," I said. "And I need to get a job."

"Ha," he said, crossing his arms and leaning against the doorframe. "No you don't. All you need to do is fuck Blake."

"Marcus," I warned. He was finding little ways to spend lately, like demanding money for new clothes when he could wash the ones he already had, or feeling weak that he hadn't eaten and needed oysters to regain his strength. "Iron deficiency," he'd said, sopping up butter and garlic drippings with his bread.

"What? We're fine. But we'd be better if you just let Blake fund your writing career and let him build you a Barbie house."

"Where Azalea House was."

"So? It'd be a totally different house."

"How do you even know that's what he wants to do, Marcus?"

"I can just tell," he said, a smile playing on his lips. "He has family money. Why not take advantage of a good situation when you see one?"

I put my head in my hands.

"Quit worrying. We're fine."

"We are," I warned again, "but we just need to be conservative."

He rolled his eyes.

Truth be told, I didn't want to go back to Florida, and living in a brand-new house didn't seem so bad. Louisiana had some familiarity to it, like the food and the places I yearned to haunt back in high school. The goth clubs, the Quarter late at night, the music, it all called to me in a way that said it would put black ribbons in my hair and make me a goddess of the night.

The Keys had its own sense of charm, of crumbling cemeteries and classic architecture. New Orleans, however, was a place where debauchery and deviance were welcomed. The Keys was a place where one was expected to become immersed in the turquoise waters and the history, all while upholding a relaxed attitude so as not to ruin anyone's family vacation.

"Why don't you just give Blake a blowjob or something and get it over with?"

"Jesus Christ, Marcus. Why don't you blow him if you want to live here so much?"

"Excuse you?" Marcus flared. His face flushed red and his eyes went dark.

"What? Why are you so mad?"

"Don't go around accusing *me* of being the promiscuous one here," Marcus said. He folded his arms across his chest and jutted his chin at me.

"Calm down," I said. "I just don't see why we can't stay here. I don't really see the appeal of staying in some cookie cutter house out in the sticks."

"What? The only payoff being that you'd live in a new house, but on Azalea House's old grounds? That doesn't sound bad to me."

"But what will you do?"

He shrugged. "Live with you and keep doing web stuff. I can earn my keep. I'm not stupid, you know. You're the one who thinks zombies are going to come up out of the yard and eat you. You're way too into all that goth stuff lately."

Now it was my turn to roll my eyes.

"We'll stay if I can hustle up some writing. Okay? I'll work something out so we can stay here in the condo, at least."

He grinned like he'd won. He stalked back to his room and slammed the door. The music blared again just as someone banged on the front door.

Blake. Of course. He was holding brightly colored presents.

Books. First editions. He had chosen wisely. Of course.

I ran my hands along the spines.

Louisa May Alcott's *The Candy Country*. Kate Chopin's *The Awakening*. Charlotte Perkins Gilman's *Herland*.

"Thank you."

"Sure thing," he said, grinning. "I called some bookstore and told the lady there you were into all that feminist stuff. So she picked those out."

"They're wonderful."

Blake eyed me, a flash of concern crossing his face. "Why don't you come and see the plans for the house?"

"Why would I want to live out there again? Blake, I hated it there."

"You hated the way it was," he said. "But you'd like it with a pool and your own office. Your own library. Think about it. It's got so much potential. You'll never think about your family there, because everything will be new. New house, new life, new memories."

Family. Why did he have to bring up family?

And why did he have to bring up a pool? I was terrified of water.

"I don't know," I finally said. "Why couldn't you just live somewhere else?" I asked, pleading with my eyes.

"You know how my dad is. I need to stay nearby. It's the best piece of land in the area, Marianne. Believe me, I know." He fiddled with his cufflinks and smoothed his jacket, as if to say, look at me. I already know lots about real estate. Look how fancy I am in my clothes.

"Besides, I need you. I need your planning, your creativity. Think of it," he said, his eyes full of fantasy and his hands framing an imaginary scene. "You drive up to a grand, modern house with beautiful gardens and a glorious front porch for reading," he said, winking at me. "You'd walk in and there would be books everywhere, floor to ceiling. We can even get you one of those sliding ladder things. And you could even design secret rooms if you want, where you could keep all your creepy books."

Something stirred within me, reminding me of the time I had crept down the secret staircase at Azalea House to discover a peephole into my parents' bedroom. All those times spying on Troy and Julia. And now I was meeting up with Troy all the time. It felt like I was cheating on Blake, even though we weren't together yet. And now we were sitting here, envisioning our future.

I had done damage, just like my mother. My charming, too much mother with her crystal voice and her drop dead gorgeous looks. The way her aura just sucked you in and left you empty. I had done it. I had choked the life out of the only person who maybe loved me.

At least Blake didn't want my money. And he wasn't even pressuring me to have sex. In a way, he was the only man in my life who didn't want something from me other than to take care of me. I could do no wrong by him. He forgave me for everything. I watched him, glassy-eyed, as he babbled about the house plans.

"So will you do it?"

"Do what?"

"Help me design the house," he said, his head cocked. "At least pick out some books I can get you so you can keep them there if you decide to come visit."

I couldn't help but smile. He'd do anything to make me happy.

"Fine," I said. "I'll throw in my input. But I'm not making any promises."

He put his hand over his heart and smiled at me as if he'd won.

"How are you doing?" It didn't feel right to ask, as if bringing up his fiancée and child was a taboo. I shrunk back as I asked, afraid of the answer.

His smile dropped. I regretted bringing it up.

"Not good. It's Christmas. They're on my mind, that's for sure. I bought both of them presents over the summer. I can't believe it's been almost four months."

"I know," I said, really meaning it. I was starting to forget what Chloe even looked like.

"But I've been in counseling. Still, coming back to my parents' house is the hardest part. I guess that's why I want to hurry up and get this house going. It'll keep me busy. I have to look forward to the future, Marianne. I don't have anything else."

He glanced at me, his eyes glossed over with tears.

"I'm sorry for bringing it up."

"You're the only one who asks," he said, wiping his eyes. "You and Marcus, anyway. How are you both doing?"

"I guess I'm already jaded," I said, half laughing. I'm doing some things that might be out of character, or they might really be a part of me, I wanted to say. Marcus is drinking his feelings away, I wanted to say.

Blake looked at me in a strange way.

"I know it's a lot of pressure to get you involved in the house plans. And pressuring you to give me a chance. You probably thought it was weird."

I didn't say anything. It was weird.

"But I'm coming to grip with things. And that means moving on," he said, lighting back up. "And I'd still like to do that with you—"

Marcus walked down the steps and made a beeline straight for the present.

"You're both smiling. I've never seen that before," he said, ripping through the paper. "Thank you, by the way. This is going to work out great," he said, patting the box and looking at Blake.

"Sure thing, buddy," Blake said. He bolted up, straightened his jacket, and patted Marcus on the back. "See you, sweetheart." He saw himself out.

I said nothing. Blake really bought Marcus a computer. I stared, hoping to melt him into the floor.

"What?" Marcus said, his tone accusatory.

"Here we go."

"You wouldn't get me one."

"Are you going to milk Blake for everything?"

He shrugged. "If you won't."

"Damnit, Marcus. We're going to be indebted to him. Hell, we already are."

A NEW YEAR lurked around the corner.

It was getting dark. I shrouded myself to blend in with the shadows, pinning my hair back into an intricate braided bun, swiping on black eyeshadow and taking my time to make sure my makeup was perfectly in place.

I mustered up enough courage to wander back to the sex shop in search of more magazines. I didn't know what answers they would hold. But something pushed me there.

"I remember you," the cashier said. "You were in here looking like a lost puppy."

I shrugged one shoulder and she found that hilarious for some reason. The shop was empty.

"What do you do?" she asked.

"Not much lately. I'm trying to find some work."

"What kind of work?"

"Writing. Journalism. That, or I guess I can start stripping on Bourbon."

I hadn't felt this comfortable talking to someone in a long time.

She laughed again, leaning over the counter, her jewelry clinking together as she did so. She had on a lot of it. Four hoops in each ear, rings on all her fingers. She looked like she could be in a music video.

She leaned down and pulled out more glossy magazines.

"You could write for one of these."

Had she read my mind? Did she know I obsessively read all the stories, all the ads? The mischievous grin on her face said she did.

I stepped over to the counter. She smelled like clove cigarettes. Her black lacquered nail pointed to an ad for an erotica writer.

"You use a pen name. Like a guy's name. Or a woman's. Whichever. I'd pick something gender neutral. Makes it more mysterious."

"So, not Marianne?"

She shrugged. "If you want. If you're not afraid. Or you could just use 'M.'"

I glanced up at her. She smirked. "My name's Victoria. But everyone calls me Vic."

I slid the magazine closer and flipped through it. "I make up stories in my head reading these personal ads." I looked up at her again. Her blue eyes glimmered. "But I don't know much about this lifestyle."

"Why don't you come back here after the shop closes? I get off at midnight. I'm going to this place after work. You should come with me."

I thought about Marcus home alone at the condo. "I don't know," I said.

"Come on," she said, giving me puppy eyes. "It's New Year's Eve."

I looked around the shop, at all the sleek black clothing, the shiny sex toys, the glossy magazines. Everything so bright and new and—

"Magazines are nice and all, but seeing it come to life is totally different. You'd learn a lot." She grinned, but something wicked played in her eyes, something riveting, something that told me she knew the Quarter's secrets and wanted to share them with me.

I didn't hesitate. "I'll be here."

The way she said 'this place' filled me with a tingly sense of intrigue. I had never really gone anywhere with a friend before. Chloe and I only went to each other's houses, and my only outings beyond the village while in high school were with Marcus or Troy. When I graduated, I spent time traveling alone, but when I landed in the Keys, it was like I needed to put my feet up and rest while avoiding people.

I waited outside as she closed the shop. We walked, the unseasonably warm French Quarter air a sensual caress.

"Where are we going?"

A slight smirk. "You'll see."

"How did you end up working at a place like that?" I asked, gesturing back at the shop with a head nod.

"They'll take anyone. I just need it to fund my art, that's all."

"You're an artist, too? I sketch sometimes, but my main thing is writing."

"I have a gallery opening next week. You should come."

"Okay," I said, hoping not to sound too eager.

We arrived at a nondescript place with double wooden doors. There was a well-dressed man standing outside.

"I forgot to ask, you're eighteen, right?"

"Nineteen." I pulled out my ID.

I wanted to ask her again where we were, but I had a feeling it was better to see it for myself. Music thumped beyond the door as the man checked our IDs.

He slid the heavy door open and we were soon swallowed by music and flashing lights. I blinked to adjust my eyes.

What I saw had my heart pounding with shock and wonder. I had almost dressed appropriately. Most of the other people in the club were wearing black. That is, the people who were wearing clothes.

I followed her, or the trail of her, through shiny black latex and squeaking leather, trying to keep my focus.

There were bodies everywhere, undulating to the beat playing or just to whatever was in their heads, pleasure pulsing through them, causing their bodies to writhe in ecstasy to the music. Some were even off to the side of the dance floor, obscured by darker shadows. A woman in nothing but thigh-high boots whipped a half-naked woman who was fellating a masked man. In another corner, two men were having sex. I tried not to stare, but the wild atmosphere had my heart hammering in my chest, almost as if the music's beat had wormed its way into my heart. It was as if everyone checked their inhibitions at the door. I swallowed back a bout of nervous shaking, and what remained was a dizzying, drunken feeling. It made me giddy.

I wanted more of this feeling.

We walked up a set of stairs. Immediately at the top was a closed off room with a glass window.

"We can see in," Vic said. She pulled something out of her purse. A flask. She took a long swig. "But they can't see out."

I moved closer. It was an orgy room, and the people standing on the outside were voyeurs.

"They…like to be watched?"

"That's what makes it exciting."

I felt so stupid, just wearing the clothes underneath, yet not really participating in something like this. I had a sudden urge to tell her about Troy, but decided against it. Would she know him? I wondered if she was better at controlling herself than I was, better at delivering pain and pleasure.

"Do you want to go in?" she asked. My chest swelled with anxiety. I shook my head and she smiled slightly, turned on her heel and went around to the side door of the room. I stepped closer to the window, mesmerized.

She never removed her clothing, but a couple immediately pulled her onto the main circular bed. Vic pushed the woman down and straddled her, pressed her shoulders down and bent to kiss her. My chest still fluttered with a strange new sort of anticipation, the kind I had experienced at the cheerleader's house in high school.

The girl's partner just watched, touching himself as the events unfolded before him. Vic maintained control the entire time, not letting the boy touch her, but feeling the girl up and keeping her still.

Watching seemed too intimate, like I was a fly on the wall in Vic's bedroom. I had no idea she was into women. Were we friends? Or did she go into the room because she needed to get off, and I was being too stiff?

That shy, nervous sensation welled up in me again, and I could not swallow it back. I was watching again, not participating, and it was almost like the sensation of being back in the closet at Azalea House, feeling out of place.

I wanted to do *something*, anything, but the petrified sensation anchored me to the floor.

I wanted to be like Vic. I wanted to do things that would please her. But in a friend way. I didn't want to hook up with her. That would ruin our friendship, wouldn't it?

Or would it bring us closer together?

I was so lost in thought that I almost didn't hear the meek words whispered in my ear. I turned around.

"Hello," said a lithe boy in leather shorts and a spiked collar. I swallowed, wondering what he wanted. He kneeled before me.

"What…"

"I am yours, Mistress," he muttered.

A couple of latex-clad women beside me burst into laughter. "You can take him into a room and do whatever you want with him," said the taller black woman. "Here," she said. She fished around in her bag and pulled out something that made a jangling sound. "You can borrow this." I didn't realize what it was until she put it in my hand. A leash.

"In there?" I asked, my head spinning.

She pointed to a hallway. "Private rooms are down there."

I looked, blinking like an idiot. A private room to do whatever I wanted with a stranger. I clinked the leash clip on his collar and pulled slightly. He followed, obedient and ready.

Once inside the room, he knelt again.

"I don't really know anything about this except for articles I read. My uh…friend dragged me here."

"Oh," he said, blushing. "You can do anything you want. I can take it."

"What do you like?"

He glanced up and looked around the room. "Anything you like."

I sighed. Why were people into this? Troy was so obvious about the things he liked and didn't like. Everything that happened with Carina the cheerleader seemed natural, carefree. How could I get into likes and dislikes when I didn't even know myself?

"Get on the bed," I ordered. Intuitively, it felt right to order, not ask.

He hopped up like an eager puppy. I straddled him, my fingers pushing the leather collar aside. I pressed my fingers into the delicate skin on his neck, that old feeling of flesh yielding beneath the pads of my fingers as satisfying as any food or drug or feeling I'd ever experienced.

His eyes bugged.

It was then that something swirled around me, spinning until it entered me, through my eyes, my nostrils, my throat. It inhabited me. It took up residence in the attic of my brain. And it squeezed the flesh, harder and harder until it divided itself into another being. Like a twin sister that dwelled inside me.

The other part of me, the real me, Marianne, could see what was happening. But the physical part of me, the occupant, had control. I screamed. The boy let out a gurgly yelp. He thrashed beneath me. I was only vaguely aware of his skin, slick with the tangy sweat of fear.

A noise. Shouting. The sounds were far away, almost like they were on a television set on the other side of a house, muffled by walls. My line of vision twisted away. I saw faces. Angry, concerned, scared.

And then I saw Vic.

"What the hell were you doing?" someone shouted. "You could have killed him."

Me. I almost killed him.

But it didn't feel like me.

I looked around the room at the sea of faces. The bass thumped away, sounding like a war drum.

Then it all went black.

"It's Y2K!" someone screamed.

Hysteric, high-pitched voices reverberated around me. I put my hands on the wall to steady myself.

A click nearby. There was Vic's face, illuminated by a cigarette lighter's glow.

"Let's bail," she said. I took her hand.

We stumbled through the dark, Vic leading the way. When she flicked her lighter again, I saw a familiar face by the exit.

Marcus.

He was standing by a breaker box with a maniacal grin plastered on his face. He waved at me before disappearing into the shadows. I saw a dim slice of light from a side exit door, then his lanky silhouette fled from the club.

That brat.

9

"It's okay. He'll be fine," Vic said. She linked arms with me and patted my shoulder.

"I don't know what came over me." I had to look down at the ground to avoid tripping. I was still shaking.

"You just need training, that's all."

I looked at her. "You forgive me?"

She broke out into laughter. "I've done worse, trust me. I almost suffocated some guy by putting a bag over his head." She shrugged. "He said he wanted it. But you have to know when to stop. I can show you a few things."

"It felt like something took over my body…" I cut myself off. No one ever understood the things I saw, what I felt.

"Hormones?" She laughed again. "We all get a little overzealous at times. Here," she said, retrieving a pen and an old K&B Drugstore receipt from her purse, "this is my number. Call me when you've cooled off and you're ready to learn more. You can come by the shop when it's closed and I can show you a few things. See you around."

"See you," I said, my voice weak. The number looked real,

her name spelled out in spidery writing, with a little devilish smiley face next to it.

I walked back in a daze.

"Marcus!" I screamed once inside the safe confines of the condo.

I was alone, though. Fine. He could black out the entire city for all I cared.

"You have mail from the other day," Marcus said at my door the next morning. I jumped out of bed and pulled on my robe, threw the door open and snatched the envelopes out of his hand. "Good morning to you, too," he murmured. But I was too focused on the mail.

My heart dropped as I read.

"What is it?" Marcus asked.

"Rejection letters."

He looked at me with a blank expression. "For the book," I said.

"Oh. Sorry. Maybe you should get some other sort of job."

I stuffed the letters in my bookcase and sighed, defeated. I resigned to write some stories for the magazine today. Maybe my adventure from the previous night would generate something. Anything. We really needed money, and Marcus making more than I was at his age was beginning to eat away at my ego.

"So," I said, looking him square in the face, "what's up with that stunt you pulled last night?"

That grin was back.

"Marcus!"

"What? It was just a prank, Marianne."

"Don't follow me again."

"You're always out. I just wanted to see where you were going."

I didn't ask how he got in. I put my head in my hands, rubbed my eyes, and shut the door in Marcus's face.

I decided to call Troy, to see if he had made it to work yet. I needed someone to tell me I was good enough, to tell me I was pretty. As I was walking to the phone, though, it rang.

"It's me," Blake said in his usual holier than thou tone of voice. "I'm in the city. Let's meet up for lunch."

He was helping us so much, I felt obligation gnaw at my stomach.

Even though I hadn't had any alcohol with Vic the night before, I felt hungover. I barely touched my food as Blake yammered away about house plans.

"I want you to help me pick out some things for the house. And I want your insight on the layout."

"Why?"

"Because it's important to me. Because I need a woman's opinion."

I almost told him to get his mom to do it, but I forced a smile and said yes.

Soon, we were back at the property, Blake chattering on about color schemes. I clutched my stomach, gritting my teeth as a bout of nausea gripped me out of nowhere.

"What are you thinking for the exterior? I was thinking something modern—"

"Yes," I said, swallowing back bile. "I think that sounds wonderful."

"What color exterior?"

I sifted through my mind. "White." It was the first color I could think of, the color I focused on when I was afraid. And now, I was so afraid, my heart leapt into my throat, threatening to steal my voice again like it always did when I was a child. But there was nothing here.

"I'm meeting the architect out here in, oh—" Blake glanced at his watch. Expensive, probably Cartier. "Less than an hour. You have an eye for this stuff. I would love your input."

"Alright." I swallowed and nodded.

"Are you okay?" he asked. "You look a little pale."

"I'm fine. Do you mind if I take a walk around for a minute?"

He shrugged. "Not at all." He turned his back and strolled away, probably thinking I needed a minute to grieve the property.

Not at all. Nausea had me trembling, and I didn't want to

vomit in front of him. As I walked away, I sputtered and coughed up bile. I spat on the ground.

That smell. A memory, fresh as the morning, hit me head-on.

It was of Vivienne's suicide. She'd been living with Marcus and me, along with her mother Julia, as well as Troy, after my parents' accident. Abusive and manipulative, she was a constant source of misery to herself and everyone around her. I wasn't surprised that day I found her hanging from the shower rod in the bathroom, but what I'd forgotten about was the smell of urine and bile. As I looked up at her, it trickled out of her mouth and stained the front of her nightgown. I stared, but the smell was what had made me so hysterical. It was the smell of fresh death.

And now, no matter how far I walked from where the house used to be, it assaulted my senses. It was all around me in a cloud. I broke out into a run towards my twin brothers' resting place.

A rumble above. When I looked up, the sky was blotted out by black clouds against a slate-gray sky. The first droplets fell, cooling my burning skin.

It began to rain, washing away the stench. Then it rained so hard my feet began to sink into the ground. When I tried to move, the mud held tight to my shoes, suctioning me further into the muck. Soon, I was calf-deep in it. I screamed for Blake, but I was cut off by a boom of thunder.

As my jeans were ripped away by roots, I felt something coil around my leg, tightening itself into a vice. I flailed around in the mud, yanking away earth and plants, but as soon as I pulled them away, they were back again, larger, stronger, as if they had been waiting, resting deep underground until the rain renewed their strength. The very earth around this place wanted revenge, wanted to make its screams heard.

I yanked the last bit of slippery bark away from my leg and bolted back to the clearing. I saw Blake's car through the screen of pine trees. It stopped storming.

"What happened to you?"

"We can't build anything here! We can't!"

"Marianne, what do you mean? What are you talking about? Come into the car. Dry off."

I panted as he held me by the shoulders.

And then he said those magic words: "It's going to be okay."

God, I needed to hear it. I needed to hear it from someone other than Troy. I fell into Blake's arms and sobbed. "I don't know. I don't know what I mean. If you build here or if I run away from it or come back to it, it always haunts me."

"This place?"

Yes, this place. The past. All of it. Maybe he was beginning to understand me. I had that parallel past in common with Blake, someone my own age, someone who never presented a problem. Maybe he really did care about me and Marcus. I pressed against him. He told me again that it would be alright.

"Come to the car," he said.

He sat on the driver's side and I sat in the passenger seat, but unlike when I was with Troy all those times, there was no barrier of age and inappropriateness, no awkwardness of our situation. Perhaps fate brought me to Troy for a lesson in lust, and it brought me Blake for a lesson in practicality.

"I'll make sure you're safe, Marianne."

Chloe's face flashed across my mind. He hadn't protected her. Or the baby.

But what good could a young teenager do? What could I have done differently?

We had both lost someone. Troy was a spoiled brat and a mooch.

Blake put his hand on my neck and I leaned into his palm. I closed my eyes and he kissed me. It was my first kiss with a guy other than Troy.

He crouched into the back seat and pulled me back there with him. Soon I was wrapped up in his whispering assurance and strong hands.

Was this what sex was supposed to be like? Tender, loving and…normal? With Troy, he just took it. With Carina, it was weird, but natural. It was different than the other times I had sex, yet something still felt missing. Even after it was over, something wild within me stirred in its cage, restless. Unfulfilled.

"We should get dressed," I said, rummaging through the clothing pile. Anything to avoid meeting Blake's sickly-sweet gaze. "That architect is coming and—"

"One thing first," he said. He reached over and rooted through his clothing, pulled something out of his pocket.

My heart dropped into my stomach. A small velvet box. I gulped.

He looked into my eyes and opened the box.

It was my mother's. He had replaced the ruby and all the little pearls around it. My head spun.

"What's this?" I asked with a constricting throat.

"It's only an engagement ring if you want it to be. I found it in the rubble and replaced some things on it, had it cleaned up."

I had totally forgotten about it. I had left it at Azalea House in haste.

"We're so young—"

"You can't deny it. We have something. You can look at it as a 'will you move in with me' ring. And I can get you a real ring when you're ready."

Oh God.

But how bad could it be?

He slipped it on my finger. Doom radiated at that ruby gemstone and crawled up my arm, a spreading burn. I swallowed it down. What good were those sensations anyway? Be practical, be practical, my brain hummed.

"What about the insurance payout from the fire?"

"I'll take care of it."

"My grandmother wants to take over everything," I said, my breathing getting shallow and uneven. "She wants to take everything from me."

"I'll take care of it."

"You will?"

"Marianne," he said, his eyes lovey dovey, "my father is the best in the business. I just sold a multimillion-dollar house. We can handle everything."

"Okay. I'll move in with you."

He kissed me softly on the lips as the architect pulled up in the driveway. He didn't need my money. He just needed… me.

After that, once the paperwork was signed, things moved so fast, it was a blur.

10

Days later, I was back in Troy's arms again.

He hugged me again in front of the condo on Esplanade, the familiar Mercedes chariot ready to take me away from all my adult responsibilities.

I couldn't resist him. He was addictive, and always swirling around my mind like some incubus. When I actually slept and dreamt, I dreamt of Troy. We had only been together that one time. Was it the intimacy of it I craved? Or did I want to do the secret things we did in the kitchen again? Pushing up against him, my hands on his neck…would that kind of power help me segway into total power over my life?

Couldn't I just practice on him?

That wouldn't be so wrong, would it?

I wouldn't be cheating on Blake. We weren't together, yet, and I didn't think I even wanted us to be. Wouldn't New Orleans be the perfect place for a music writer anyway?

It seemed right in so many ways, and damned in all the wrong ways.

Now that my mind was more focused on him, that same veil of pheromones swirled around us.

"Where do you live?" I asked as I nuzzled into his chest.

I didn't mean to blurt it out. But I had to know.

He pulled away, held me by my shoulders, smiled in his typical devilish way and said, "Warehouse District. You should see it."

We drove there. Troy stood back and watched me as I dug through shelf after shelf of vinyl.

"Have you eaten?"

I shook my head. He didn't say anything about my weight, which was another thing I liked about him. Everyone else made some snide comment or said they wished they were this skinny. I wasn't even trying. The weight just fell off.

We talked about the book. Vivienne. Julia. Then, he gestured to my neck. Lower than that.

"That's an interesting top you're wearing. It's leather."

I shrugged.

"It…reminds me of something."

"I thought it might."

And then it just happened. I sauntered over to him, pushed him against the couch, and grabbed his hands. He ran them up and down the sides of my waist, feeling the leather. He pulled my hands over his throat. I hesitated.

"Do it."

That was all I needed. I squeezed, his flesh hot beneath my fingers. He squirmed under me, breathless. I moved over his crotch, feeling the hardness there. He tapped my arm and I let up.

We played this game for a long time, me squeezing him and dry humping him, then letting him up so he could feel me up again.

But it was safe. We never took our clothes off.

It was safe.

Right?

I liked it when he was totally still, dependent on what I would do next.

"So you're really into this?" he asked again as we straightened out our clothes.

"Yes," I said after thinking about it for a beat. "But you didn't—"

"Get off? Sex isn't always about getting off."

"It's not?"

He reached out to me. I took his hand and he led me to his bedroom. This time, he let me do everything I wanted. It was nothing like that time back at Azalea House, when he slipped into my bedroom on my eighteenth birthday and he did everything to me. I didn't say no that time, because part of me wanted it, too. But it didn't feel right.

It was then, in Troy's bedroom, that I finally figured out why. This time, I was the one in control. He lay back and let me explore every inch of his body, hardened by exercise and chiseled by this new healthy lifestyle he'd been leading. My hands left his neck, traveled down his chest, explored his torso, further down, following the soft trail of hair down to the apex of his thighs.

Something took over me, savage and wild, even free. I saw concern etched into his face.

"We can do this however you want," he said, reading my mind.

I pinned his arms by his side and moved on top of him, taking him inside me, fully mine.

Late that night, I walked through the courtyard, everything aching, high on the power, when I smelled that perfume again. It mingled with something metallic and tinny. I winced and ran my tongue over my teeth.

"Slut," a female voice whispered, but it was rattly and raspy. I spun around. Waited.

Nothing but chattering out on the street. A siren from an ambulance a few blocks down. But there wasn't anyone else in the courtyard.

I turned to go inside, but something or someone grabbed me and pulled me.

I was going into the pool. A push. And then I was enveloped by the harsh cold.

The sensation hit my lungs first. I wasn't sure if I tried to suck in air or if it was the cold of the water, but it burned. I headed up and flailed, gasping for breath.

I could feel Vivienne's presence. Her jealousy. It was just like the time she pushed me into the pond outside Azalea House.

"Go away, you bitch!"

I couldn't think of anything else to say. Shaking, I got out and stumbled towards the condo.

It was real. I wasn't going out of my mind. Someone pushed me into the pool.

"What the hell happened to you?"

Marcus was curled up on the couch, a half-eaten pizza on the coffee table.

"Someone pushed me in the pool."

"Who?"

"Vivienne."

Marcus tilted his head and stared at me.

"It's true."

He said nothing, unblinking.

"I'm going to take a shower," I said.

She was there, too. Her energy, the same negative energy she always brought into a room, judging, jealous and nasty.

I showered, still shaking, not quite getting warm enough under the steaming stream.

I had to go back to Azalea House and see what the hell she wanted. If anything, to exorcize her from that place. I'd have to bring the Ouija Board, and talk to her alone. But what could she do? Kill me? I would rather die than live with her tormenting me, invading my life like this.

I called Troy the next morning.

"I need to borrow your car. Please."

"Where are you going? I can drive you."

I sighed. "Shopping?"

"Nice try," he said. I could tell he was smiling. "You're going to do something shady."

"No," I said. "I mean, I was going to try to get some photos of the area around Azalea House."

"Oh. In that case, you're on your own. Take it."

It was half true. I did want to do a couple of paragraphs on the weird history of the house, but delving too far into it wasn't an area I wanted to go into very much. It would make me sound crazy, a stigma I always felt like I was fighting lately.

I told Troy I wanted to use the dwindling light because the golden pre-sunset haze made for magical photographs, but I knew the forces of the plot of land would be stronger at night. The full moon, bold and bright in the sky like a new quarter, allowed me to see well enough.

I sat down in what used to be the garden. Vivienne had a fit right before she killed herself and dug up or chopped down most of it, but some of the benches and statues remained. The statues always gave me the creeps. I'd look at them, then look away, sure I could feel their eyes following me, mocking my fears.

I put the board I'd found amongst the burned rubble on my knees, the planchette in the center. When I rested my fingers on it, it immediately shuddered, like it had been waiting for me.

I half-screamed and yanked my hands away. This was always easier with Marcus, but it was clear he was done with my bullshit about ghosts.

The planchette quickly spelled out, "I-L-L S-T-O-P Y-O-U."

"Why?"

"Because I hate you."

It wasn't the board.

It was a voice behind me.

I didn't turn and look. But I could smell her, stale designer perfume, sweat, urine, grime…and that memory came roaring back, of finding her in the bathroom that day, hanging, swaying.

"I'm banishing you from here," I said. "You made your choice to leave this world. So leave."

It was quiet, save for the distant night birds and frogs croaking down at the overgrown pond.

Maybe I had done it. Maybe I really had banished her. Maybe I was getting some sort of control over all of this.

"I'm going to take him from you. You'll see."

I stood up and spun around, trying to catch a glimpse of her. But there was nothing, nothing at all. She was toying with me, fading in and out of realms in a game of hide and seek.

Shaking, I drove back to New Orleans. Who did she mean? Was it Marcus? Oh, how she and Marcus duked it out, the worst of enemies. Looking back on it, sometimes she tormented him more than she messed with me. She knew it bothered me, that I was protective of Marcus.

It had to be Marcus she was talking about. I stepped on the gas pedal and sped back towards home.

When I arrived, I was stunned to see Blake at the condo. There were beer bottles littering the coffee table.

"There you are," Blake said, chipper than usual.

"I was out doing research."

"In Troy's car, by the way," Marcus said to Blake. What exactly was he trying to start now?

Blake pressed his lips together as I dropped my bag on the floor, scolding Marcus with my eyes. I hated that I did it, too. It would only make things worse if Vivienne were trying to harm him. It would only help drive a wedge between us.

"I came by to see if you wanted to go to dinner," Blake said. "But you stayed out so late."

"Yeah, well, I took my time."

Blake eyed me with a hint of suspicion. We weren't even dating and he was already asking about my whereabouts. I bit my tongue, reminding myself we were staying at this condo while paying next to nothing in rent.

"I'm sorry I missed you," I managed to say, "but it looks like you two have been having a good time without me."

Silence. Awkward silence. A wash of something strange passed through me.

"I'm tired," I said. "I'm going to bed."

"Wait. Stay up with us," Blake said.

I smiled and started up the stairs. But Blake stayed, chatting with Marcus, who was making a point to speak and laugh loudly.

I should have been pleased. I guessed any normal girl would

be. A man who got along with family was a dream come true for most. Especially a man who could calmly take care of things, who was patient, generous.

Vivienne must have been pissed about me messing around with Troy.

That does it, I thought.

I had to stick with Blake. He was the safer choice anyway.

Troy represented a past I wanted to leave behind. Blake was the future, full of possibilities.

11

That night, I had a dream of a great big white house with floor to ceiling windows, clean and fresh and new. The lush lawns accented it. There were white flowers everywhere. Roses. White ginger. White azaleas.

Then the house took on the appearance of some sort of skull, a creature I didn't recognize. The windows looked like eyes, and the columns like great big fangs. It started to roar with a certain sort of fury, a thousand voices screaming all at once. Then it fell black, and I saw pale hands holding something, prying something loose. A hammer. Black again. Then red, everywhere, red, as if the entire dream eclipsed into memories of Azalea House.

When I jumped awake, it was still dark. Blake was passed out on the couch. I jogged out into the courtyard, past the lush plantings and the dripping lion's head fountain, out onto the street, as if trying to run away from the horrid events in the dream.

I crossed Esplanade and walked into the forbidden territory adjacent to the French Quarter, an area where crime festered like an infected wound.

Never cross Esplanade, my mother would say to us on the few trips we took to the city. It's too dangerous.

The city on this side sagged and drooped, sad and used, an old and worn-down place. The sweltering heat did nothing to improve the atmosphere, as if hell seeped up into the asphalt and cobblestone streets and haunted the city.

I dragged my feet. It had rained earlier, and the runoff dripped off balconies and onto the street. In one place, leaks were so intense they had worn the stucco off the side of a building, leaving it looking like melting makeup.

I was then in a part of the city ravaged by kudzu. It crept across the sidewalk, overtaking several houses.

Had I brought this with me? All the suffocating things that still held me to Azalea House, the demon and the vines that tried to hold me down?

A group of goths sauntered past me, laughing, veiled in clove smoke, all perfectly made up, draped in shadows.

Where were they going? I followed them until they disappeared behind a dark entrance, swallowed up by pounding beats and synth. I scanned the room, looking for Vic.

I couldn't help but wonder about her. What made her leave home? Was she a child like me, locked in a castle of a house, the wild animal in her stirring, howling to get out and make a life for herself? I resigned to ask her all about her past.

Surely they didn't have an uncle who bought them an inappropriate birthday present, a white lacy bra and panty set reserved for brides on their honeymoon. Surely they didn't sneak off to the mall and exchange it for a black bustier, and surely they didn't fool around with older, attractive step-uncles.

I left the club, not knowing what to do with my hands, back to the normalcy of Blake and Marcus.

Around every corner, lone wolves flitted away, chased away by the rising sun. I looked down the street to see a man with a Jimmy wedge breaking into a car. I locked eyes with him. He paused briefly, letting the shame quickly wash over him, before he kept trying to pry the lock open, as if I were no longer there.

Everywhere I looked, I caught a glimpse of the underworld, but I could never quite reach it. Maybe someone was protecting me, or maybe New Orleans didn't want to open up its secret oyster shell and allow me to see the pearl inside.

"Girl, you don't need to be over here!"

It was some woman, scantily clad, in towering heels, tottering towards me.

"Why? What's here?"

I had to know more. I had finally escaped the confines of Azalea House. I was teetering right on the precipice of the underground world I so longed to see. I wouldn't give up. I had to find a way to keep this condo and stay down here. I told myself it wasn't to see Troy. I fought that feeling, swallowed it back. I had a friend here now, I had a book to write, articles to delve into, a job to complete.

She looked me up and down, her fake eyelashes fluttering, taking me in, deciding if I was worth it.

Could I have both worlds? Hell to play in, and heaven to stretch out and relax? Daddy always called that having your cake and eating it too. But what was the point of having cake if you couldn't eat it?

"What's wrong with *you*? You on something? Huh?"

"On something?"

I looked down at my hands. They didn't look like my hands. And I had an unlit cigarette wedged between my fingers.

Something was happening to me. Two inner voices—one striving for evil deeds and one trying to right my wrongs, fought inside of me. New Orleans brought my darkest secrets to the surface, encouraging the worst in me to emerge. But the old Azalea House property was trying to kill me, or trying to absolve me of my sins by bringing up the past and trying to tie me down. It felt like it wanted me to be buried in its ground like every other tortured soul who had passed through there.

"You looking to score? You looking for a pimp?"

"What?" I asked. The lady looked me up and down, shook her head, and tottered away.

I wanted to tell her I just wanted to see what was on this side of New Orleans. And I thought I found it. Esplanade just split it in two, dividing what was deemed good and shiny from what was bad and sinful.

I wandered back to the condo, wanting to be alone, but I knew Blake would be there waiting for me. No matter where I turned, there was someone there, wanting something from me—my time, my money, my body. I couldn't just be. I couldn't just exist as a friend. I had a friend at one point, and now she was dead. I just wanted uninterrupted time for me, no brother spouting off shit about his narcissistic problems, no extended family beating down my door for whatever scraps I could give them, no male suitor trying to fuck me or get whatever they could out of me, attention or energy. I wanted none of it. I just wanted to be alone.

Images of walking out into the Azalea House grounds' swampy area flooded my mind, sinking, down and down, until the until the alluring appeal of the cool mud swallowed me up and overwhelmed me. Drowning like my twin brothers. There was so much to juggle, it seemed, so much to life that I didn't have a grasp on. Plenty of other young women under the age of twenty-one in my hometown were getting married. What was so different about me all this time that made me not want to do the same things as other people? Other women would kill for this much attention, attention I thought would eventually kill me.

I was almost at the gate when I noticed a bright red BMW parked in front. It still had the stickers on it.

"It's yours. Happy birthday."

Blake was leaning up against the wall, waiting for me.

"I went up to your room, but you were gone. I was about to come looking for you."

I blinked stupidly. "Vivienne had one like this."

"Oh," he said, standing up straight. "I didn't realize that. I'll return it."

How was it already my birthday? Surely, he meant this as an early birthday present. But when I looked around, Japanese magnolias were unfurling, their citrusy, floral scent filling the air, signifying spring.

"No," I said. When I looked at the car, all I saw was blood. "It's fine."

"Really?" His face lit up again.

I forced a smile. "Yes. Really. Thank you, Blake."

"Now you won't have to borrow his car again."

His car. He couldn't even say his name.

"I have some things to do," he said, looking at his watch, "but meet me in the village tomorrow. They have the foundation down, the framing up, everything. You'll love it."

That fast? When did they get started building the house? How much time had passed?

"Get some sleep," Blake said, his face washed out with concern. "You look tired."

Lying in bed, my exhaustion immediately took me to a different place. I had dreams about my mother, things I had forgotten about, strange things she did before she died. After I had brought up the twins, she fell into long bouts of depression that lasted for days. Normally, she'd either keep Azalea House sparkling clean or have someone come by to take care of it, but when she was in these moody episodes, it fell to the wayside. Clothes would be strewn all over the floor, her bathroom products scattered everywhere, dishes piled up. Marcus and I would do them as she slept in her dark room, alone. The more I thought about it, the more I remembered that she and Daddy were never really around each other. They had good times, yes, but I wondered how much fighting and making up they did over the years. Whatever it was like, they sure did a good job keeping things secret.

Even though she was locked away in another room, her low vibrations permeated every corner of the house, like her spirit was haunting the hallways, wanting everyone else to mourn her life with her. But there was nothing to mourn. She asked for all this, she was born to be famous and sing, she had that sparkle, that charm. If she didn't want it, why did she pursue it so hard?

I inherited more than my mother's money. She also bequeathed me her depression. I should have been happy about the way things were going for me. I never had to work again if I didn't want to, never had to deal with family again if I didn't want to. Never had to lift a finger. Blake would take care of it all. But it was a life of no ambition. And when you're not growing, you're dying a little more each day.

I didn't realize how much it affected me until much later, when we moved into the condo together, after I had visited the remains of the house. How tumultuous their lives had been, hiding from people who wanted to scrutinize them and fabricate lies, and dealing with their own inner demons while being married and in a band together. Maybe they had kept it together just to keep up appearances.

Troy called. "Julia's talking about doing an interview," he said.

"What?" I sat up in bed.

The truth about my mother's affair still hadn't come out in the press. Fucking Julia! She was always after attention, anything to take away from my mother's glory. I could feel it coming.

"I have to get the book out first."

"I know." I heard him sigh into the phone. "I've been distracting you."

The world knew Julia drowned my brothers, but they didn't know why. If Julia landed an interview from prison, who knew what she'd say? I felt like I was playing chess and didn't know her next move.

"I thought I would tell you before you heard about it in the gossip rags," he said. "When will I see you again?"

Family, always weighing in on me. Making my decisions for me, telling me how to dress or what I should do. Take good care of Marcus. Do this, do that, give me part of your inheritance, sleep with me, do this for me.

These days, it seemed Troy didn't want anything from me except that true part of myself, that part that wanted some sort of control over my life. He wanted to tease it out, to help me become more complete.

If I was to be the head mistress of the new house, I would have to keep visiting it again, to take it over and try to tame it.

As I DROVE to the village, an ominous dark cloud formed on the horizon.

When I arrived, there was an electricity in the air, so strong my flesh prickled and my hair stood up. Blake wasn't there yet. Everything was still, the only sound faraway rumbling from angry storm clouds. I walked past the foundation, down the overgrown trail to the graves where the twins were. Everything was covered in either poison ivy or kudzu, like a swamp monster's green hair, like it wanted to strangle the life out of any remnants from that place. I could barely make out the indentations of their graves underneath the overgrowth.

I thought of Vivienne. Her angry face was forever imprinted on my mind that day right before she committed suicide, when she tore up the garden in a fury. Destroying things for attention came naturally to her, much like upsetting me. She was fiercely jealous for reasons I still didn't understand. She had everything—expensive clothes, a new car, support for her modeling career. But she had to have it all. If I got any attention from anyone else—Troy, the cheerleader, even the unwanted attention from Blake in high school, it was too much for her. That her jealousy drove her to kill herself still haunted me.

I sat down, thinking I'd need to clear the ivy if we built a house here. Perhaps, even if I never moved in with Blake, the twins would be safe here. Maybe I'd even plant something nicer for them. It did help knowing that someone I knew was buying the land and taking care of it. I felt a pull to stay there, so I did.

The first tiny droplets rained down, and distant thunder rolled. Even though it stung my skin, I lay back and relished it, thinking of all the evenings I'd come back here just to escape the house.

It wouldn't be like that ever again. I'd be living with only

Marcus and Blake. I'd have my own bedroom, my own study, hell, even half of the house if I wished. We'd fill in the pond and we'd put a pool out back. I'd get over my fear of drowning.

I began to get lost in the thunder and the drizzle, drifting in and out of daydreaming, when I felt something encircle my wrists.

I opened my eyes. I'd become entangled in some of the invasive vine again. I reached over with the other hand to pull it off.

But I couldn't. My other hand was bound. When I lifted my head to look around, vines were creeping all around me like snakes. I opened my mouth and let out a half-scream that was cut off by more vines.

I flailed and said a silent prayer to make this stop. I was wrapped like a mummy, those vines coiling around me, pulling me down into the ground with all the other decaying things.

It wasn't long before I shut my eyes. I had to. Dirt filled every orifice, my ears, my mouth, and I was enveloped in silence and darkness.

When I regained consciousness, my chest burned for air. I shifted in the earth and found there was some give, but the earth's consistency was slicker. Mud. It had rained even more.

I shifted, moved and thrashed until I grew exhausted and passed out again. I gained consciousness several times to break free of my bondage. When I saw light, a new sense of energy filled me again, and I scrambled until I broke free, gasping for air and pulling the vines off me. They left angry red streaks behind.

The faint sound of laughter. I looked back only once, horrified at the broken kudzu I was leaving behind, terrified that she had somehow done this.

Vivienne was my guilt. She was my past trauma, my abandonment issues, my need to be validated. She was like my evil twin, my shadow self.

I ran away from the graves, bramble and branches scraping my skin. I had been out there all night. The sun was reaching the horizon, casting an early golden shade over the overgrown grounds.

What difference did it make if I was here or any other place? Spirits house themselves in people, not places. I may as well tame this place once again, make it my own, drive the dark forces out and master it. It would be the ultimate form of control for me.

Confident, but sore from the binds left by the vines, I drove back to New Orleans. Blake could do whatever he wanted for all I cared.

"I want to ask what the hell happened to you," Marcus said over his cup of coffee, "but part of me doesn't want to know."

"I want to use some of the money from the sale as a down payment for this condo. I need a sanctuary, some place I can be alone while I'm writing this book."

I could tell he wanted to protest, but he seemed to weigh things by the way his eyes shifted around. "Okay," he finally said.

There were more beer bottles scattered around. Blake had been here again, and they had been bonding over drinking.

"He was worried about you," Marcus said, reading my mind.

"So you both got drunk instead of looking for me?"

"Marianne," he said, closing his eyes again. "You don't exactly say where you're going. He went to the village to look for you. The car was there. But you weren't. You were supposed to meet him there, remember? He came back here and we talked."

Distrust trickled through me, but I pushed it aside, unsure if it was intuition or just old wounds opening up again.

"You talked? You talked!" I began laughing so hard, I doubled over. Somewhere, part of me frantically wondered why I was doing this. What was so funny? "You fucking liar! I'm going to kill you!"

It was like watching my hands through a window. I lunged, grasped his shirt, knocked him to the ground. He screamed and writhed beneath me.

"Marianne! Let me go!"

The occupant in the attic of my mind stepped aside. Marcus's eyes bugged. He backed away, wedged himself into a corner.

"Just clean this up," I finally said after I caught my breath.

I ran upstairs and cried in the shower. I didn't have to live there if I didn't want to. Blake wasn't forcing me to do anything. I could simply design the house, stay there a couple of days a week, and come back here.

I had sought approval from Troy. But I had approval right here, with Marcus and with Blake. Troy just compounded the issues I had by planting seeds of doubt in my mind. Maybe Blake did worry about me and wondered where I went. Maybe he and Marcus were really concerned about me and not just laughing it up and having beers and partying. But it always seemed that way.

Blake had a camaraderie with Marcus. I felt empty, alone, like I was branded with something that said, "Available woman. Take her."

I poured out some of my frustrations in my writing, painting Vivienne as a pathetic attention seeker, which was more or less true. I wrote down some of her good qualities: hard working, wanting to please her mother, always diligent with her grades and appearances. But so much of that led to her demise, too. She worked for her mother, so Julia could brag and tell everyone her daughter was something, that Vivienne was well to do in her own right, not because of Spellbound Hearts. All of it really *was* Julia's fault.

12

Weeks passed. I think. It only seemed like a day or so since I—or someone—had knocked Marcus to the ground.

I rolled out of bed to get ready. I was supposed to meet Blake at the construction site that day.

A wave of nausea passed through my body as I had my first sip of coffee. Not unusual when I didn't get enough sleep.

But this was a psychic flash. Something happened out there. I hopped in the BMW and tore out of the Quarter, a/c blasting, on Interstate 10 in no time.

By the time I yanked the wheel into the driveway, the nausea had bubbled up into my throat. I opened the door and puked up that morning's coffee before I parked closer to the foundation of the new house.

"There's been a horrible accident," Blake said, jogging around to the driver's side of the car, and when I turned my head, I understood his rush to avert my eyes. "Don't look!" But I had already seen it.

Blood. All over the concrete foundation, still fresh and spreading in petal-like pools.

"Some scaffolding broke and…"

"He was crushed," I finished.

The dream I'd had about the house turning into a skull. It was a premonition.

I almost asked Blake about the hammer. But I kept my mouth shut, for fear I'd throw up again.

"This is a bad sign…" I murmured, not really meaning to say it in front of Blake.

"Sign of what?" He took hold of my shoulders and squared me towards him. "Tell me."

"I…I…" I gulped.

"Oh, I didn't know *you* were coming out today." It was Marcus, his voice unusually musical for someone whose house was already tainted with an accident.

"I wanted to check on how things were going. Blake just told me."

Why was Marcus even here?

"Oh. Yes. It's awful! I'm so shocked." Marcus shook his head, one hand on his face, the other wrapped around his torso.

"Marianne," Blake said, his face twisted with concern, "perhaps you shouldn't be here. It's too gruesome. Everyone's packing up and the contractor is giving them some time off anyway after the accident."

"Alright," I said. I drove away, leaving Marcus and Blake standing in the driveway. I looked up in my rearview mirror in time to see them stepping towards each other to exchange words. Marcus threw back his head and laughed.

I expected the nausea I felt to pass as I pulled out of the driveway, but it tightened into a hot iron ball instead. The sun set behind me, sending a streaming kaleidoscope of pink and purple into the blackening sky. The dark outline of New Orleans beckoned with its nightly secrets.

I woke as the sun streamed in through the blinds, my brain feeling like it was stuffed full of cotton.

But hadn't I just driven back? How had I gotten back to the condo, in my bed, and it was already morning?

Nausea knocked on my door again, and I rushed to the bathroom to relieve it.

My skin felt wrinkled and dry. There were angry black streaks of mascara dried on my face, and my lips were smeared with red, like I had been a zombie on a rampage last night.

I scrubbed my face clean, drank water, and set out with my recorder and notebook. I was determined to get some good, honest work done today, despite how awful I felt.

The pages I wrote were a jumbled mess.

I will get inside you. I will be you.

I had written it over and over again.

I had an interview with another bar owner.

I stood up straight and walked towards Decatur, where all the hustle and bustle made me dizzy. The doughy smell of beignets drifted down through Jackson Square, along with turpentine from the artists and incense smoke from the tarot card readers there.

A cold hand on my arm made me yelp. When I looked down, there was a dark hand with red nail polish and lots of sparkling rings.

"There is someone else inside of you, love!" I looked into the woman's eyes, some tarot reader trying to intimidate me into a reading. "Something that dwells within you, something awful!" She pulled me towards her table draped in purple with chicken feathers and crystals, incense swirling in the early spring breeze.

"No!"

I pulled away from her and ran the rest of the way through the Square, weaving through tourists.

When I walked into the cool, dark bar, it provided relief from crowds and strange psychic energy. "There she is," the owner called. I nodded and followed his lead into the back office.

"May I record you?" I asked, even though we'd already discussed it. He nodded, his eyes sweeping from my legs up to my breasts, then my lips, then back down again. He wedged a cigarette in between his lips, his eyes still on me. I shifted in my seat and pulled my dress down over my knees.

"Tell me about when Spellbound Hearts came here to play."

"That was years ago. I might need a drink to remember." He reached down and opened a file drawer, then retrieved a bottle of something amber-colored. He wriggled it my way and I shook my head, ready to begin.

"Okay," he said with a sort of scoff and an eyebrow raise, as if my refusal to drink offended him. I looked around.

He had locked the door.

"Well, Janelle was really kind of carefree. She came in with some booker they worked with, uh…"

"Monica?"

"Yeah," the owner said, his leery grin widening. "They were really flirtatious and kinda hanging all over everyone, you know." Once again with that grin that seemed to be splitting his face in half.

I jotted down notes, ignoring him, but my hands began to shake.

"You kinda look like her."

"Who?"

"Janelle. Long kinda reddish hair, and those legs."

I looked up and through him. And then his hand was there, on my knee, then pushing back the skirt. I rolled the office chair back.

Bang! Bang! Bang! "Keith! Someone's here to see that gal."

"I can tell you more later," he said.

I pushed him away and fumbled with the lock, pushed past the bartender and into another layer of cigarette smoke. Troy was leaning up against the bar, waiting for me.

"How did you know I was here?" God, I was relieved to see him. I threw my arms around him, nestled my nose into his familiar smelling neck. I heard him let out some sort of amused huff, then he bear-hugged me.

"You told me last night, remember?"

"I don't remember. Let's get out of here."

"You were acting weird, strutting around. You drank too much. Don't do that again. Honestly, you were acting like Vivienne."

I pulled back from him to see the expression on his face,

something to tell me he was kidding. It was tightened into annoyance.

He wasn't kidding.

"Oh. Troy. Something's wrong with me." I put my hands on my stomach and dry heaved.

"Come on. Let's get you back to my place."

Once we had traversed the nauseating bumpy streets and arrived at his place, I spent the next hour dry heaving in the bathroom.

Troy left me on the cool bathroom tile. It felt soothing on my burning skin.

"Come on," he said, shouldering his way into the bathroom. "You need to pee on this."

"I am not going that far, Troy," I groaned. He pulled me off the floor and waved the box at me.

"You need to take this."

I reeled. A pregnancy test.

"No."

"Yes. And if it's mine, you're leaving Blake."

I stared at him, woozy, but he got up and left and shut the bathroom door.

I didn't want to take it. But blackouts, nausea…what else could it be?

The tarot reader's face came to mind. Something inside of me…

"Marianne," Troy called from behind the door, "drink some water and take that test." I rolled my eyes and took it. But I already knew.

Just like my mother. Using one man and playing another.

❧

"I can't just leave Blake," I said. We were sitting in Troy's kitchen and he was making me a healthy meal. God, how things had changed since those long days at Azalea House, Troy wandering around the old kitchen, drinking and making things like chocolate chip pancakes. Now he was experimenting with different vegetables and some sort of rice I'd never seen before. His skin glowed, and he looked so young and vibrant. I was sure I looked like something that had crawled out of the Mississippi River.

"Do you want a man to control you?" he asked as he stirred something on the stove. "Or do you want to be in control? Because you could have anything you want."

"He's not controlling me."

"He's building you a dream house. He's financing your career."

"Sounds like I'm the one in charge. It is the perfect situation."

He grinned. There was something all-knowing, almost sad flickering in his eyes. "You wait. I know people like Blake. They always expect something in return."

"And what could *you* offer me?"

"Freedom. He wants to lock you away in a castle. I don't want to control you. I want you to be free. To do your own thing. To be yourself."

"I can do that around Blake. And who says I'm not in control? He's doing everything I want at this point. And Marcus is going to live with us."

"Marcus," he said, laughing. "Of course."

I crossed my arms over my chest. "What is that supposed to mean?"

"Tell me," he said, "how well do they get along? Does it seem like they're always together?"

I thought about the last few times I'd seen Marcus. It was like every time I met Marcus or Blake somewhere, they were always together. My mind swarmed with flies of doubt. What exactly were they doing? Talking about me? Plotting about the family fortune?

"Troy. Tell me what you mean."

"Nothing," he said. I could tell he was trying to stop grinning. I put my hands on his chest and pushed.

"Hey."

"What do you mean by that?"

"Nothing. I was just teasing you. I'm glad your fiancé and your brother are getting along. Really. That's the way it should be." His expression eclipsed into something more serious, and I felt myself relax.

"Blake's not gay or anything. He was a bully because he was going through a rough time in his life."

"I didn't say that. I'm sorry. I was just teasing you. You're so serious all the time, you know."

"We're keeping this separate, Troy. I don't want to talk about Blake or even Marcus around you."

"But...you're family to me," he said, inching closer despite my hands on his chest. He put his hands around mine, his face full of feeling.

"That's the way it has to be if we're going to keep seeing each other."

He said nothing, but I knew I bruised him in a way that only I could.

13

Both men were pulling me in different directions, Troy allowing me to explore the darker corners of my mind, and Blake wanting me to live forever in the daylight. But I wouldn't be able to see Marcus if I decided to stay with Troy. Blake could offer me a perfect life, free of shame.

Memories of the immoral things Troy and I did, formed into icepicks and probed my guts with sharp stabs of anxiety. I reached down and clutched my stomach. If it was so wrong, why couldn't I break away from him?

Marcus and I were still vulnerable kids in a lot of ways, me trying my best to take care of a precocious teenager who had just freed the shackles of his abusive past and disability. He had changed and worked to build a life he was accustomed to. Why would he leave Blake's side after they had built up a chummy relationship? And what was that shit in the driveway, anyway?

"The restaurant owner and his journalist girlfriend," Troy was saying. It did sound very cool. A lot better than playing housewife with Blake. I felt like myself around Troy; the shame was always eclipsed by how carefree I could be, like he had teased the demon out of me.

You reminded me of Vivienne.

How could I crush that memory of her, hanging from the rod in the bathroom? She'd died there in an awful way, her absolute fury eating her alive and winding around her throat. I thought about her rage the day before she'd died. I'd seen her out the window, yanking up the beautifully landscaped garden, her body covered in dirt. I'd seen her like that many times. It was like she was born with some kind of hellfire, hot and explosive.

Maybe she couldn't cope with anything blossoming and beautiful in her world, as though everything tried to outshine her. She always had to make sure she was at the center of everything.

But didn't I feel that way around Troy, too? Something brought it out in everyone, right? It's just that Vivienne couldn't contain hers as well as I had. But maybe I was paying the price now for being contained for so long.

"I can't leave Marcus," I said.

"Marcus is doing fine. If Blake is such a good friend, would he really throw Marcus out in the street? It's time for you to be your own person."

"It's wrong what we did."

"Mari, the divorce from Julia will be final soon. I promise you that. Then there's nothing wrong with what we're doing. It might even bring your work more attention."

I put my head in my hands. "Just what I'm afraid of." I looked up at him. "You don't think what we did back at Azalea House was wrong, Troy? That it led to where we are today?"

He broke eye contact. "Maybe. I don't know. You can't help who you love."

He looked at the floor as if he was struggling with something to say next.

"I don't like Blake for you, Mari," he said, raking a hand through his hair. "He just wants you as a trophy wife. He won't let you be the person you want to be. You know that."

"Don't tell me you haven't met other girls down here."

"No," he said, squaring his shoulders to me, "only you."

I could not do this. I could not do what Momma did to

someone who'd loved her so much. Blake loved me.

I longed for Momma's quiet resolve. I could barely remember how she looked. Her face was fading away. Nothing but green eyes left, framed by reddish hair. Her perfume had faded away, too.

"Marianne, I promise."

God, why? Why did he call me Mari when the sun was still up, then Marianne when it set? It's like he also saw this great split in me, obvious as a New Orleans sidewalk.

"I need a night on my own," I said. "I need to think."

"What is there to think about? You're here now. It feels right, doesn't it?" He stepped forward and tipped my chin up so I could see into his eyes. Dark, seductive eyes that spellbound me and seduced me away from logic. I mustered up enough internal strength to gently push him back.

"I need time."

I should not have looked back at him, at his glimmering eyes and blank expression. It was enough to plunge me into another bout of sadness and confusion.

I left Troy's place with a conflicted, uneasy feeling twisting my heart. My body burned for Troy, but my brain hummed with possibilities of a normal, comfortable future with Blake. I sat in the darkness back at my bedroom in the condo, as if the dark would blot out the rest of the world and help me find a clear, blank canvas.

The next morning, I drove back to the house to see its progress. The framework was up. All one level. No pond. No stairs. Sprawling. A wraparound with a pool courtyard in the back. Very modern. I had chosen white everything. Clean, new, fresh, but with some Italian elements. So not too modern. It was everything I asked for, exactly the way I asked for it. I didn't want it to be too trendy or too Julia. Timeless.

But when I blinked or saw something out of my peripheral vision, it seemed like a skull. Just a nasty part of my mind poking through the clean upgrades. And fitting, considering I had dug through this very earth and found the graves of two twin brothers. I was seeing things. Remembering. Ruminating. That was all. And the thing with the worker was an accident. Accidents happen no matter where you are, even when they tend to find you.

I walked up to the site. Everyone was gone for the day, but Blake's car was there, along with one I didn't recognize.

At first.

Where had I seen that green Jaguar before?

I walked the path to the back.

They had put out a table.

I saw the back of her head first. White and coiffed, like icing. Blake and Marcus looked up at me. Marcus narrowed his eyes.

Lily turned. Her gray blue eyes cut me, icepicks.

"Hello, dear. Blake was just telling me about this house. Congratulations. You've finally developed into a more socially acceptable person."

As if expressing the thought made it so, talking to me as if I were a second-rate person.

"Well? Say something." Lily turned to Blake. "She's always had trouble, you know. I'm so pleased you've taken her under your wing, Blake. She's always needed help."

Enough, I thought, turning around and storming off. And what about Marcus? Why was he sitting there, white wine and ice in his glass, listening to whatever venom she was passive aggressively spewing across the table? And if Blake really loved me, why didn't he say anything? This was to be his house now, wasn't it? And as man of the house, he should have his say!

Troy would have said something. He would have at least come running after me.

I stood by my car, heaving, trying to regain control.

Lily strolled up, her head held high.

"Whatever you have to say, the answer is no," I choked out. Her mere presence felt like claws wrapped around my throat.

"You should be thankful I agreed to come," she said, her red talons clutching her purse. "Your fiancé's father paid me off."

I blinked stupidly. What did she need the money for, anyway? She and Ed certainly had enough of it already.

"I know you've been with Julia's husband," she whispered, her tone frigid. "You used to watch him through the hole in the wall, didn't you?"

I looked up at her, at those tomb gray eyes, and swallowed back guilt. "What?"

She opened the car door to the Jag and tossed her purse inside. "Bessie used to like to spy on her guests. You forget, this house has been in our family for generations. I know a few secrets myself."

"Julia knows," I said, before I caught myself. Something in the devilish glint in Lily's eyes told me Julia had found out about that damn hole in the wall.

"Ha!" Lily said, looking me up and down. "Now she does. My own kids never knew about those damn stairs. I made sure of that, otherwise Janelle would have been all over the place, tormenting the guests. But I damn sure told Julia before you had her locked away. You write your little book, dear. But Julia's story is going to be much better. She and I will see to that."

She climbed in with feline-like grace, started the car, and threw gravel up as she backed out. Once she had driven close to me, she rolled down the window. Her eyes were covered with sleek sunglasses. "One other thing," she said with a slim cigarette between her red lips, "stay the hell away from Troy."

With that, she roared down the driveway.

Blake came strolling around, hands in his pockets. "Hi," he said.

"Hi? How could you just come around here and say that to me! You know I can't stand her!"

"Maybe you should try and get along with the family you have left, Marianne."

"Why? Because it looks good? Is that all you care about?"

"Of course not," he said with sharpness cutting through his voice. "You should know that by now."

"I'm tired of everyone treating me like a goddamn helpless child! I'm tired of your stupid Barbie doll fantasies in this ridiculous place! I'm tired of being perfect for you! I want to break up, Blake. You're nothing but a fucking fake, and I see right through what you're trying to do. Tell me, Blake. Did Chloe flee from you in the middle of the night? Where was she going? She had a lot of stuff in her bag, didn't she?"

"You stop this right—oh God," he said. I followed his eyes down to my thighs. I was bleeding, covered in blood. It was so much it spattered onto the gray driveway.

A vicious pain ripped through my abdomen. I imagined something eating through my insides, tearing at it with tangled skeleton teeth.

"The baby," I said, falling back onto the car.

"What—" Blake's voice faded, and all I heard was the wind rushing through the overgrown grounds, howling like a tortured soul.

Everything went black, but I felt something warm and viscous in between my legs. Pain bloomed in my right shoulder and my abdomen, which drew me in and out of consciousness.

I was vaguely aware of what was happening. A strange sense of loss began at that spot in my womb and clenched my heart. It flowered around my brain, too. I had been confused at the prospect of a child, but too afraid to face the reality. After I had seen the positive lines on the test at Troy's, I stored it away in the attic of my mind with the demon and all the other things I didn't want to deal with.

But now, as I danced in and out of the rooms of consciousness, I began to accept that truth, a truth full of numb, cold grief.

I woke up in the emergency room.

"Why didn't you tell me?"

It was Troy's. I knew it was. But Blake thought it was his. The hurt look in his eyes told me so.

Or was he thinking of Chloe, his dead fiancée, the blonde of his dreams who he had shaped into the perfect figure, as if out of clay? Did he miss playing God? Did he ever shed tears when he was alone, his perfect woman and the perfect baby they'd created, all crushed to death, his dreams crushed alongside them? He had to be thinking of them, especially now that he was with me. He had sat here before. When I looked into those eyes, sometimes I saw the high school bully who would stop at nothing to get what he wanted. Then they would change, shine with light and empathy, and he would crinkle the corners of his eyes and convince me we could be in this fairytale together—the thin line between love and hate.

But I didn't want to be a part of some pity campaign. "I didn't want to tell you because I'm still not sure I want a life with you. You're pushing so hard. It seems like you're trying to gain popularity by taking on cases. Like Marcus and his disability."

"Marcus is fine now. You're letting Lily get to you."

"She *does* get to me! Don't you see? And you seem to be playing on all this. When Lily mouthed off, you just sat back."

We exchanged a long look until a brief expression of annoyance shadowed his face.

"I need you to stand up for me against people like that, Blake. That's the most important thing to me. I need someone who is on *my* side."

"You know what? Fine, Marianne. Give up the dream house and the life I can give you and your brother. Just throw it all away." He stood up to leave.

God, how dramatic. "Don't leave. Don't be upset. I'm always suspicious."

Oh God. Please let Troy understand that this is the way it has to be.

Blake turned, and in his profile, I saw oceans of pain pass through his face. Oh, what had I done? I really was like my mother, just doing whatever the hell I wanted, when I wanted, with no regard for other people. Was I going to make Blake pay for all the pain my mother had caused us?

Confusion and indecision twisted my heart once again. I was selfish, just like my mother. The guilt of obscuring the truth from Blake festered in the void in my womb. Freedom always seemed to lead straight to anarchy.

"I'm sorry, Blake," I said. A vision of being a carefree writer in an interesting city with the man I loved passed through my mind.

I blacked it out, leaving a new canvas. How could I just give up the real me, though? I didn't want a boyfriend who wasn't creative in some way. I didn't want anything to come between me and my goals, and yet here was a man who would offer a stable life, who was hurt by my venomous words and by the selfish way I acted.

The rain intensified, beating against the windows and drowning out the hospital sounds. Blake returned to sit by the bed and I drifted off several times, only to awake with a start. He stayed there, staring off into space as the rain hammered down.

"You think you're the only one who suffers," he murmured in the dark, a secret cutting through the air. I barely heard him. "I loved Chloe."

"You told me you were only after her to get to me."

"You don't understand," he said, finally looking at me, the anguish bubbling through in his voice. "Maybe that's how it started, but people grow close. We developed a love for one another that you didn't see. And with Marcus, we had a little family."

"That you shut me out of!"

"You shut yourself out. You shut yourself out by continuing to see Troy all the time, too."

I recoiled and drew the covers up closer. "I do not."

"Marcus saw you. You don't think he worries about you? You don't think I worry about you? After everything your family put you through. That your aunt put you through. All that pain. And yet you choose to be near her husband? Why?"

Being near Troy felt so intoxicating at times, he made me forget about everything else. That was the magic trick of his charm. Was I unconsciously getting some sort of revenge against Julia? Was he? I didn't even realize I was doing it. I'd spent so much time trying to forget that maybe I was pushing the memories away for my own selfish reasons. Who was I, really? Was I this sensitive, creative person who had a hard time connecting with the 3D world? Or was I, like Marcus said, just like my mother, vengeful and uncaring, ready to fulfill my desires no matter the cost?

14

Once I recovered, I told Blake I had to go back to New Orleans to finish some interviews.

His eyes narrowed to suspicious slits. "You insist on staying there quite a bit. My family home is expansive. Marcus loves it there. Why don't you stay there until you're waiting for construction to finish?"

"Good for Marcus. But I have work to do."

Leaving Blake behind, I went straight to Troy's apartment. He pulled me into a hug.

"I lost it," I whispered into his shoulder.

He hugged me even tighter. "You're under a lot of stress. Do you want a drink?"

I met his eyes. They went dark, full of mischief. "I don't know."

He put his hand under my chin. "That's not an answer," he said. He grinned and walked to the counter to make me a screwdriver. Those first sips reminded me of those days in the kitchen at Azalea House. Even though I didn't really care for orange juice all that much, those moments of comfort flooded back.

I cradled the drink in my hands and watched him in the small kitchen, my back against the wall.

"I never see you drink anymore," I said, watching him in a daze. "Why do you have alcohol around?"

He flashed a quick smile. "For you. For friends."

I opened my mouth to say something else, but nothing came to mind.

"How do you spend your days lately, Marianne?"

It felt like a loaded question. Troy wasn't always easy to read. There was something accusatory behind his eyes, as if he were trying to intentionally make them vacant and uncaring, but there was a world of turmoil behind the calm, like a storm cloud on the horizon.

How was I spending my days, exactly? I was watching the house being built, stressing over wall colors and subway tiles, plumbing lines and electricity wiring. And... Vivienne. I swallowed back the rest of the drink.

"That bad, huh?" He laughed and reached for my cup.

"No. It's not. It's just..."

"You're bored."

I said nothing, as he took my glass to refill it.

But he spoke the truth. Blake's life was so different. Wealthy but out of the spotlight. Nothing to care about but sports and real estate and building the perfect home. It was tough to argue when you didn't even have to think.

Troy inched closer until I could smell his cologne.

"I missed you. I know it's wrong to say, but I really have. I feel like, I don't know..."

"We had a connection," I finished for him. It was really true. However taboo it was, it was true. In that moment, I didn't care that he was married to Julia, or that he was technically family, or ex family, whatever you want to call it. Maybe that was part of the appeal. Or maybe it's because we had something in common, being locked in that lush estate together, locked away like dolls in a dollhouse, with only each other to turn to. We were both wrapped up in worlds we wanted to escape and had both wrenched our way out of the shackles that bound us to our pasts and that place.

His smile formed slowly. "We did." He reached out and touched my bare arm, sending shivers through my flesh. "It's not too late. You could stay here. With me. I don't make much, but I could support you. The restaurant is picking up. I'd be there most of the time anyway if you needed your space."

I glanced around. He lived well. There were pictures of him with friends at Mardi Gras, people he reconnected with after Julia. His place was full of art from friends down in Jackson Square. To Troy, with love. They were all personalized.

My mind wandered to a life here, surrounded by likeminded people, people who stalked the night and stayed up late and howled at the moon. People who poured themselves into their creative work. Compared to Blake's stifling air of money, it seemed like comparing the Louvre to mass produced needlepoint at Wal-Mart.

"Blake proposed to me. Kind of." I said it without even thinking about it.

He glanced down at my ring. I had been taking it off before visits with him, but I forced myself to wear it this time. It felt like a vice, completely devoid of my mother's energy.

"That's quite a rock. It was your mother's."

His eyes flickered with something soft, like amusement mixed with sorrow.

"You really want to be locked in another castle in the same place your parents died? What happened to getting away and starting something new?"

I hung my head and looked at my feet.

"I know you burned Azalea House down. I know why, too."

Something acidic bubbled in my stomach and its tentacles reached my chest. He knew?

"Why would I do something like that?"

"So you would never have to go back. It was freeing. Wasn't it?"

He really did know. And I felt like he knew me. Really knew me, like I could say or do anything and he would still adore me. I looked into his eyes and something passed between us, an understanding and acceptance.

He stepped closer and his familiar smells filled my nostrils and wove a blanket of comfort around me. Drawn to his warmth, I put my arms around his neck and we stayed like that, locked in a stare.

He did it first. I should have known. He inched forward and closed his lips around mine. I let it happen.

Then those words rang in my ears: "You're just like your mother."

I pushed him away.

"Marianne," he said, his eyelids fluttering, "you don't have to marry Blake. There are other options."

"He's setting me up for life," I said. "Marcus too. I have to think about Marcus. He's still my brother."

He sighed. The disappointment dropped across his face like a theater curtain. "I can't give you everything you want, then," he said.

He studied me for a moment without breaking his embrace. "But I think I can give you something. Something you're lacking." He slid his hands down my back slowly, his fingers gently wandering across my hips until they reached my hands. He weaved his fingers into mine, gently, methodically, pulling my hands up to his neck. He pressed his palms into the back of my hands, inviting me to squeeze his throat. My fingers fell slack around his neck. I didn't know if I could do this.

"Do you do this with Blake?"

I shook my head. Of course not. With Blake the lights were always off during sex. The heat disappearing with the light, as I struggled to feel beautiful in the dark. To feel desired. Blake had a way of making the bedroom feel like a boardroom, with sex simply something to be scheduled in between other obligations.

"But you miss it," Troy said. "Having control. Exploring."

I wanted to keep my head still. But I could feel the hellfire raging inside me, and I nodded 'yes.'

"He doesn't have to know. Ever." He took my hand from his neck and led me to the bedroom.

This was what I really wanted, this part of Troy, the Troy who gave himself over to me and let me use him like an artist's canvas.

"You can tell me what you want me to do. And I'll do it."

That same demon that had me saying yes earlier unfurled into its true form. It was like another person inside me, another being that was not Marianne, but part Marianne, a character I was still developing inside my head. Someone unafraid of her desires, someone who spoke up and held her head confidently. I stood up straighter and looked him up and down.

"Take your clothes off," I told him.

Glee filled me when his face didn't change, but something in the way he welled up made me proud of myself for saying what I wanted and for saying it with authority.

I crossed my arms over my chest and watched him, making no move to remove my dress.

Once he was undressed, I stood there looking at him, every plane and detail of his muscles. He made no move to cover himself and obviously, he was enjoying himself. Had he really put that in me? Jesus. It seemed bigger now just looking at it.

"You're enjoying this, too."

He flushed red. "Of course I am. You should see yourself."

Normally I would have blushed, too, but that demonic character reveled in being in control, of telling a man what to do. Was this what I was looking for to overcome all the things that clamped my tongue down, that made me hide all of myself?

I walked over to him and ran my hands over his smooth body almost like a blind person, exploring every detail. Trying to file it in my mind.

My fingers moved to his neck, skimming up and down along his carotid, from his jaw to his collarbone. I traced the lines and contours of his throat, studying every inch. He wanted me to touch him there. His erection pressed against me, needing it.

"This is dangerous," I whispered.

"That's why we both like it."

And I knew he was right. This had been our escape. This is what made us feel alive when everything was dying around us.

And then I found myself wanting him inside me, to fill me in the way things like a new house or money or material things could never fulfill me. I yanked my belt off and fastened it around his wrists, securing them to the bedpost. I was going to give him what we both craved, and waves of pleasure prickled my skin as the realization dawned on him and showed through his ecstatic expression. The thrill of that god-like power rushed through me as I imagined squeezing and squeezing him, his life in my hands, in charge of his pleasure and pain. With just enough pressure I could put him out like a finished cigarette. On top of him, I took all of him inside me, letting it ebb and flow until a full tsunami crashed over me. And him, too. I collapsed on top of him, my skin tingling. I untied him from the bedpost, and he wrapped his arms around me.

Was this what sex could be like? I experienced it a bit with Carina, that no judgement sex, good times and carefree, but not like this. Not like I wanted.

Part of what made it so wonderful was the intensity and passion of it all, almost tangible. But after the tingling subsided and the orgasm washed over me, the guilt came fast. Blake had proposed. I said yes. I glanced over at the ring on my finger and it caught the sunlight filtering through the bedroom window. Tears welled up in my eyes and cascaded onto Troy's chest.

"What is it?" he asked.

"I can't do this. I shouldn't have done this."

Julia's last few words to me before she was taken away for questioning rang in my ears again. "You're just like your mother." God, there was so much strife between them, and Julia hung on to it with her claws, even after my mother died.

"Julia was right," I said, reaching up to wipe my face. "I am like my mother."

"No, you're not. People aren't completely good or bad, Marianne. They're people."

"But I shouldn't have cheated on Blake."

Troy rolled his eyes, then reached up to smooth my hair back away from my face. "I wouldn't worry too much about Blake. For all you know, he has his own things going on."

I studied his face. "Then why would he want to marry me?"

"Your name. He bought Azalea House, essentially. That says a lot about a real estate guy. Now he's made a name for himself off of you."

He was hiding something. I could sense it. Before I was able to tease it out of his mind, he put up walls.

"If you know something—"

"I don't."

"Troy. You do."

"They're just rumors, I think."

I sat up and gathered my clothes. "You're trying to manipulate me into staying with you."

He grabbed my arm and tried to turn me around to face him. "I'm not. But think about it. Why do you think he and Marcus are so close?"

Fear and doubt bloomed in my chest, but I swallowed it back and got dressed. Blake? No way. He was with Chloe before me. And now me.

I hooked my bra back on and slid into my panties. He wrapped his arms around me.

"Troy. Stop."

But he kissed me in places no man had kissed me before, gently lighting the hellfire inside me again, then turning it higher. And once again, I succumbed to his charms.

I stayed the night.

His apartment, protected by its brick walls and windows overlooking a private courtyard with a pool, felt intimate, even more private than the new house. No one knew I was here, except for Troy. Troy would never blab to the media about where I was.

It would be just as damning to the media for him as it would be for me.

I left in the morning as the new light came in through the old warehouse windows, dappling the hardwood floor. I danced around it as I collected my things, as if the light would purify me too much and make me want Blake.

I worked the rest of the weekend until my wrists ached, striking the keys in a frenzy until my fingers felt numb. Still, I couldn't get Troy out of my system. It didn't even require his touch anymore. Just the thought of him let my demon out of its cage. I resigned to see him one more time before heading back to the village to check on Marcus.

I called. No answer. I called the restaurant.

"I'm not sure where he is, darlin'," some waitress said. "He was supposed to be here today."

My insides went cold. I took the BMW and punched the gas through red lights, partly because I wanted to see if Troy was okay, partly because I welcomed a peace that only death could bring me.

I knew this feeling of disturbance. I felt it all the time at Azalea House. I could feel adrenaline searing my chest and my stomach, the only heat in my frigid body.

As I pushed his apartment door open, an emptiness overcame me. It felt like a tidal wave of quiet, as if the air hadn't been disturbed for days.

I walked into Troy's bedroom. The first thing I saw were his bare feet. There was a stool off in the corner of the room, as if it had been tossed there as an afterthought.

My chest constricted.

I stepped forward, hoping he was just provoking me, using danger as a toy the way we liked.

But I knew as soon as I saw his bloated face that he was not. There was a belt wound around his neck. My belt. The one I had used to tie him to the bed.

Horror and dread filled me, weighing me to the floor. I pulled my knees tight to my chest, hoping to soothe myself. I bit my lip until I saw red.

When my vision cleared, I noticed something next to the bed, gleaming on the wooden floor. Round and full, white and glistening like the moon. Was I going crazy? Was it dark outside?

I reached out to grab it, blinking back tears as I held it between my fingers. A smooth, white pearl. I rolled it between my fingers, using the smooth surface to soothe me.

But I was soon shrieking again. Nothing could soothe me.

I don't know how long I screamed, but neighbors showed up.

Then police.

Then more people.

Then someone zipping him up in a body bag. Carrying him away on a gurney.

Then the crowds dwindled.

"We'd really like you to come in to answer more questions," said a smirky detective who'd introduced himself as Gabe Ledeau.

This was it. They were going to find out that it was my belt. They were going to arrest me.

Jesus. In prison, what if I had to come in contact with Julia, of all people? Wouldn't that be the ultimate slight against me for Vivienne? Being face to face with her mother again?

I threw up right there in the kitchen, on Troy's immaculate counter, where he had just stood recently, making us something to eat.

This was how I was going to lose Marcus.

This was how Vivienne was getting her revenge. Torturing me. Just like she had done as a living person.

The police asked me the same pedestrian questions over and over, probing for a discrepancy, a hole in the story of a woman spurned.

"What time did you arrive again?"

"And how did you get in?"

"And when was the last time you saw him?"

Numbness. I answered each question at the police station in a zombie-like state, still questioning whether it happened at all. Seeing his face…his poor, bloated face, and his extremities, reddish purple, like they were going to burst…

Mechanically, repeatedly, I explained that I'd walked in and found him. Yes, it was my belt. No, I didn't remember leaving it there. Yes, I had seen him a few times over the past few months. No, we weren't lovers. Were we? Did two times count? And all the other stuff we'd done together? The things I didn't remember?

"You don't remember?" Ledeau asked again. His elbows were on his desk, his hands steepled, his brows drawn together.

"I've been trying to finish this book. We're building a new house. And I'm looking after my teen brother."

"Been under a lot of stress, huh?" He smiled.

Oh, shit.

Blake was sure to hear about this. And Marcus.

What motive would I have to kill Troy anyway? Maybe I should have asked for a lawyer. But what did I have to hide? Nothing. Everything.

Fear froze me as their eyes followed every tiny movement I made, but there wasn't anything they could put me away for at this point. Other than the belt, they had nothing. Dried, caked makeup scratched at my eyes. I was sure I was playing the distressed friend well, with streaks running down my face, but the detectives didn't seem to think so.

Maybe it was time to bury that part of me that danced with the dark. It would have to die with Troy. Even if this was what I needed, what I craved, I would have to accept that I wouldn't get it from Blake. Demons didn't like being locked up like princesses in faraway castles, in spaces with edges polished to a shine so bright that no shadows could exist, too clean for its dirty secrets.

I had been justifying things with Troy by those insinuated rumors.

But how did he know? Had he witnessed something specific?

I had only one more night to think about how to act around Blake when I returned on Sunday.

I left as the church bells sounded, reminding me of what vows

I may take in the future. Oh, didn't everyone do something bad, as Troy said? If it was just sex, was it so bad? Was it wrong to love Blake in one way and to love Troy for what he let me do to him?

I wondered if the hellfire had been extinguished forever now. All Blake wanted to do is protect me from danger, the danger that fuels the fire. The safety felt smothering. The power that made me feel alive was gone. When Troy died, part of me died with him.

15

Blake was relaxing in the living room condo when I walked in, his socked feet hoisted up on a footrest, reading a magazine. He never read books, claiming they wasted his time. But magazines, he said, were very important. They contained trends, people you needed to know about, places you needed to visit—or in his case, scope out real estate for rich people.

Marcus was seated diagonally from him, reading a PC magazine. I stopped and studied them as I let my purse hit the floor. The whole thing felt staged, like they'd planned to be sitting like that as I walked in, uncaring about what I'd been up to all weekend.

The Saints were on television, and Blake occasionally looked up from his magazine to whoop when they did something right, and sneer and boo when they did something he didn't like. Marcus watched with rapt concentration, mostly glancing at Blake before he reacted. Looking for cues on whether he should be happy or not.

"Since when did you like sports?" I asked. They both turned around and looked at me.

"Oh," Blake said, "we didn't hear you come in. Did you get everything you needed?"

We. Always we.

"Yes," I said, my voice strange and gruff. I had been screaming and moaning all weekend, and I hoped they couldn't tell my throat was raw. Marcus raised an eyebrow, always intuitive. "I got a lot of work done. Marcus? Since when did you start watching football?"

"Since I met Blake."

"My man here has many layers, sweetheart."

Saccharine sweet.

And…my man?

"Whatever," I said. "I'm going to write." Or rather, mourn Troy, I thought.

"Babe," Blake said, "why not just sit here with us?"

"Yeah, sister. You don't always have to hide."

"But I need to concentrate," I said, backing away. "And I have a space for my typewriter and—"

"But you hand write a lot, don't you?" Blake reached for the remote control and muted the television. "See? I can keep the volume on mute, and we'll still know what's going on." He patted the cushion next to him on the couch.

"Fine," I said. I settled in with my notebook and a pen and started writing some backstory.

It was only still and quiet for a beat or two.

"Yes! Yes!" Blake screamed.

"Touchdown!" Marcus yelled, meeting Blake's enthusiasm.

If only Blake was that amped up during sex, I wouldn't have been running off to see Troy.

I gathered up my things and stomped off to my room, where the typewriter waited like an old friend.

"Women," Blake muttered, just low enough for me to hear as I headed up the stairs.

This was what life was like with Blake and Marcus. Them bonding, me feeling trapped, caught in between secrets and lies.

"Marianne," Marcus said, his voice tight, "what?"

I swallowed back that same strange bile taste as I stopped on the stairs. "Troy is dead. I found him this morning."

Blake and Marcus both looked at me, then at each other. I put my hand on the stair rail to steady myself.

"I'm going to take a bath."

I had to get that taste out of my mouth. The smell, too. No amount of gargling or toothpaste would get rid of it.

I stared at myself in the mirror as the bath water ran. I had been with Troy only a few hours before his death. What was he doing? Why was he like that, hanging in his closet, with my belt of all things?

An instinct inside me reared its head and told me it was something sexual. It was some desire I was not around to fulfill, something he had to sate. Only it got to him. It killed him.

I splashed my face with cold water and looked at my reflection again. It didn't look like me. It looked like...

Vivienne.

Her cold eyes. The high cheekbones versus the rounder face. Was it the weight I lost? Right before my eyes, my face shifted again. I looked like me.

But someone else was in the reflection now, standing behind me.

Vivienne.

She was standing in the doorway, dressed as she was the day she died. My limbs froze.

I forced them to move. I rubbed my eyes and looked again. She was gone.

We all went to bed without saying a word. They didn't even say they were sorry. His name unspoken. They didn't even ask how it happened.

My Troy. My forbidden love. Fate brought us together twice. And now lust took him away. Lust had gotten us in trouble before, too. Fate and Lust, dark sisters.

I awoke hours later. She was back.

All I wanted to do was close my eyes and curl up into a ball under the covers, but each time I blinked, she moved closer, until she was crouched at the foot of the bed. I opened my mouth to scream. Nothing came out. And then I found my jaw was locked in place.

She stank of piss and bile. Her nightgown was stained just like it was when I found her in the bathroom that day. Her eyes were rimmed black, the veins blood red, vomit trickling down her face. She crawled on top of me, her frail weight making a faint impression on the comforter. But I was frozen. Normally I would have sent her sailing across the room. She was so thin, but I was locked in place, held down by some force.

She drew closer until her wretched decay hit me full force, her deathly secretions oozing out of every orifice.

"You did this to me," she said. "You made me do this."

I tried to scream, tried to shake my head. No. It wasn't true. She did this to herself. She wallowed in her own misery and there was nothing anyone could do to help her.

She inched closer and bared her teeth in disgust. Her fingers probed my mouth until I heaved. She laughed, plunging her fingers in deeper, triggering my gag reflex. I sputtered and gagged a few times before she withdrew her fingers. And then I mustered up the energy to finally scream.

Blake was up in a flash, fumbling with the light.

"What? What?"

I glanced around, knowing I would find something, anything to prove she was there. But there was nothing.

"I thought…"

"You thought what, Marianne? I have a meeting first thing in the morning. Are you trying to keep me up?"

"What's going on?" It was Marcus, standing in the doorway, rubbing his eyes.

"I thought I saw something."

Shame washed over me. They were looking at me like that again.

The lights were soon off again, and I struggled to find a comfortable position. When the alarm rang in the morning, I was greeted with that same wash of sickness I experienced from

Vivienne's fingers. I darted to the bathroom and threw up what felt like a week's worth of food.

"You've got to stop this," Marcus said at breakfast.

"Stop what? Stop grieving Troy?"

He shuffled the newspaper he was reading and shot me a side-eye glance.

"I really saw something," I said. "She was in my bedroom, Marcus. Why don't you believe me?"

"I believe *you* believe you saw something."

"What about all those times on the board?"

He set his coffee down. His blue eyes flared black behind his glasses.

"What?"

"Don't mess with that thing, Marianne."

"Why not? You don't even believe in it anymore."

"It taps into your own subconscious. I don't know if you want to go there right now."

Now it was my turn to shoot him a disapproving stare.

"Whatever is behind it, is it really something you ought to do alone? Talking to Ouija boards by yourself? Why not go out? You have a car. You can go somewhere at least, bring a book and have some tea."

"I can do that here."

"Exactly. Blake and I are your only company." His eyes flickered and I picked up on his thoughts for a split second.

Unless…

"I do talk to people. I've been interviewing people for the book."

"Uh huh," he said, sipping coffee. "How'd that go? What the hell happened to Troy, huh? Did you also knock him down to the ground and threaten to kill him before he died?"

Oh, God. His tone. What did he know? There was no way he could know anything, though. Marcus wasn't in tune with the spiritual world like I was. He couldn't pick up on other people's thoughts like I could.

Or could he?

"I don't know," I said, raking a hand through my greasy hair. "I found him hanging in his closet."

"Autoerotic asphyxiation," he said in such a nonchalant way, I wasn't sure I heard him.

"What?"

"I said what I said."

"Aren't you upset? He lived with us and—"

"I am not!" he roared, standing up. "And you shouldn't be, either! You should be grateful for what you have, not running off and doing whatever the hell you want!"

"Fine," I said, hoping it would fend him off. "But you seem to be overly concerned about me."

He shook his head in a pitying way, then picked up the newspaper again.

"I am. You should make more friends."

"What about you?" I said. "You hardly ever leave the house, either."

He snapped his head back to me. "I have online friends, you know. And," he said, jutting a finger at me, "don't forget. I left. I went out into the world before you did, dear sister. I met people. I made friends. Yes, your *faggot* brother made friends."

"I'm sorry. I didn't mean what I said."

Jesus. He had a point. Maybe I did need to get away from the board. After all, dwelling so much on Vivienne's death certainly wasn't doing me any good. I wouldn't be able to stand on my own if something happened to Blake, and I didn't want to live the rest of my life cooped up in another house. How had I let this happen?

Vivienne. I could hear her jeering laughter in another room just as I sat there with Marcus. I sat up straight and strained my ears over Marcus shuffling the newspaper.

"Why do you even care?" he continued. "All Troy wanted to do was fuck you. And it looks like he got what he wanted, didn't he?"

I fumed and clenched my fists.

"I see I'm right."

"What difference does it make?" My voice was so loud, my throat seared and Marcus recoiled. "He wasn't blood related."

He scoffed. "Like that matters."

I clenched my jaw.

"You were underage. It's not your fault. The fact that he gave in to his own dark desires is his fault, but it's *your* fault for not writing and getting wrapped up in some murder mystery again."

"I cared about Troy. He loved me."

Marcus took a swig of something that looked like a mimosa. "He loved your body."

Shuffling down the hallway again.

Scratch, scratch.

"Do you hear that?"

"There you go again."

But then, I smelled it. Acrid. Sour. Sickly sweet. Flowery Gucci Rush perfume mixed with vomit. It was her.

"She's here," I said.

Marcus slammed the newspaper down.

He opened his mouth to say something. But his eyes said it all.

I darted upstairs and threw myself on the bed, letting it smother me for a moment, lost in that sensation of not being able to draw in a breath of air and thinking about how Troy must have felt.

Alone. He must have felt alone. What was he doing with a belt around his neck in his closet?

I couldn't let this one go. It did not seem like Troy at all. I knew him. I was one of the few people in the world who really knew him. Did I love him? I certainly acted that way. You always love the forbidden ones. I knew I didn't love Blake. I was using him, and this was my punishment.

I wanted to tell Marcus I think I killed Troy. But what would he say? He'd say he deserved it, just like Uncle Joseph deserved it when Julia poisoned him so he wouldn't get any of the money from the sale of the house. Marcus didn't care, as long as his needs were met, and he could drink his life away.

Even if Troy did commit suicide, it was Julia's fault. Julia's fault that my brothers died, that Theo died, that we suffered so much while they were there at Azalea House with us, in our house. Everything was her fault. People like her lorded over everyone's lives, telling them they were sinners, that they were bad or wrong for the things they desired. What an invasion of privacy it was, to have someone take over our house. She did what she wanted with it. And Troy was my only ally in that time, someone I could confide in and trust. There was Marcus, but there may as well have been oceans to separate us. I could rely on him and tell him things when he was still at Azalea House, but him running away drove a wedge between us, one that could never be put away.

I wanted revenge for the world taking this part of me away, condemning me to this purgatory. But on who? Julia was already away, Troy was dead, my parents were dead, I got everything I wanted. Even Vivienne was gone, though she still tormented me. If I could let it all go, maybe I would feel normal, like I had gotten justice.

The truth was, if I wrote this book exposing everything Julia did, it would be some sort of revenge. I could tell my truth, my parents' truth, the story of me and Marcus locked in that horrible house.

&a.

THE HOUSE WAS ALMOST DONE. I hired an expensive interior decorator to finish everything for me. I didn't want to see the progress. Signing that paperwork filled me with remorse.

Things were moving too fast.

I had created another hell house. Without realizing it, I had picked a facade the color of long dead people, of bones, the windows with arches like questioning eyes, watchful eyes. It was different from Azalea House in so many ways, but both houses had taken on an almost lifelike quality, watching and waiting, amused that we were all suffering so. I chose white because it reminded me of freshly washed, bleached sheets, a new beginning.

But from the end of the driveway, its reincarnation looked menacing as ever, its arches like the eyes of a skull, its windows like teeth. Ivy Manor. The ivy I'd chosen to wrap around the lattice work now reminded me of something left in the woods to decay, something that ivy would wrap itself around and drag back into the wild.

"Ivy is poison," Marcus had said. "Ivy wraps around everything and suffocates it."

And he was right. Everything about that house weighed in on you, the walls, even the largest rooms seemed to entomb you.

I wanted the pond filled in, for it to be overgrown and unseen. But nothing would grow there. It was too swampy, and it quickly filled with saw palmettos. When I walked down there, the ground was still soft, like it would swallow me. With every step, something rustled and moved along with me, water moccasins, serpents that blended in so well with the foliage, it startled me into running back into the house. I would always be haunted by something dark there, no matter what we did with it, reminding me that the past could never be erased, no matter how many coats of white paint you use.

16

I woke up hours later to blinding light. The whole day was behind me. Now the sun shone straight into the dining room, announcing the late afternoon.

What day was it?

When I wandered out of the bedroom, I noticed it was different.

This was not the condo.

Was this the new house? Everything was white and blinding. I squinted and stumbled through the house.

"Jesus Christ, Marianne. We need to get you to the doctor." It was Blake, standing in the hallway, his business suit perfectly ironed.

"What happened?" I croaked. I was so thirsty.

"You started tearing your hair out," Marcus said, appearing out of one of the rooms.

I let my eyes adjust. He had dark crescents under his eyes. Worry lines etched in his forehead.

My fingers were twined with webs of sticky hair. It was everywhere in tufts, balled up on the bed, sticking to my neck, in gobs on the floor.

"Oh God," I moaned. My scalp burned.

Blake studied me with horrid disgust. My looks were the trophy he got to carry around town. Without them, he couldn't take me out and my value diminished to him. I hadn't seen myself in a mirror, but I already dreaded it.

"It was her. She was *in* me. I could feel it. I could smell her!"

"Take this, please," Blake said, handing me a pill.

It was hard to swallow, but once it dissolved, I felt like I was floating.

Patches of hair were missing from the sides of my head. Everything on top was still intact.

Marcus slipped into the bathroom and observed me while I assessed the damage.

"If you shave the sides, you can style it into a mohawk," he said with a slight smile playing on his lips.

I couldn't help but smile back. "I'm sure Blake would just love that."

Marcus shrugged. "You never liked being his little doll anyway. I don't know why you let him dress you."

We met eyes just then. We both know it was trudging up an old memory of Uncle Joseph buying me that virginal white lingerie set when I turned sixteen.

"You must have been scared," I said. "I'm sorry."

"I don't like this. Whatever is going on with you. I just want it to stop."

"Me too."

"I believe you now."

"What do you mean?"

"This place does things to you. You even sounded like her. Like Vivienne. Like you were...I don't know... possessed."

Vivienne would have taken delight in something like that, to be able to control another person. Was that why I was always so compelled to run to Troy? After all, didn't it always seem like she was near him or trying to impress him?

"I've been losing track of time lately," I said more to myself than to Marcus. Now that I reflected back on it, the days blurred together, and I couldn't pick out specific memories from when we started working on the house.

"Maybe it was a bad idea to build a house here," Marcus said.

"You think?"

He pulled up a chair and sat behind me, sectioned off my hair and trimmed the sides. "We really are going to have to shave this to make it look right."

I nodded, not wanting to look at myself in the mirror.

"I don't know what I was thinking, letting Blake build a house here."

"Don't think too much about it. I think one of the reasons you're having...difficulties...is that you're overthinking all this. Maybe the past isn't inside the house. Maybe it's still inside you. Maybe you would have been haunted no matter where we ended up."

Maybe he was right. But how could I stop thinking about all the bad things that had happened here? The longer we stayed at Azalea House, the more terrible secrets were revealed. Who knows how many buried whispers were still out there?

Troy. I could turn to Troy about this.

I met Marcus's eyes in the mirror. They went cold with something I didn't recognize. He shaved the sides of my head in silence.

When he was done, I stuffed suitcases with as much clothing as I could muster. All my black clothing, anyway. The preppy stuff, the stuff Blake picked out for me could stay here and collect dust for all I cared. I still wasn't sure why I was doing it. Was it guilt? I kept imagining Troy's death until I wasn't sure if I witnessed it.

I yanked the preppy clothing from the hangers and threw it in a pile. All the shoes that didn't suit me went on top of it. I opened the door to Blake's closet and began tossing stuff inside. He could deal with this shit if—

I froze. A lady was standing in the closet.

My hand trembling, I flipped on the light.

But it wasn't a lady at all. It was a dress. A really short dress on a hanger. There were heels in front of it, too. It was placed out like it was ready to wear. I stepped forward. Pearls. A pearl necklace was out on the hanger, too.

I thought about the pearl I tucked away in my purse.

Holy shit.

I inched forward to examine the clothing. The dress was too large for me. The shoes were, also.

"What are you doing?"

Blake. He was sheet white.

"I should ask you the same thing. What the hell is this?"

Slack-jawed, he finally spoke and said, "It—It's not what it looks like."

I grit my teeth. "Then what the hell is it?"

"I—well."

"This isn't my size. It's not your mother's size, either. It's not even Lily's size!"

"Jesus, Marianne!" Blake said, turning away. "Your hair."

"What was she supposed to do? Leave it patchy? You should be complimenting my hairdressing skills," Marcus said. He appeared in our bedroom.

"I'm changing rooms," I said. "Then I'm out of here in the morning." I stormed past them both, grabbed my purse, the luggage, and my car keys. Blake trailed me.

"I don't think it's a good idea. I think we should be getting you into bed and scheduled for a doctor's visit in the morning."

I pushed past him without saying anything.

"Let her go," I heard Marcus say as I slammed the door.

I wandered around the new house until I found a guest bedroom.

Fuck them both and their camaraderie. I supposed any other sister in the world would have been thrilled that their brother and fiancé were getting along, but it made me anxious and spiteful. The closer Marcus felt to Blake, the further away he felt to me.

That dress was so big. Those shoes.

What the fuck was going on?

❧

THE NEXT DAY, before anyone was up, I took the BMW to the church where Julia used to go. I rode with the top down, the heater on full blast.

I sat in the parking lot, smoking a cigarette, the brand Vivienne liked. I sat and smoked and stared at the church, its steepled roof, the arched windows that looked like eyes, and wondered if I'd been here before.

It looked a lot like the new house.

A blue minivan pulled into the parking lot.

"That's quite a car," a skinny, older man said as he got out of the van.

"I hate it." I took a deep drag and flicked the cigarette into the parking lot. The man kept the same smile on his face, but his eyes followed the cigarette butt for a second.

"Is there something I can do for you?"

My fiancé is gay or bisexual or a crossdresser, and I'm possessed, I wanted to say, but instead, I said, "I don't really know."

"Why don't you come inside for a few minutes? The church will be empty, and we can talk."

I looked him up and down. The skin on his hands was crinkly and spotty. He stooped. There was a light dusting of white hair on his face. He smiled again.

Inside, the church was cool, the lights soft. Something moved in my stomach, almost animal-like.

"I'm Pastor Bob Broussard, by the way," he said.

"I'm Marianne Easton."

The slut, a voice in my head said.

"Ah, Easton. Let me guess," he said as he settled into the pew next to mine, "you're having trouble adjusting to your new home."

"Yes," I said. "In a way."

The look on his face put it all into perspective. So you're having trouble adjusting to changes, it said. Don't we all.

"I feel like something won't leave me. I'm missing chunks of time. I am seeing my deceased cousin around every corner. She won't leave me."

His expression shifted from friendliness to concern.

The sunlight filtered in through the church's windows. Dust motes floated in the air. I thought for a second, he might fall over dead.

"I think I can help you. Close your eyes, Marianne."

I did.

"I want you to imagine a bright, clean space. Breathe deeply and relax."

I tried. Still, I did not feel relaxed.

I was in my old bedroom at Azalea House. I was lying on my bed. The bedroom was decorated like it was when my parents were alive.

In that bright, clean space, something scurried into a corner.

"You're completely relaxed, and nothing can harm you in this space. There is nothing to worry you, nothing to trouble you," Pastor Bob said.

Vivienne laughed from the dark corner.

"This is your safe space. Whatever is there with you is only there because you allow it. You are in complete control."

I didn't feel in control.

"I want you to imagine a cord that connects you to your cousin."

I looked down. A greasy, green vine was attached to my belly button. The other end of the vine was attached to whatever was hiding in the dark corner.

"Now," Pastor Bob continued, "I want you to imagine cutting that cord, Marianne. I want you to cut the cord that connects the two of you."

I looked for something sharp. I could not find anything.

Vivienne appeared from the corner, holding the shears she had once used to destroy the gardens at Azalea House. She smiled, something black and viscous oozing from her mouth.

"The cord is cut. Look down and see that it is cut."

In a flash, she scuttled across the room and settled on my chest, the black substance dripping into my eyes, my nose, my mouth. Before everything went black, I saw the slimy, green cord connected to her navel, too.

"Imagine a healing white light, filling you, surrounding you."

All I saw was black, the dark corner spreading around me, suffocating me.

"Come back out of your safe space. Listen to my voice and follow it back to me, to the church."

I opened my eyes.

"Do you feel any better?"

"Yes, Pastor Bob," I said. "I feel much better."

Only it wasn't me who said it. It was Vivienne's sing-songy, sarcastic voice. But it was coming out of my mouth.

17

I drove straight from the church to New Orleans.

Maybe I really didn't have anything to do with Troy's death.

Pages of fact and fiction shuffled in my mind.

I wasn't wearing pearls. I think.

The pearl wasn't dusty. It was smooth. And there was a little trail it had left in the dust, too.

But it had to have been me. Images flashed through my mind of egging him on, of his face as I choked him, still and red, flushed with desire and pain.

Vic was standing outside the condo, leaning over, looking into the courtyard as I pulled up. What was I going to say to her?

"There you are!"

Did she look pleased to see me? Emotions fogged my brain. I couldn't even read street signs, my eyes were so swollen from tears.

"I, uh—" I wrung my hands, trying to decide if she was trustworthy enough. Should I tell her what happened?

"Oh my God. Your hair is different!" she said, touching the shaved side of my head. "And you look...different."

To my own surprise, I didn't blush like I normally would.

"I'm still figuring things out," I said, absently reaching up to touch my remaining hair, "but I think I'm on the right path."

"I heard about that guy you were seeing."

I nearly fell back on my ass. "How?"

"Our world is a very small one. The subs around here gossip constantly."

"I feel…"

"Guilty?"

"How did you know?"

"I can see it in your eyes. And your car is filled with suitcases. You're not responsible for his perversions, girl. Were you there?"

I blinked. "I can't remember."

Her face fell. "Let me come inside with you. Look, if you're thinking of leaving, you'll only make it worse."

My hands shaking, I pulled out the key and opened the gate to the courtyard. All was quiet inside, except for the faint trickling from the lion fountain. It seemed there were no other residents home, either. A tiny bead of relief formed in my stomach; at least I could give Vic an idea of what was happening before I was arrested.

"Did you get called in for questioning or something?" She lit a cigarette and offered me one. I took it. It tasted like dirty mint, but the scorching sensation distracted me enough to focus.

"No. I was the one who found him."

"You found him," she said, smoke curling around her face. "So that means you weren't there, right?"

"I don't know. I've been losing track of time."

"Shit."

"I know."

We stared at each other for a moment. She scanned me, reading my face. "Do you remember anything at all?"

"No. I was there that weekend. Then I went around and ran some errands and worked. When I came back, he was dead. But I don't remember anything that happened during that time where I was out, the time before I found him dead."

"Look," she said, blowing out a thick stream of smoke. "You

tell those fuckers, if they ask, you tell them you were with me, you got it?"

I nodded.

She took another deep drag off her smoke, those piercing eyes penetrating me.

"You'd do that for me?"

A slow smile formed on her face. "I might need something from you later. You never know."

God. Someone else who needed something. But I said, "Thank you."

She nodded, forever cool.

"What if I did kill him? Like, accidentally? I mean, that time at the club…"

"Shit happens. Like I said, you can't let yourself feel responsible for these perverts. They do themselves in. For all you know, he did it himself. Now, stay your ass here. Go about things as planned, like you usually do. Write whatever shit you're working on, go out, get coffee, all of that. Act normal."

That memory of the dominatrix and the lawyer sprang to mind.

She leaned back into the chair and lit another cigarette, glancing out the window, probably to figure out when the sun would go down. It occurred to me this was the first time I'd seen her in daylight. She seemed even more otherworldly, her skin paper white, set off by her glossy black hair.

Could she have done this? Was she helping me or getting me to help her?

"Let me stay here," she said in a sharp tone, "you'd want to do that anyway, right? Have a friend stay with you while you're in mourning?"

I nodded.

And I would find a way to go through her shit to see if she was involved with Troy, too.

But it turned out, all Vic had was a shopping bag full of black clothing, black makeup, cigarettes and a toothbrush. I'd have to figure out a way to invite myself to her apartment to see if there was anything to link her to Troy.

Troy. Oh God. His blue face…

There was a moment where, when I was pushed into the water, that the cold shocked me and chilled my intestines. It was an overwhelming sense of dread and stillness, letting the frigid water consume me, getting my bearings. That's how processing Troy's death felt.

My body stayed that way for days, that turned into weeks.

I opened my mail to find a rejection from the agent.

"I'm sorry," she said, "but I just don't see why anyone would want to read about an indie new wave band from the 80s now. Thanks for sending it, though."

The shock deepened and the wound felt like I'd poked it with a stick. What did she mean? I thought for sure this was definite, that if Blake's family knew this agent, it was a sure thing. Plenty of people wanted to read it. It was an interesting story. Wasn't it?

Marcus stopped by while Vic was at work.

"Look!" he said, gesturing at Blake's car out the window, "Blake taught me how to drive. He's even letting me borrow his car while he and his dad carpool together. Isn't that cool?"

I didn't say anything. I knew what he was implying. I should have been the one teaching him how to drive.

He said nothing else negative about Troy, but I could tell part of him was relieved that Troy was gone. It meant I was at the condo more.

"Send it to another agent," he said after I showed him the rejection letter.

"Do you think it's pointless? Maybe she's right. Maybe no one wants to read it."

"Don't you think people love drama? Besides you can refute everything the gossips are talking about."

"What? That Momma had an affair because Theo was good looking and charming? That's why she did it, isn't it?"

Marcus shook his head and looked out at the pool area,

probably hoping for warmer, brighter days where he could sit out there and not take care of me.

We still hadn't talked about how I'd walked in and found him. Marcus probably didn't want that sort of detail. He was ready to move on. With Julia in jail, Troy was the last link to Azalea House. He wanted to break free, to do everything right so he could live his own life, free of me.

Blake and I spoke at length at first, him saying over and over that he was sorry, that I didn't deserve to lose another person in my life. He played the role of the concerned, empathetic white knight. Perfectly played.

But I still wasn't having it. I very much enjoyed spacing out for hours, pretending to listen, but spacing out and thinking about other places. The sex shop. Memories of sexy things with Troy. Listening to music, replaying it in my head, playing lyrics over and over from my favorite bands, or thinking about Depeche Mode, or thinking about sifting through all my albums back at Azalea House. Hell, I even thought about the mall sometimes.

Anything to avoid thinking about how I'd found Troy, naked and hung with my black belt.

"Marianne?"

I looked up to see Marcus, angry, looming over me.

"You listening? You need to go to a mental ward or something?"

"Of course not!"

He continued to stare. Ghost mewed from his window perch, concerned.

"I'm fine," I said, hoping to encourage him to leave so I could daydream again. "I just need time."

I needed to blow off steam some kind of way. I needed to prowl, to control…to choke again.

I switched permanently from cloves to regular cigarettes, Vivienne's brand, enjoying the cauterizing sensation it had on my throat. I felt like I would smoke anything, anything that would give me even a temporary feeling of being out of my body. I did not enjoy just being in my body. I wanted out.

I began wandering late at night, where I would see Troy on the streets, only a glimpse of him. Some lookalike or his ghost, I never knew. But it twisted my heart to see it.

I would never have anyone like Troy, would never have that kind of connection. I was an outsider in a world I desperately wanted to live in.

18

I went to the sex shop that night to meet Vic.

"God," she said. "You really do look different."

"Such is life," I said, shrugging. I pulled something off the rack, some lace-up crop top that was sure to accentuate my cleavage. I wasn't sure I wanted that.

"Oh honey, you in that? They'll do anything you want," Vic said.

I put it on the counter and fished my wallet out.

"Look, I'm serious about this party. You should come. It'll help you get over your…friend."

"I don't know. What if I cross the line again?" But who else was I wearing these things for? Myself, of course, it gave me some sense of control. But what good was it if it gave me a power I couldn't control?

I felt nauseous, like someone was poking at my innards with a stick.

"You need to eat something. Let's go get some oysters and raise hell at this place." She fished out a flier from a drawer beneath the register. A scantily clad woman in cat ears had her heel dug into a man's back. He was wearing puppy ears.

I shrugged. She was probably feeling sorry for me. "You were going to go to this anyway, right?" She gave me a strange look. "Okay," I said, resigned.

The vibe was much different, this time playing sludgy synth music that could have been out of a 70s arthouse film. The colors were much more monochromatic this time. Graveyard-esque.

Vic waved at the girl at the entrance, and we bypassed a line of people that stretched to the next block. We proceeded past the pay area and into the womb of otherkin all dressed in black, or barely dressed at all.

Everything melted together in inky rivulets.

I slinked my arm behind the bar and grabbed an open bottle of vodka.

"Marianne," she laughed, nudging me. I handed her the bottle and watched her suck it down, dazed already.

Honestly, I wanted to have a secret more than anything. Expressing my sexuality, having something apart from the responsibilities of caring for Marcus and dealing with Blake's advances felt freeing, like I could be myself, the future unburdened by the past.

I longed to disappear into some city again, like I had when I first left the house, places where no one knew me, desperate to get away from that look of pity. "Oh, we're so sorry you grew up with hippie musician parents who were probably always high or something, swathed in cheating scandals and murder. Bless your heart, you poor thing."

Or sometimes it was, "Oh, you lucky little bitch, to grow up with so much money and that you had this and that." What people didn't ever acknowledge or feel sorry about was the fact that we didn't have parents anymore, that we were doing the best we could with what we had. The roulette wheel always landed on pity, anger or jealousy. Never respect. But in kink, it always landed on respect. Respect just for me, just for being present and confident in my body. If I had control over anything, I had that. Kink wasn't a game of chance. I was a winner every time.

The sneakiness wasn't a downside. The taboo may have even

been the best part of it. Even now when I look back, it didn't matter what I was doing, if I was breaking in or talking to ghosts, just doing something I wasn't supposed to be doing was thrilling. I suppose that's what I got for growing up in the middle of nowhere, a boring place, where everyone did what was expected. I made things up, I overexaggerated things when there was nothing there. Maybe it was pure intuition telling me about the twins, and that it wasn't ghosts at all. The things my intuition uncovered, things I didn't want to face head on, that I knew were hanging around like death's odor. The stormy, on and off moods between my parents, the way my dad disappeared, the way my mother used to lock herself in her room and ignore me for days on end for the slightest things. She was so sensitive, but it's because she was judging herself, not because other people were judging her.

I had control over my body. I could make myself slight, so I could ease into corners or slip through shadows, unseen, observing like a black cat.

I always envied them. They came out at night and slinked through the Quarter, their bodies lean and in tune with their surroundings, not an ounce of waste or worry. The only way to know if they were there was to look for them specifically. And no one would be out looking for me specifically. No one except for Troy, really.

My mind drifted to him. How he made me feel. How he would have loved this place. Could he have killed himself? Did he really die at the hands of intense lust, because I couldn't give him all he wanted?

An obscene thought of Julia escaping prison crossed my mind, but it could not be so. Of course, she could have had someone on the outside pull a favor for her. But why? Troy was her trophy, her conquest, the one thing she had left over from the ashes of Azalea House.

Maybe it was Vic. Maybe Vic was obsessed and jealous of Troy, wanted to control how I did things, wanting to be the ultimate mentor. I always got strong "listen to me and let me be your priestess" vibes from her.

But the worst possibility of all was me. I could not get a grip on my brain, no matter how hard I tried. I flashed in and out of reality a million times a day, without knowing how I got to one place or how I ended up in another. I had constant headaches on top of that, so the moments I was actually in reality were totally distorted, as though I had taken some sort of drug.

But not feasible. I must have been the one to do it. I must have been there and encouraged him to do it. Maybe I had done the same with Vivienne.

Why couldn't I remember anything? Everything was a dream state, and I floundered around between semi-wakefulness and a dream world.

"Do you want to play?"

The voice, the heavy synth of the music playing, and Vic pinching me, it all brought me back down to reality.

Right. We were in another BDSM club.

I turned and faced him. Oh, how he reminded me of Troy. The confident stance, the little glimmer of mischief in his eyes. He even looked like him, tall and olive skinned with brown eyes, deep eyes. I shrugged and he led me to a small room with a large wooden X and a lot of gadgets.

"I'm still new to this," I said, and a wave of disbelief coursed through me. Normally, I would never admit something like that, for fear of being judged, but it was again like something possessed me to say it.

"I'll show you around."

He pointed out all the various whips and canes, torture devices and chains, but none of it really caught my interest.

"I don't really need any of that," I said.

He shrugged and smiled a little. "It doesn't hurt to know."

"But you like being hurt?"

He smiled wider. "You're good at this. Show me what you like."

I looked him up and down. Did I want to go down this road with a stranger?

"Get on the edge of the bed. Sit on your hands."

One thing Vic had told me was to make sure my words were orders, and not phrased as options. If they didn't want to participate, they could just say no and leave.

He obeyed, and I straddled him. Already, he was hard. I put my hands around his neck.

"This is what I like to do."

I squeezed.

"Wait," he said, straining.

I saw red. I felt pressure around my hands, yielding flesh, squeezing, hot…

I was vaguely aware of him tapping me on the arm, but something came over me. Excitement or possession, I didn't know. I was enjoying his straining erection and the fact that I had caught him off guard.

Before I knew what was happening, my ass hit the ground and I was jolted back into reality.

"You crazy bitch!" he yelled as he rubbed his neck. His voice was gravel-like. Several people filed into the room.

"What happened?" someone asked.

"She tried to kill me!"

I looked around, dizzy. "I didn't."

It was then that Vic walked into the room. Her face was flushed, her hair sticking out at wild angles.

She pulled me up off of the floor.

"What the hell happened?"

"I don't know," I said, glancing down at his erection. "He seemed to be enjoying the fact that I'm a crazy bitch."

She giggled, and then she led me out of the room and down the stairs.

"What's going on? I told you. Don't worry about that guy."

I sighed. What wasn't going on?

"Just lots of stress lately."

"I think you should train as a sub before you get too far into this Domme thing."

"But I'm not into that."

"Sometimes," she said, looking off in the distance as we

ambled through the night, "the way to gain control is to give it up completely."

Vic brought me back to her apartment. It was plastered in pictures of goth rockers. She lit black candles.

"Maybe back there, it's not for you. Maybe it's for people like me."

She lit a cigarette. Again with that faraway look.

"Maybe I want to be like you," I said.

She snapped her head in my direction. "No, you don't."

She smoked while I looked around her apartment. It was very similar aesthetically to the clubs we'd been to. Hardened candle wax covered the tables. Black draped over everything, over lamps, chairs, the walls. If I walked, I had to look down at the dark hardwood floor to avoid bumping into everything.

I sat back in my chair. She looked over at me from across the room, the faint yellow glow of the candles illuminating her alabaster face, leaving it looking even more ghostly white. Her icy eyes studied me, prying me open.

Slowly she stood up, her hips snaking towards me, wavy and watery from all the colorful things I'd consumed. Music pulsed from the stereo, something I didn't recognize. I had been consuming as much industrial and goth stuff as I possibly could to impress her, but I couldn't recognize the music or any of the musicians that covered her walls defiantly—their genderless haircuts, beautiful cheekbones and exquisite makeup adorning waifish bodies, smirking in the face of society's sexpectations. Taunting the status quo with their androgyny.

"Dye your hair… tattoo yourself… pierce your nipple," she said, flicking my piercing. I resisted the urge to wince. I didn't even realize I was topless. "It's never enough, is it? You still can't escape yourself. There's no escape. Well…" Her dark lips quirked into a grin.

"Death," I finished for her.

She lifted her thin brows and smiled a little wider, impressed I would know. But I knew much more about death than she realized.

She put her palms into my chest and squeezed my breasts. My own hands tightened around the armrests of the chair, resisting the urge to grab at her. I needed someone, anyone, to take me in the way that Troy let me take him: full of passion, animalistic and wanting. But I already knew Vic intended to make me wait.

"Why me?" I asked. I just said it. How stupid. Like part of me was trying to kill the mood she had created.

Her eyes misted over, like she was about to cry. "You never smile. Not like all the other girls who come in."

I could only watch her as she continued to sway and tease, rubbing her body against mine. I gripped the armrests tighter, my nails etching lines into the wood.

In rhythm with the music, she rocked her hips and peeled her latex top off with expertise, revealing more tattoos and pierced nipples. A black-and-white tiger prowled down her sternum towards the botanical jungle etched into her lower abdomen.

"You can escape everything," she said, her voice hardly audible over the increasing bass of the song. "Except yourself."

She pulled me into her velvety embrace, hard cold steel and soft skin, cloves and sweat and the rubbery scent of latex. Blue black, squeaky, slick, just like I'd imagined it that day I'd seen it on my aunt. And soon we were grinding up against each other, her on top of me, me under her ministrations, submitting, breathless as the beat wore on. Our climaxes peaked simultaneously, as if we were cresting over the top of a roller coaster together, resulting in a release that seemed to shed a buildup of emotions in me. She held me in her arms, and we stayed in comfortable silence.

As we caught our breath, the first gold glints of the sun began to creep in through the dark velvet window shades.

"What are you running away from?" she asked.

I gave her the brief version, but I told her everything. How could I not? In her strong, sinewy arms, I felt safe, myself, something akin to what it was like with Troy.

"I miss him," I said. She held me tighter. I expected some lecture about incest, waiting for a judgment that never came. Here, among all the androgynous people with dark masks, among the black candles and drapes, I was myself. "I don't want to go back to Blake."

"Then don't."

"I have a brother to look out for."

"He can handle himself."

I supposed he could. He had, after all, lived on his own for a time while I was still at Azalea House. But I couldn't just leave him with Blake. I would have to find a way to keep the condo.

"It's autoerotic asphyxiation," she said, blowing a smoke ring. I turned over and looked at her. "Your *friend*," she said with a slight smile, casually, as if she'd seen him in the mall.

"What do you know about it?"

"When you cut off the air supply, they say it makes for a stronger orgasm. That's why guys like being choked. Sometimes they call it breath play."

"Do you think he killed himself?"

She shrugged and stubbed out the cigarette. The lights from Bourbon Street filtered in through the dark room, giving her a sultry, red glow. "If he did, he probably didn't mean to do it. Sometimes, these guys keep pushing for that high. They want to see how long they can last."

I put my head in my hands, then raked my fingers through my hair.

"It's not your fault," Vic said. She lit another cigarette, mixing orange flames with the red light. "It happens."

"I think he was murdered."

She looked at me, the flame still lit, the cigarette wedged between her lips.

"Who would murder someone like that?" She lit it and looked at me through the flame, her eyes lit up like amber jewels.

I shook my head and looked around at all the stuff in her apartment. A lone saxophone blasted some tune I vaguely recognized.

"What makes you think he was murdered? I know you're new to this, but accidents like this can happen with this lifestyle."

"I know they can. But there was something strange there at his apartment, something I don't think that the detectives noticed."

Vic lifted her eyebrows and looked at me through the veil of smoke.

"I found a pearl on the floor."

She grinned. "He was banging someone else, huh? A classy chick who wears pearls?"

I shook my head. "I feel like he would have told me that."

"And what would you have done if he told you? Bedrooms can hold a lot of secrets, especially when they get in the way of what a man wants."

I looked at the floor.

"What about you?" I asked. "Do you keep secrets?"

"What do you mean?"

"Anyone ever die on your watch?"

"No. Never."

I believed her because I wanted to.

Some sludgy beat began down the street from the apartment, probably something from one of the strip clubs, sounding out of place with the morning sunlight streaming in through the window.

We slept the day away. When I awoke, it was late, already slipping into the hours when trouble could be found in every shadowy corner.

"Let's go out. It'll make you feel better."

"Not tonight."

"Come on," she said, flashing her signature mischievous grin, the same one that always reminded me so much of Troy. "We'll have fun." She came around the corner, dressed in her figure-hugging mini dress, black stocking and heels, and let me drink in her slinky body before covering it with a coat. She took my hand and I followed, hypnotized by her feline movements.

19

New Orleans was a different animal after midnight. The early drinkers were rowdy, the serious ones getting ready to begin the evening. The black-clad crowd ducked in and out of clubs playing sludgy metal music or dark wave beats, smoking clove cigarettes or drinking absinthe. Then, there was our crowd —dancing on the fringes, disappearing into clubs disguised by hidden facades.

It was dangerous, even to walk with someone. Everyone in New Orleans had a story. Vampires, lurking in the shadows, ready to slice your arms open and drink your blood from the wound, or even lick it off the asphalt like a hungry stray. Muggers poised as regular passers-by, ready to pull you into an alley, not caring about your money, but wanting solace in your body. Vic and I only got stares and catcalls. Looking back, it's a miracle nothing serious happened. Vic was like a black cat that brought good luck.

We took another side street, not the one to the regular club we'd been visiting.

"Where are we going?"

"It's a new place," she said, keeping her eyes peeled to the streets. "New to you, anyway."

Her tone made me feel as if she still didn't take me seriously, that she still thought I was green and inexperienced.

The vibe was different, uninviting, like the walls were caving in all around us. The claustrophobic air of the place was compounded by all the staring people, who circled around me like I was a piece of fresh meat. Vic wandered away into the bowels of the club so quickly, I lost sight of her.

I felt a hand on my arm.

"You look like you could use something to take your mind off things," said a man's voice. I turned around to face a barrel chest. When I looked up, I staggered backwards. This man was tall. He wore head-to-toe black, like most people there, but his towering presence was menacing. A strobe light flashed across his face.

The cop from Troy's apartment. He was here, staring me down.

"I'm just—"

He put a hand over my mouth and one on the back of my head to shush me. I struggled and tried to push him off, but it was like trying to move a wall of steel. How had I gotten into this mess? It was supposed to be the other way around, not him trying to dominate me.

He laughed, his voice richly toned. I felt something cold snap over my wrists and he flipped me over his shoulder like I was simply a rag doll.

"Put her down, Gabe."

"She came in here unaccompanied. She's mine."

"She's with me," Vic said. "Uncuff her and put her down."

I landed on my feet and the guy produced a small key and undid my handcuffs. I shot him a nasty glare before following Vic.

"What is this place?"

Vic turned a little to shout over the music. "Sadists' club. Keep up with me."

I followed Vic into a back room. She had a man tied up there, spread eagle, his hands and feet tied to a St. Andrew's Cross. He was completely naked but withstood the worst of some instrument. Angry streaks crisscrossed his skin in random patterns.

"My friend's here to watch. She's a real wild one," Vic said. She picked up a cane and *thwack!* It smacked it so hard against the man's skin, the noise echoed in the room, and I winced.

"V," I said, but she didn't appear to hear me. That was what she said she wanted to be called at these places. She unleashed a fury of smacks to the man's genitals, a violence I hadn't seen in her before, and he squirmed and moaned through his gag.

She beat him so hard, she left merciless bleeding gashes all over his body. The man wailed through his gag, yanking on his binds and skirting out of the way in a vain attempt to avoid the cane.

"V, I need to talk to you."

"About Gabe? Don't worry about that dumb fuck. He's only trying to rile you up."

"It worked. What's he doing here?"

"He's into this stuff. Was on the case because of the nature of…*the crime*." She shot me a sardonic look. "These sick little pigs will do anything to get their rocks off. Even risk death. Ain't that right, piggy? Squeal for yes!"

The man squealed, followed by a feeble attempt to cry. Tears streamed down his face now. *Thwack!*

I backed away towards the entrance.

The cop, the wall of steel, was behind me.

"So, you *are* into this stuff, aren't you, honey? I knew you were."

I found a way to escape through the tiny gap he left, his accusatory tone and Vic's pleading voice trailing behind me.

Was she the one who did it? Was the cop in on it? Bedrooms held endless secrets.

Jesus. I needed to get away from the city for a while. As crazy as Ivy Manor was, at least I was familiar with its ghosts. That nagging feeling of checking on Marcus tapped me on the shoulder, too.

All the lights were off at Ivy Manor, its bone-white outline barely visible with no moon. The BMW's headlights reflected off the arched windows and I cursed myself for forgetting to shut them off before turning in the driveway. Blake or Marcus likely noticed.

I opened the door with as much caution as I could muster, which ended up creating more noise than I'd hoped for. I crept into the kitchen, hoping to snag a nightcap before bed.

"Where the hell were you?"

I jumped. It was Blake's voice. He was sitting there in the dark, waiting for me.

"I went out with a friend." I reached for a lamp and Blake kept his eyes on the bourbon in front of him, the ice melted long ago. Ghost squinted and blinked at me from underneath the table, then began his mewling greeting, winding around my ankles as I went to the bar.

"You're always out with friends these days."

"I didn't realize I was under a curfew," I said, not looking at him, focusing on pouring my drink instead as my hands shook. How dare he act like a parent.

He was up and across the room before I could turn around. He grabbed me from behind and spun around, causing my drink to slosh around. Some of it landed on the floor and Ghost darted back into the shadows.

"You seem to forget who is in charge here."

"In *charge?* You can't be serious." I laughed at the audacity and took a sip of my drink. Blake snatched it away and set it on the counter.

"Your nails are black?"

I laughed harder and picked the drink back up, stepping away. "I'll leave if this is how you're going to be."

Just then, Marcus emerged from the back, squinting at the light and shuffling in his slippers.

"What's going on? Are you two fighting?"

"Oh, Blake here is upset that I'm going out and wearing black nail polish, apparently," I said, not able to contain my laughter.

"You *are* going out a lot," Marcus said, making his way to the bar.

"And you're drinking a lot," I snapped. "You're not twenty-one yet."

"Neither are you."

"You seem to forget," Blake said through clenched teeth, "I'm taking care of both of you. I gave you both a place to live. The least you could do is tell me where you are, when to expect you so I don't worry about you."

I slouched against the counter. Maybe he did care. And he was right. He was taking care of both Marcus and me.

"I'm sorry," I said. "I'll tell you from now on. I just needed to blow off steam. The past couple of months have been rough." And now, I think Vic might know something about my boyfriend's death, I thought. Oh, how I wanted to vent to Marcus about my ideas like I did when we were younger. But these days, it felt like Marcus and Blake were allied against me, reminding me of the toxic bond between Julia and Vivienne.

Marcus huffed and shot me a look.

"I'm really tired," I said, hoping to escape from the tension. "I think I'll go to bed."

Blake kissed me on the cheek. Marcus flashed me a disapproving look before I left the two of them alone in the kitchen, drinking together again.

I drew a bath and finished my drink there, letting theories tumble around in my mind.

I let the idea of an accidental death settle in my brain for the time being, just so I could sleep. To hell with Marcus and Blake. I slept in one of the guest bedrooms that night.

But my dreams were clouded with Vivienne moving in on Troy, about how she used to nuzzle up to him to get his attention, and how now, she was closer to him than I was. They were both dead.

Troy seemed to be a gifted secret keeper. It made me wonder what else he kept quiet.

I dreamt about Julia behind bars, scheming to get back at me. She had to suspect me. I thought about her face twisted in anger, her nails digging into her palm as she thought about ways to make my life miserable.

The logical part of my brain knew I should go speak to her, to see what she knew about this fetish he had. I was sure she had some sort of knowledge to help shed light on his case, but facing her? Could I do something like that?

It would be a juicy bit for the book, too, to talk about how I'd gone to see her locked up. I could confront her about all kinds of things. Would she talk to me?

I made a plan. I talked to Blake about where I'd be. Just back at the condo to do more interviews.

But the look in his eyes told me he knew what I'd be doing: going out again with strangers.

That should have been the least of his worries.

20

No Blake at the breakfast table. I got dressed and packed my bags. I ventured deeper into the house, my boots echoing on the tile. Still no sign of the two of them.

I sighed and opened the door to the bedroom Blake and I shared in better days, ready to temporarily shed the veil of sex and sweat, cloves and latex as I said goodbye to him.

Marcus sat straight up in bed and gasped so loud, it roused Blake. He lifted his head, his eyes slit against the light.

"Oh, shit," Marcus said.

Acid bloomed in my chest.

I fled the house to the sound of laughter, teasing laughter, filling my head. I put my palms over my ears and stumbled out of the house.

Blake called after me. He had thrown on a robe, but his nakedness, the same body he'd shared with Marcus, was under there. I couldn't bear to look at him.

"Stay away from me!" I screamed. Birds flew out of trees and into the dawn sky. My voice echoed throughout the property. I climbed into the car, and he grabbed the door, wrenching it back as I tried to slam it.

"Marianne, wait. Let me explain."

"There is nothing to explain. Let me go!"

He threw himself on the hood of the car. "No! You can't leave!" He was wailing like a pathetic child.

I started the car and roared out of the driveway, steering wildly back and forth to throw him off. Finally, he let go and tumbled down into the grass. Good. Too bad I hadn't killed him.

Marcus didn't bother to chase me. At least Blake tried. Marcus clearly didn't care. He should have said something, should have apologized. I gunned the car out of the driveway and had to swerve to avoid missing the ditch. The car fishtailed before I finally gained control. My god, I had almost careened into the same ditch my parents died in.

But then, my heart flipped from acidic anger to hollow hurt. Was what Blake and Marcus did any different than what I did? I lied and cheated to fill my own needs.

God, Troy. I missed him. I missed the comfort he gave me.

I drove back to Vic's, doubling my speed, racing through red lights, ignoring the horn blares from traffic. So what if I also died in a car accident? Who was left to care?

My usual stoic face fell when she opened the door, dressed in only an oversized t-shirt.

"Oh, honey," she said, her eyes changing from sleepy to shocked.

"Blake and Marcus," I said. Understanding flashed in her eyes.

"Come in."

She slept. I didn't. I blinked back tears the whole day.

I knew she was awake when she stretched out her lean body and spooned me. She pulled me in close and nuzzled my hair. I pushed into her.

"You gonna leave him?"

"I don't know." I twisted the ring on my finger.

"I'm not gonna tell you what to do. But let me tell you a story. I can tell by your accent that you come from a small town."

"Is it that obvious?"

"I'm telling you this because I'm from a small town, too."

She lit a cigarette, staring at the ceiling, her eyes going glassy from the memory.

"I went to school with this girl. Angela. Good grades, went to church, her boyfriend went to the same church and lived nearby. They'd been dating for a few months. She told me one day, crying, that she was pregnant. It seemed so shocking. She told me, barely wanting to say the words, that she intended to end it. Her dream was to go to college, somewhere out of state.

"Anyway, Angela said she was going to tell the boyfriend after school and ask him to help pay for an abortion. When I saw her on Monday, she looked awful. I asked what happened, and she told me he had come by with his parents on Saturday. He'd proposed in front of them all and "accidentally" revealed her pregnancy. Her parents would disown her for an abortion, so he trapped her.

"Angela had to marry him just after her eighteenth birthday. She had the baby a few months later. Never went to college. Had two more as the years went by. Until one day she dropped off her kids with her parents, saying she had to run errands. Then she drove off into the Amite River in the middle of the day. It was ruled an accident. The autopsy revealed no alcohol… but that she was pregnant again.

"This is the future they want for us. A boy picks a girl. And he can burn any dreams or opportunities she has to the fucking ground to get the wife and family he wants."

I knew she was right. Blake was the type who was caring, as long as he got what he wanted.

"Stay here with me," Vic said. "I can teach you how to make money. You can be my understudy. It's the best way to learn."

Would it be more of what we did that night? That tease, that exquisite pain she'd shown me, that vulnerability? Would I be able to do something like that, to allow her to see the things that brought me pleasure and pain? It seemed so embarrassing.

I nodded, and she responded with a satisfied little chuckle.

"What does an understudy do?"

"Help with my subs. Watch. Listen. Learn."

"So I don't have to crawl around like a dog or lick your boots?"

She laughed. "Only if you want to. And if you like it, you can take some of my subs. I'm too busy anyway. I want to do my art more."

I wanted to devote more time to something, too, besides being Blake's trophy and pretending everything was roses all of the time. Writing brought me pleasure, but I couldn't seem to break in.

"Does it pay well?"

"Hell yes it does! I'm about to quit the sex shop and do that full time as my real job. It can pay about two hundred an hour."

"But you have to have sex with the guys."

"Nope," she said, sitting up to light a clove. She stuck one in my mouth, too, then raised her eyebrows in anticipation. I got the message and lit hers before mine. If this is what it took to live with Vic, I was at her disposal. "They might ask for it. But if they do, tell them they're not worthy of your pussy."

I blanched. She howled with laughter. "Darling, you've got to learn not to be so embarrassed all the time. And consent. You've got to get consent before you go around choking people all the time."

She stretched and rummaged through clothing, pulled on something loose and black. When she bent over, I could see the silver jewelry in her nipple shimmer. "I've got a full day of work," she said, pulling on matching black leggings. "Make yourself at home." She tossed an extra key on the bed.

What to do now? I had some major decisions to make. But thinking of a free life, being myself, thrilled me and made my brain thrum with excitement. No more self-confinement. Freedom.

I went back to the condo to pack some things. Marcus's room was dark but for the small blue light of the computer, an electric humming filling the room. He had decked it out to his interests: modern, cold and stark, but with dust everywhere. I sneezed. I had been waiting on him so long, catering to his needs, that he didn't know the first thing about keeping things clean.

I went back into my own room and began throwing all my black clothing into a suitcase. All the preppy things could stay. Blake could wear them if he was so obsessed with them.

But there it was again, that feeling of being watched.

Something rustled deep within the closet. Something dark passed by my peripheral line of vision. Just when I thought I'd put everything to rest.

"That place is the vortex to hell. It's on the wrong ley line, and it pulls things in. I saw it before I slipped on the edge of the tub and broke my neck."

It was Vivienne again. I couldn't see her, but I heard her voice. My heart galloped. My skin iced over. I waited until all I heard was the humming from Marcus's computer. The air conditioning kicked on.

I continued to cram things into my suitcase, trying not to think about Troy.

This wasn't my fault. Couldn't be my fault.

Yet, how had he gotten my belt? I didn't remember leaving it there.

What if Vivienne could block my memory, control me, use me?

I raked my fingers through my hair. When I pulled all the way through, my hands came away covered in spiderweb-like strands of hair.

I could feel my mind cracking, splintering off in different directions, wanting to go to different places, one wanting to bring Troy back, one wanting to run away with Blake, one wanting to run away by myself, even without Marcus, and be by myself.

I retreated to my closet, the darkest place in the condo, and curled up into a ball. The voices all spoke, simultaneously lulling me into a stupor and splintering my mind even further, a webwork of personas forming. One was my mother's voice. After she and Daddy died, I missed them; I loved them; I pined for their presence. I even had vivid dreams that Momma was still alive, that she was just on a solo tour. Some dreams were about the accident as I imagined it, and that when we went to her funeral, she was in pieces, tossed into the casket haphazardly.

"She was such a mess that we couldn't piece her back together," the funeral director would say.

There in the closet, though, Momma's voice started saying things I hadn't thought about in years.

"But really, Marianne, why don't you talk? Why do you hide away when people come over? Where do you go?"

She was sympathetic about my mutism but made no effort to understand it. Sometimes, after family gatherings, she would pull me aside, exasperated, and drill me about why I did the things I did.

I never wanted to talk to her about Joseph. I still didn't know why.

"Marianne, you could do so much with your life if you would just *talk*," she would say after I'd sat there, completely mute, looking for patterns or things that looked like animals in the marble counter. I listened, but I didn't.

You should know, you should know, I'd think over and over.

I hated her for not knowing. I hated her for asking too many questions. I hated her for not asking enough questions, the right questions.

I dialed back through my childhood, thinking about interactions between my parents. Daddy knew. He had to. From the random clearing I'd found in the woods where he could look out over the pond, to his hesitation to talk about the twins, to his distance, I had a strong feeling he knew my mother had an affair with Theo, her sister's husband, and that the affair resulted in the twins.

Vic was scheduled to work late into the night, which meant I was on my own. I slept in the closet that night, my things half-packed, part of me wanting to stay at the condo and find some sense of familiarity, my mind still grappling with going back to Vic's and being her understudy.

It felt like something was always holding me back from freedom.

21

"You need to come home," Blake said.

He had called the condo twenty times before I finally broke down and picked up.

"Blake," I said into the phone. "There is no way."

"Your grandfather passed away."

Another day, another funeral. Fog covered the treetops in a thick frosting. Granddaddy wanted to be buried next to his favorite daughter, the one he thought could do no wrong: my mother.

If he only knew.

Marcus sidled up next to me, a pleading look on his face.

"Not now," I whispered. I wanted this all to be over with so I could go back to my shadow life in the city.

"Lily is staring at you."

"I know. I can feel it."

I knew if I met her eyes, I would see nothing but pain, nothing but cold revenge in those steely, bleak orbs of hers. Had this whole deranged trait come from her side of the family? I couldn't imagine it coming from Granddaddy, who was always so nice and fair to us. I couldn't imagine how Ed and Lily met and stayed around each other all those years.

Glancing over and seeing my parents' graves twisted my heart in a strange way. I was more sad about missing them.

I wanted to interrupt the funeral service at once and scream at Lily to stop staring at me like that, that her son was a pervert, that her daughter Julia probably poisoned him so she could have more of my parents' money, that it wasn't my fault my parents were dead and that Vivienne was insane and couldn't deal with her issues.

The funeral ended, and Lily stalked towards me.

"I need you out at the house. Tomorrow," she said. "I'm moving and I want you to clear out the rest of your mother's things."

There was something off about her. Besides the lack of grief in her face, she looked different somehow.

"Well?" she said, her face twisting into anger.

I glanced at Marcus, who gave me a little shrug. Why couldn't he do it?

"Fine," I said. I avoided her eyes and pretended to look for something in my purse.

The following day was the first time I had been to my grandparents' house since my parents died. Memories flooded back. Lily screaming at Momma in the driveway, telling her how we were messed up. Momma throwing some dessert across the room at Lily's comments about her not taking her life seriously, after she'd returned from some tour.

"Don't touch that," Lily snapped. I moved out of the way, eyeing the piece she was referring to, an old statue. "And don't stand next to that!" A lamp I had almost backed up into. "It's Italian."

The house was so cluttered with stuff, I had to turn my body to the side to shuffle through all the junk. There were things from Azalea House Momma had collected from tours. Little trinkets, small statues, masks, artifacts. Lily must have scooped them up during the time they stayed with us, right after Momma and Daddy died. Lily must have seen me looking at them.

"And don't even think about touching those," she said with a sneer. "I have every right to those, and you know it." I looked her up and down, not holding back my expression of disgust. "They might be worth something." I rolled my eyes. She thought everything was worth something.

Maybe she didn't want to let Janelle go. All these things represented the best of her, all the traveling she did, all the money she spent. I knew the worst, the cheating, the lies, the deceit, the things that drove Julia crazy.

I proceeded through the living room. There were family photos on the shelves. Seeing Momma and Daddy again seized my heart, but there was something else.

Troy was in a few of those photos. But his face was scratched out now.

"What's this?" I said, picking up one of the frames. It was from Easter, the first time I ever really had a conversation with Troy.

Lily snatched it out of my hands.

"I said don't touch anything!" she screamed.

"But why is Troy's face scratched out like that?"

"He is no longer a part of this family!" She tried to place the photo back on the shelf with shaking hands.

"In that case, my parents aren't, either. And neither is Uncle—"

"You stop it right now," she said, her body shaking with madness. "I know what you did. Julia told me. Troy should have been put down like the dog he was long ago!"

I stepped back as if her comment had the ability to move me physically. When I did, I took her in again. Her outfit. Her jewelry.

"You're not wearing your pearls," I said, more to myself than anything.

"Why would I wear pearls to clean the house? Come on!"

Now her hands were balled up into fists, just like Julia used to do. I took another step back. "I called you over here to clear out your mother's things. I could have just set them on fire! I'm doing you a favor! Now, go on!"

She trailed after me, ranting about how ungrateful I was, but I couldn't get that image of Troy's scratched out face out of my head.

I ignored Lily and went up into the attic. I covered my nose and mouth with my hand, my throat already constricting from the dust assault.

"Hurry up," Lily barked from behind me. She was ready to get Momma's useless things out of the way to make room for more things she deemed worthy. I put on the gloves Vic gave me and got to work. Lily eventually grew restless and marched back downstairs. I was left on my own.

Two white boxes stood out among the junk. I opened them. They were full of clothes, early 90s clothes. Winter clothes. In my mother's size. Everything still had a tag attached to it. The style was completely different from what she usually wore around Azalea House. I rummaged around the clothing.

Under a trench coat, there was a letter.

Just come up here. I know how my father can be. You'll find another guitarist here, I'm sure of it. Ring me when you get to Logan airport.

Logan airport? In Boston?

I know how my father can be.

The envelope was addressed to my mother. The return address was indeed Boston. The name at the top said L. Hume.

I sat the clothes aside and put the letter in my pocket. I piled up the things for donation and put the clothes in the trunk. I didn't know why. They weren't my size, and they were totally outdated.

When I got home, I washed everything. It was all upscale and European, nothing like the hippie boho stuff she wore at the house when we were kids. I put on one of the outfits, one black blouse with obscene shoulder pads, as well as black trousers. I pinned everything in the back and reread the letter.

Boston.

Just come here.

I know how my father can be.

If Lily had answers, she wouldn't give them to me. I had another option, though.

22

The roads to the woman's correctional facility stretched out for miles, the journey taking me through isolated parts of Louisiana I had never explored before.

The traffic lessoned and I found myself isolated on the drive, with nothing but the hum of the engine and needly pine trees on either side of the road. A sign indicated the prison was a mile away.

My heart began to pound in my chest like some feral creature looking for an escape. I pulled the car over before dizziness came over me. The lump in my throat formed next, that familiar knot that kept me from speaking. I gripped the steering wheel with sweaty palms and took deep breaths until the physical sensations subsided. It took almost an hour.

This was worse than when I rode my bike out to meet Carter Leblanc, the man accused of killing my twin brothers.

I drove on until I got to the jail. I went through security in a numb daze.

When Julia came to the inmate's phone, I almost didn't recognize her. I had never really seen Julia without makeup, and she looked pale, her eyes sunken deeper into her face. She seemed vaguely rat-like and wild.

"I'm writing a book," I said. "I want to give you a chance to be heard."

"You've got some nerve coming here after ruining my life," she sneered at me. "Why should I tell you anything?"

"Julia, look," I said, my palm sweating into the handle of the phone, "you're already in here. You may as well tell me."

She rolled her eyes.

"I mean, what do you have left? You lost so much. Your husband. Your sister. Your daughter. Troy." And my brothers, I wanted to say.

"How about my life, child? I have lost my life. I'm in here for god knows how long. I'll probably never get out."

"But you can use this as an opportunity. You can make your voice heard through this book. And maybe it'll get a lawyer interested in your case, and maybe your sentence will be reduced."

She cracked a smile. Her teeth were yellowing. "Ha! Right." She hung up the phone and stood up.

"Julia!" I screamed, pounding on the plexiglass. The guard eyed me. "Let me help you!"

I pleaded with my eyes. We couldn't end on this note. I needed answers about Troy.

The thirst for freedom was too much, even for Julia. She took her time sitting back down and picking up the phone again.

"I know hurt people hurt people," I said. "I know you did what you did because my mother betrayed you."

Her stern face faltered, as if she was cracking.

"What about Janelle? How was she hurt?"

"Abel was no angel," she said, "but the past is in the past for a reason. If you're so smart, you figure it out."

Damn her. I knew I would get nothing from her. She quirked her lips into a devilish smirk, as if pleased she skirted the question.

"If you have any ideas about Troy, tell me. Please."

She sighed and looked off in the direction of women shouting at each other. "I don't know."

"Anything would be helpful."

"He was into stuff like that. But as far as I know, he wasn't stupid enough to hang himself. But he did drink. Did he have alcohol in his system?"

I shook my head. It was one of the many endearing things about the new Troy. He stopped drinking. Julia probably didn't know that.

"He used to go to a place on Dauphine for kinky stuff. Do you know it?"

"No," I said, thinking of Vic. I never even thought about exploring other places without her. It was time to expand my horizons.

"Your time's almost up," the guard snapped.

"Julia? What place on Dauphine?"

She looked over her shoulder, at the chaotic world on the other side, as if it would offer some relief from her past.

"Time's up." The guard began to walk over to Julia.

"Julia!" I hated the desperation in my voice. Damn her. She knew what she was doing.

"Forbidden Gardens."

She hung up the phone and left without looking back.

23

I had some idea of what to expect. But this?

I kept it from Vic. I went in a low-cut black dress, fishnets, stilettos like daggers, thinking they might protect me from the poisons of Forbidden Gardens.

But nothing could protect me from its sharp thorns, ready to hook into wide-eyed newcomers.

It was an unassuming place. I stalked up and down Dauphine, looking for any sign of it. There were no indications of it. The directions I coerced from the crossdresser at the adult shop on the other end of the Quarter led to a locked courtyard. I paused and looked in. It seemed like a typical New Orleans residence, its gardens tropical and abundant, lion head fountains spouting a trickle of water on either side of an oval-shaped pool.

"Yes?"

I looked around until I spotted a camera pointed in my direction.

"I—"

I swallowed and composed myself, drawing up to my full height, teetering on the stilettos.

"Orchid."

It was the code word the crossdresser told me. I waited, the seconds ticking away in my head. I stepped away from the gate, ready to turn back—

A buzzer sounded. I opened the gate and walked through before whoever was in charge decided to see right through me and turn me away.

The courtyard was a jungle, so lush I wondered if predators lurked under draping greenery. I walked through the double doors, trying to replicate Vic's catwalk, pretending to know what I was doing and where I was going.

I slipped behind a curtain and found myself in an enormous mansion with sky high ceilings and painted black walls. The club Vic and I had been to seemed exclusive, but this?

Women wore chic leather outfits that hugged their dangerous, cinched in curves, the men in elaborate harnesses, suits or G-strings that cost more than my inheritance.

This place was excessive. Everything from the subtle blue lighting, meant to enhance the shine of latex and leather, to the sleek bar, screamed money. Who owned this place? Did Troy and Julia really come here together?

I could see her doing it, dying to fit in among the elite, Troy trailing behind her like some purebred prize pet.

Little theatrics unfolded in every corner. Near the entrance, a large man in an all-black suit sat with a wiry boy bent over the man's knee. The boy was about my age, I guessed, with much longer hair and skimpier panties. The man gripped a fistful of the boy's hair and brought down a flurry of hard spanks on the boy's bony ass. I winced, held my head high, and continued to walk, not sure what I was looking for.

By the bar, a small group of women in black latex barked commands at a group of crawling people. When I inched closer, I noticed they were all wearing collars and leather dog masks.

I sat down at the bar, already overwhelmed. When I turned and looked around, two young women in pigtails and Catholic schoolgirl uniforms were being paddled by a bespectacled, stern-looking woman. I could hear the thunderclap of the wood reverberating as it struck their bare flesh. As the scene played out, a tall woman with dark skin and long, wavy hair grinned as a man in a pink frilly dress kneeled beside her.

Something clicked beside me and when I looked, a silver case was presented to me with a hand-rolled cigarette sticking out. I took it and put it to my mouth and suddenly, I was surrounded by lighters. I turned in the direction of the case and accepted a light from a small, wry boy. It was the white-haired boy from earlier, the one who was taking the beating.

"Hello, Mistress," he said, shyness woven into his small voice. "I'm Ari."

I tried to hide the shaking in my hand by taking a deep drag. I needed to come up with a Mistress name, and fast.

"M."

The boy smiled, his lashes fluttering. He dropped to the ground and kissed my heels. I tried not to let my eyes widen. The whole time with Vic, I had been a voyeur. This place was making me feel like a complete amateur.

Ari rose and leaned up against the bar, close to me, his white hair cascading around his bony shoulders.

"Mistress M," he murmured, so close to me I could feel his warm breath on my neck, "pleased to meet you. I've never seen you here before."

I took a deep drag on the cigarette. "First time. I usually go over to the warehouse district."

Ari threw back his head and laughed, a tiny musical tinkling. "Ah. Leather and Lace."

"And this place is a little…"

"Different? This place draws a serious crowd. L&L is for voyeurs."

Like me, I thought.

"But I can tell you're more than just a voyeur," he said, his grin stretched wide across his narrow face.

"How so?"

"The way you walked in. The way you acted when everyone

around here offered to light your cigarette. Everything about you."

"How long have you been coming here?"

"Years."

"Really," I said, shocked. "You look young."

"Eighteen. But I've always known what I wanted." His eyes glittered.

Nerves threatened to seize my stomach. I changed the subject. "I'm writing a book on places like this," I fibbed. "Specifically about the dark side of it all."

"I could tell you all about that. I've seen some things."

"Oh?"

"Oh yes," he said, fluttering those blond lashes of his again. He leaned in a little, and I got the distinct impression this was a tit for tat kind of thing, that I'd have to give him what he wanted to get information.

"What can you tell me?"

"Oh," he said, tossing his hair over his shoulder. "Just some things."

"How about you buy me a drink and tell me about it?"

He grinned and ordered the most elaborate drink possible for us both. I rolled my eyes, thinking the obnoxious fruity drink would be worth it if he knew even the smallest detail about Troy.

"Did you hear about the guy who supposedly died of autoerotic asphyxiation over in the warehouse district?"

"Mmm," the boy said, slurping the drink. "I did. He came in here. Liked his liquor, too. Never thought he'd be into that. He was more into women having their way with him."

I took one more of the cigarettes the boy offered.

"But how would you even know if he wasn't getting off by himself by tying something around his neck?"

The boy narrowed his eyes for a brief second, as though insulted by my questioning. "Maybe he was," he said, "it's pretty easy to do that if you're as experienced as he was. Or at least, he seemed to be. Most of those guys start off with women and then when they can't get their fix, they seek it in private."

"What was he into here, specifically?"

"I watched him do a few scenes with that older woman he ran around with. They mostly did verbal stuff, light play. Sometimes the most exciting part for people like that is to be watched. She really loved having an audience. But I never saw any marks around his neck." Ari pursed his lips and shook his head. "Never. Usually with guys like that, you see something."

"But a lot of people engage in asphyxiation in private," I said. "Maybe she didn't know about it."

Ari shrugged again. "I don't know. You don't usually go straight to that. You have to work your way up to it. Men tend to have a very elaborate setup. Usually there's porn around or a video camera, something like that."

I couldn't help but shoot Ari a suspicious glance. "Were you there or something?"

He grinned. "No. I just thought I'd give you some creative ideas for your book."

Maybe Troy was just exploring though, and it was a freak accident. After all, he was so young. But that stool. It was too far away for it to just tumble out from under Troy's knees. And that single pearl. Why was that there?

"You know," Ari said, "you should see if there are autopsy records. See how drunk he was, or if he was on something."

"He was clean," I said. I caught myself. Ari clearly didn't recognize me, or else he would have said something. Right?

"Huh," Ari said, staring off into the crowd. "Anyway, we'll have to get more drinks if you want me to tell you more. Or we could…"

My heart pounded. "What?"

"Play?" He lifted his neatly sculpted brows and grinned. I hesitated. "Come on," he said. "I'll show you exactly what I like."

Ari linked his arm into mine and led me into the bowels of the club, the pulse of music growing into a mere thump behind us. Crowds stopped and stared, but I held my chin high and pulled my shoulders back. Still, I felt like I wanted to melt straight into the glossy, black tile. But as we walked, something washed over me, the essence that liked to come and turn me into a monster.

Finally, we came upon a room with a square stage in the middle. It was surrounded by velvet purple couches. Several people lounged, drank, and smoked cigarettes. The music here was different. Instead of pulsing house music, the tone was sludgy, the beat reverberating around the room in slow thumps.

I refused to listen too closely. Instead, I tried to take in everything that was happening and to learn as much as I could. But the monster was slipping into me like I was a mere outfit for her to parade and show off in.

"Slave Q," Ari said to a short and demure genderless person who had materialized in front of them. "Please lay out some instruments for us. I have found myself a beautiful Mistress, as you can see."

Slave Q bowed. "Mistress…?"

"M," I said, hardly believing my own ears.

"Pleased to meet you," they said, and scurried off to the stage. I watched, hoping to appear mysterious instead of ignorant, as Slave Q laid out a black cloth bundle on the stage. They undid a bow and unwrapped a sparkling collection of blades.

"Ari," said a female voice behind me. "Who's this?"

"This is a new dominant I'm excited for you to meet," Ari chirped. "Mistress M, meet Lady Dionne. She runs this place."

Lady Dionne held my gaze, and my worrying mind struggled to make eye contact. I held it a beat longer than my normal comfort levels and Lady Dionne smiled, her dark eyes glittering as she regarded me. The low light in the room reflected off her rich brown skin. Her raspy, deep voice and regal stance were the only indicators that she was older.

"Pleased to meet you," she said, looking me up and down.

"And you as well." I bowed my head briefly to show respect. She flashed a blinding white grin.

"Mistress M and I were about to do a scene. Would you care to join us?"

Lady Dionne regarded me once more, her brows slightly lifted in question.

"I would be honored, Lady," I said.

Ari motioned for me to join him as Slave Q scurried away, disappearing into a crowd of onlookers. My nerves flared thinking of them watching us, but as Ari accompanied me on stage, the nervousness dissipated and the monster took over, eyeing the blades as if they were candy. With Lady Dionne beside me, I felt even more confident. It was everything I wanted, to explore this side of myself, to see if I was really possessed, and to engage in this shadow side of myself. I inhaled and let the demon out to enjoy her playtime.

Once on the stage, Ari shed his clothing to reveal fine etchings of pink and white that covered his body like artwork. He was completely shaved except for his head and eyebrows, and there was a ladder-like piercing along the underside of his penis.

Lady Dionne took charge as I observed. They had done this many times before and moved around each other with exquisite choreography. Ari lay back on what looked like a dentist's chair. He spread his legs and Lady Dionne secured them with black silk ties to the bottom of the chair. She did the same with his hands. I watched carefully, taking in all the details.

She bent and selected a blade from the bundle and motioned for me to do the same.

"Now," she said. "These are all quite sharp. Dig in too deep, lose control, and you'll cut him. You may draw a little blood, but maintain control at all times."

Control. That's what I sought, right? I watched her handle the knife with careful pressure. She dragged the point along Ari's torso and he hissed in a great breath of air, then shuddered. I followed Lady Dionne's lead and Ari's cock twitched and hardened.

As Lady Dionne demonstrated, I followed. Something great and powerful uncoiled within me, the old Marianne sloughing away like a snakeskin, the new girl stepping in with a sense of power and control, something almost alien to me.

Was I really possessed? Or was I finally inhabiting my own body?

Everything that happened from that point forward was like being in a dream, like my Marianne brain didn't have control over my limbs or the words coming out of my mouth. How had I gone from completely mute to finding my voice, to teasing someone like submissive Ari and knowing intuitively that he liked what I was doing?

What if I wasn't possessed at all? What if these two people lived within me and now they were finally both alive?

I dragged the blade across Ari's alabaster skin as Lady Dionne showed me, leaving behind pink trails. I dragged down across his groin, and he moaned and bucked his hips.

"You slut, you like this, don't you?" I said involuntarily, the words spilling out as naturally as an exhalation. I pushed the shock of its ease back down, burying it with the old Marianne.

Lady Dionne smiled with approval. She picked up one of the black candles that decorated the stage and tilted it slightly to let the wax dribble on Ari's chest. As the hot wax reached his skin, he hissed and moaned. I followed her lead, mesmerized by the pebble-like pink marks it left behind, how it decorated his pale skin in stark contrast.

We teased him until he writhed in his binds and begged for mercy. Lady Dionne cackled and released him slowly.

"Join me on the sofa," she said. I followed, praying she approved of me.

She sat, taking up room on the sofa, her arms splayed out on the back, her legs crossed. I tried to slightly mimic her posture. Ari fled to my feet and kissed my heels, then remained in a kneeling position.

"So." Lady Dionne said, popping a slim cigarette in her mouth. Several slaves stepped forward and she chose the light from a tall, slim dark-haired man. They exchanged knowing smiles. "I hear you're a writer."

"That certainly got around fast."

Lady Dionne laughed, exhaling smoke in puffs. "These little

slaves talk like they're in a sewing circle. Way too much. What do you write about?"

"Erotica. The lifestyle. My next story is on autoerotic asphyxia."

"Belting," she said. "Huffing. Fly me to the moon," she sang. I nodded, even though I'd never heard any of those terms. "It's very controversial. A lot of men do it on their own."

"Like the case over in the Warehouse District."

Lady Dionne lowered her eyelids and regarded me, her face blank.

"You're new to all this," she said with a grand sweep of her hand. "Why not be my understudy? You could come in and take a percentage from my sessions. You have a few natural dominant tendencies."

I swallowed, keeping my chin high. "Maybe," I said. After all, it would be useful to have my own money, to not have to rely so much on Blake's allowances. He would likely be cutting me off soon anyway. Besides, I had no idea what was going to actually happen with the book since I'd been so wrapped up in figuring out what happened to Troy.

Dionne smiled, flashing teeth so white, they were like a beacon.

"Good," she said. "Experienced men know to come here, or to hire a good dominatrix for things like that. That man came in here all the time, you know." She looked me up and down, as if gauging my reaction. "I hear he was alone."

"You don't think anyone was there?" I asked. "Maybe something went wrong, and she left. Maybe she was afraid."

"It could have been a fluke. Or an accident. I even heard someone here say they were sure it was a suicide."

"Suicide?" I nearly yelled.

"I'm sure you're aware of his wife and that…scandal."

My heart pounded in my ears. Dionne smiled, her canines seeming unrealistically sharp.

"What if it wasn't a suicide, though? Why would he play such a dangerous game alone?" I asked.

"Secrecy enhances the risk," she said. "The police were here, of course, questioning all of us. When something like that happens, we all become suspects. His door was open, unlocked. A partner, if present, can react if there's an emergency. He was naked. There was no evidence of ejaculation, nothing there to clean it up… Or so I've heard."

"What about neck burns? Wouldn't you have noticed something like that previously?"

"Sometimes they place protective padding around the rope, like a towel. A belt. If you really want to know," she said, taking a drag off her cigarette, "go back to his apartment. See if there are grooves worn on the closet rafter."

I blinked. "What do you mean, go back?" My heart leapt into my throat.

"My dear," she said, "I'm not stupid. You're the niece, aren't you?"

I sucked in a breath like I'd been stuck underwater. Dionne laughed.

"Your secret is safe with me," she said. "But you may want to keep it from the slaves here. As I mentioned, they like to gossip. But you should talk to Spot. He knows all about it. Ari, go get him. I know that little slut is here."

I watched, playing it cool while Ari sashayed off into the crowds. He returned with a meaty guy, very handsome, with a dark ring of bruises around his neck.

"Tell Mistress about what you like," Lady Dionne commanded.

Spot gulped. "Choking. I also like when my Mistress pretends I'm a bad dog and yanks on my choke collar."

His voice was so quiet and raspy I had to lean in, wondering if I'd heard him correctly.

"How does it feel?" I asked, mesmerized.

"When I'm alone?"

I nodded.

"It's like being a slave to lust. It commands me. Usually without warning, too, like these popup thunderstorms we get here in New Orleans." He pronounced it like a local, saying it all in one word. "I can actually hear it when the oxygen to my brain is cut off. It's like hard rain hammering on a window. Then I get intense tingling sensations. Everywhere. Then I can't breathe or scream, and it becomes more exciting. I can look down and see my stomach suck in and out with no air."

Shock sent tingling sensations through my body. How horrible. I couldn't help but think about Troy dying up there on his closet's bar.

"I wish I could be satisfied with just my Mistress choking me with the collar. But my desires are out of control."

"That's because you're a slut," Lady Dionne interjected. Spot lowered his gaze and flushed, but there was a tiny smirk on his face.

"I really don't want to die because of it. I don't want anyone to find me like that."

I swallowed, understanding. Troy didn't either, I was sure.

Why did we have to live this way, traipsing about through the shadows, hiding our deepest fantasies and sharing only with other people in this lifestyle, whispers in the night, in hidden, password protected places? I thought of my mother having an affair with her brother-in-law, the things they did, the twins that resulted from that affair. What demonic thing led her astray from her marriage? Was it a demon at all, or was society's notion of the perfect family flawed? I still couldn't wrap my brain around it all, but I knew that marriage to Blake felt wrong. I had gotten into it too young, and now, even if I left him, it would be too late for me. Every time I came to a place like this and hid my ring in my purse, I felt like a fake, a traitor to myself, to the crowd that surrounded me, and especially to Blake.

Looking at Spot, my heart swelled. The tortured lines in his face, the worried wringing of his hands, and the bruise around his neck, a person struggling with his desires. Troy knew what he wanted—rough sex with a partner in control, always someone else to guide him through his pleasure. He didn't strike me as someone playing with fire. He danced through the piercing heat, unafraid, unashamed, with Julia guiding him and then later, me. Part of his pleasure came from someone in charge, to take an interest in him and tell him what to do. He saw that in me and helped me find myself. He certainly didn't seem to be caught up in secrets and lies.

Lady Dionne looked at me, her observant eyes reading me. "You look like you're having an epiphany," she said.

"You can read me well."

"It's part of my job. Work here with me. You'll learn a lot."

How could I refuse? It would drive Blake mad, I would learn a lot, and I could earn money for myself without having to stress too much about the book. It would allow me to keep the condo, and allow me a way out of Ivy Manor, a doorway into the city, away from the judgmental eyes of my ancestors. And I could still learn with Vic, too.

"Alright," I said.

"Wonderful," she said, rising. I took it as my cue to leave, so I stood as well. Ari stood behind me. "We can start tomorrow."

"You must have impressed her," Ari said once we were back down the corridor. "She never takes on understudies."

I shrugged. "Maybe I am a natural dominant. You going to tell me more about Troy or what?"

He fluttered his white eyelashes and smiled. "Yes. I was interested in the case because the police said it was related to this lifestyle. I work in records."

I turned to him. "Records?"

"Yes. It's a silly job for Orleans parish. I mostly listen to music while I scan police records into our system."

My eyes widened. "No kidding."

"Yep. Most of them are ridiculous reports. But some of them are really interesting."

"I think I met the perfect sub."

He turned pink and fluttered his lashes again. I decided I liked when he did that.

"Will I see you tomorrow, Mistress?"

"I'll be back around the same time," I said. "Be good."

He smiled and threw himself at my feet, kissing them with relish.

Everything could burn at Ivy Manor as far as I was concerned now that I learned about Marcus and Blake, but I had to go back and grab all the notes I left there. I drove in a tired daze back to the house, New Orleans like a glowing beacon in the rear-view mirror. Every time I left it, it was like leaving an appendage behind. I belonged there, I knew deep down. It was my home; not Ivy Manor, with ivory slate and buried whispers. I decided I liked things at face value. New Orleans was so open about its dark past, even its graves were on the surface, eccentricities were welcome, and debauchery was expected.

At Ivy Manor, it was a different story.

24

It was always the same when I got close to Ivy Manor. That sinking sensation crept up in my throat and closed around it. Was this how Troy felt right before he died, as lust and death came together as one? Because I sure felt like I was about to die every time I got close to the house.

New house, totally different interior. Except so many people died there and what Vivienne whispered in my ear held up.

You can never change it, she had said.

I walked into the new white bathroom and broke out into gooseflesh as soon as I closed the door behind me. It was like standing in the path of an air conditioner.

Even with the new house, and the open space, I still saw things. And felt them. There were good ones, and bad ones always came through the strongest.

It was early morning, but Marcus was by the pool. Blake wasn't anywhere to be found.

"You," I snapped. The little bastard had the audacity to sit there with a mimosa in his hand, sunglasses perched on his face, splayed out in his pool chair.

"Damnit, Marianne. What are you doing here?"

"I came to get my notes. And don't you play the victim. You knew exactly what you were doing."

"You don't love him."

"And you do?"

He looked out at the pool and said nothing for a long time. "I thought you knew."

"Troy mentioned it in a roundabout way."

Marcus scoffed. "You've lost your mind. I saw it when we were in Azalea House, but it's so obvious now. I mean, you're seeing and hearing things that aren't there."

"It *is* real. You weren't around in the woods that time. And don't forget what happened back at the condo, too."

"You're sleep deprived."

"You believed me once."

"I think you just have a lot going on. A lot of stress. I read about it. People can disassociate, they say. Like, a split personality…or whatever." He gave me a dismissive wave and sipped his drink.

"Where's your boyfriend?"

He gulped. "Work."

"I'm going to rest here for a little while. Then I'm packing some things and staying in New Orleans."

He got up and trailed after me. "No. Wait. I didn't mean to be so harsh. You'll just have to get used to a new house. And the situation I'm sure you knew was happening anyway. Once you accept that, life will be grand. That's all it is. It's just time," he said, trying to keep up with me in the hallway. There *were* new house sounds to deal with, and the whole matter of not feeling myself. I felt nauseous and lightheaded.

"It's not about you and Blake, it's that you're *underage*, Marcus. And you both lied to me."

"Right. It's always about you. I forgot."

"Marcus, I'm trying to keep it together here. It's taking every inch of restraint not to kill you."

"If you're trying so hard, you may as well hear the truth. We were talking about me, not you. Don't interject with your own shit."

I stood back and crossed my arms over my chest, resigning myself to be quiet. I needed to know why he'd been so defensive, and he was giving me reasons right now.

"You think Vivienne was awful to you? She was horrible to *me*. Beating me every chance she got, snide remarks about being gay. You got off easy."

"No, I didn't."

He shook his head and narrowed his eyes at me. "You did. You ever hear of projection?"

I opened my mouth to say something, but I didn't know what he was talking about, so I kept quiet.

"Never mind. You should know the reasons. In many ways, we were financially privileged. We had the basics. A nice house, too. You should have seen some of the places I stayed." He had a sudden faraway look in his eyes, his nose wrinkled as if remembering smells. "They were awful."

"I thought you said you were staying with friends."

"I did. They would do things for older men. For money."

"Marcus—"

"No," he snapped, his eyes blazing. "I worked from internet cafes. I didn't make much, but it was something. Enough to get a room every now and again. But not enough. The work was inconsistent. I wrote Chloe a letter. She wrote back. I got it right before I was about to leave for the next place."

I bit my lip, jealous that Chloe knew where he was, that Marcus relied on her and not me for help. But who could blame him? I had been so selfish, staying behind for Troy and not running after Marcus. But he wouldn't have stayed, not for anything.

"She sent money without me asking. Said it was from Blake. That he was sorry. That his nose was fixed. That he would have punched him, too."

"And you forgave him? Just like that?"

"No. Not at first. We wrote back and forth a lot. I was able to get the place in the Keys with his money. I'm sure she coaxed him into it, made him see what he'd done. Soon, he became like a brother, and she was like a sister. We started talking on the phone."

That cut deep.

"So you see, dear sister, he was helping you, too, even before you knew it."

"But why?"

There was that faraway look again. "Some people lose a part of themselves. When they find it, it seems too wild, poisonous and terrifying. But when they look closer, they find that it is a part of their true selves, and they never really lost it at all."

I scoffed. "What the hell does that mean?"

He looked at me with wide eyes as if I'd told him I was going to kill him.

"You both lied to me," I flared. I curled my fingers into fists until my nails bit into my palms. Marcus flinched. "All that time you were pressuring me to get with Blake, that was so you two could have a secret relationship. You used me. You both did."

"I'm sorry," he said, his voice quavering.

"You're sorry you got caught, you selfish little brat. You gaslit me into thinking I was the bad one, when it was really you this whole time."

"People aren't either good or bad, Marianne. They're just people. So what if Blake tried to make himself right again by helping us? Maybe he realizes how shitty he was in high school and he's trying to become better. You have to give him credit. Most people don't even try, don't even have the ability to see into themselves. Some of our family had plenty of opportunities to change their tune after our parents died, and they didn't, did they?"

I grit my teeth.

"Maybe he is trying to be better. Chloe saw something in him, didn't she?"

Something strange danced across his face, something satisfied, something victorious.

Chloe and Blake had been his saviors in a time when he was really struggling. To a teenaged boy on the run, it was sure to mean a lot.

"But you still had a choice, Marcus. You deceived me. You lied. You went behind my back. You both did!"

He shrugged, so nonchalant I wanted to slap him. "Maybe I learned it from watching you."

"Oh, Marcus. Come on. Did Chloe run away after she caught you two in bed?"

"What? No!" But his face revealed the truth he couldn't say out loud.

Marcus followed me with a list of excuses, none of which I heard. I went to my room, slammed the door in Marcus's face, and plopped down on the new bed.

A keen sense of cold washed over me, icy as sleet. There was the buzzing in my ears again. I had been drinking whiskey to fend it off, to dull it, but some days it would not go away.

"You're becoming like your mother. Never satisfied with what you've got."

Bile inched up into my throat.

"Marianne, come into the bathroom again. I can make you pretty."

I shook my head. The bile bubbled around my tongue. I sucked some of it up through the back of my nose and sputtered.

"Come into the bathroom or you won't like what's coming next."

The tight, cultivated accent. The venom in those words.

I tip-toed into the bathroom, already wincing at what I knew I'd find.

The bathroom had somehow gone from modern and white to how it had been before at Azalea House. Claw bathtub. White hexagon tiles on the floor, green tiles by the bathtub. Stained glass blue and green window.

And Vivienne, hanging from the steel curtain rod, her hair hanging from her face, her gown soaked with urine.

Her face lifted. Black flowerets where her eyes were. Black lips.

Her face waxy, veined with the darkening filigree signs of death. She screamed at me.

"I can make you pretty again."

I ran.

"Maaaaaariaaaaaanne… I'm heeeere. I'll get yooooooou."

I'll get you. I'll get you.

It trailed after me, imprinting into my mind, spreading like an ink stain. The twins were silent. It was only Vivienne's voice, powerful enough to drown out everyone else's.

Just like she was in life.

I bolted out of the bathroom and started packing more belongings. To hell with this place.

"I'm going back," I said to Marcus. I stuffed things into my suitcase and mashed it down. It still wouldn't close.

"Well, I'm staying here."

I whirled around to look at him, my hand still pushing down on the suitcase. "You're staying here? With Blake? Why?"

He shrugged. I turned my back on him again and bit my lip to avoid saying something rude. Sometimes, he really could be such a teenager.

"Well, I'm going back to New Orleans and staying permanently."

"You can't actually do that. Legally, I mean. I'm not eighteen yet."

Now I did look at him. What the hell was this? "What do you mean? You can stay here with Blake since you're such good buddies."

"No," he said, looking quite pleased with himself, hands behind his back. "Not yet. Not legally. You two aren't married yet." He rocked on his toes.

"God, Marcus. I'm having a tough time here. I saw Vivienne again. And you and Blake? You're underaged, for—"

"Like you were with Troy?"

I stared at him, my mouth hanging open.

"You need to let go of the past, Marianne. Grudges cause all kinds of illnesses. What if you get cancer by worrying about all these dead people?"

"Shut up," I said. Defeated, I flipped the suitcase over on the bed, leaving a pile of frilly black things.

I went out through the greenhouse and into the backyard and stared out at the pool. I thought all these different touches would change things, like they'd chase old ghosts away. Was that what Julia was thinking when she remodeled Azalea House? Hadn't I done the same thing, thinking it would chase away the dark?

I went inside and packed a weekend bag. When I walked out, Marcus and Blake were on the front porch, laughing and drinking. Damn Blake for always indulging him. Sometimes, it was like he was trying too hard.

"I'm going to do some research at a record store in New Orleans."

"Great, babe. Will you be back?" A pleading look touched his eyes.

"Maybe." I hopped in the car as Marcus frowned.

Damn them *both* to hell for leaving me out all the time, for having a good time while I was miserable. They could deal with Vivienne's nasty wrath for all I cared.

I peeled out of the driveway, angry at them, but even more angry about myself.

All my life, I felt like I had no control. We were imprisoned in that damn house, day after day, with nowhere to go except for the grounds and school. Those were the only safe places, especially according to my mother.

She was trying to protect me. That's all it was.

I wish she would have just come out and said it, though. My entire life, I stood in the background while my parents did their thing. Day in and day out, they devoted their lives to recording and practicing. It felt like I spent many days searching for my mother, only to find her locked away in some room like she didn't want to be found.

I finally knew why. She felt control in being alone. There was no one around to judge her about her affair with Theo, or why she let the twins out of her sight.

Where could I find my control? I didn't have it with men, that was for sure. It always seemed that men wanted something from me. Sex or money or something I could not give. Even Marcus depended on me, even though I didn't see him as a threat. He had built up a life where he did his own thing, building web pages and making his own money, establishing his own independence. But what was I doing? I told myself this whole time, I was recovering from trauma, escaping all the pain of Azalea House by living in a totally different area, a change of scenery where all that turquoise water would blot out the memories.

But what was I doing to establish some sense of control in my life?

When I arrived at the condo, I looked at myself in the mirror, at the gradually deteriorating physical body. I no longer had curves. I had become lithe, and my hair had grown nearly to my ass, curling in the way Daddy's used to, shining in that almost auburn hue that Momma had.

I could control my clothing. Back at Azalea House, Momma always had us wear dated clothes. She said it would keep us from attracting too much attention. I never really thought about clothing until after they died, until Marcus started wearing all black and Vivienne stepped out dressed to the nines every day, just as one would expect a fashion model to do.

I could change my clothing. I went into my closet and pulled on an all-black outfit, something different than the clothing I kept at Ivy Manor.

I found Marcus's clippers in the bathroom and shaved the sides of my head again.

I could take control of my body, my brain, my life.

I fell asleep in my clothes, exhausted, my stomach growling. I curled into a ball, hoping the position would comfort me somehow. Outside my window, the sky turned seashell, shocking pink, the sunset enhanced by the pollutants in the Louisiana sky.

I woke up to a noise. It was totally dark, the outlines of the bedroom barely visible. I sat up, the blood in my veins coiling with something acidic.

There was the noise again. The window was rattling, like someone was trying to get in.

I did not want to look, but I inched forward on the bed, taking my time to glance in the direction of the noise. I could only make out a figure in the window, staring my way, their stance upright and very sure of themselves.

Then, the figure transcended all boundaries. They were *in* the room, standing by the window.

Shock iced over me in a cloak. I scuttled, crab-like across the bed, and thumped onto the ground.

I looked up, ready to face the attacker.

They were gone.

Frantic, I switched on the light.

No one.

I put my hands in my hair, ready to tear it out, trying to wish away the inevitable.

I went downstairs and made a sandwich, downing it without chewing much. I ate it so fast it sent me reeling with nausea. I scrambled to the bathroom and heaved up everything, until I could taste the pits of my stomach.

I slept on the couch the rest of the night, waiting for the light that couldn't come fast enough.

25

"Troy wouldn't kill himself."

Gabe Ledeau sat back in his office chair, put his hands behind his head, and grinned. His legs splayed out, his knees almost touching mine. "There was nothing around him, nothing up his ass, no weird clothing, no mirror, nothing recording him. No mask, no covering of the face, no duct tape or gags in the mouth. No bondage of genitals."

"You didn't know him." I scooted my chair back away from him. I had been to a few sessions with both Lady Dionne and Vic, and finally had some sense of using my words.

"I'd like to get to know *you*."

I smoothed my clothing. "I'm here in a professional capacity, Detective Ledeau."

"Alright, honey."

My skin crawled, but I pressed on. "If this was a regular thing for Troy, there would have been more marks on that closet rod. There weren't. I knew him. We played this choking game together. If he was pining for that, he would have waited for me. And if he couldn't wait, he would have done it in some way to be safe."

"Look," he said, "you can crush the trachea at about four

pounds of pressure. The head weighs about ten pounds. All it takes is a little slip, and then you're screwed. He could have kicked the stool across the room while he was struggling. It's a quick death. You can lose consciousness in about ten seconds. People tend to video tape themselves and that's how we know."

"But Troy didn't videotape himself."

"You'll start having convulsions at about fourteen seconds. And then there is something called decerebrate rigidity, where your arms and legs are extended, your wrists are extended. That's a nerve response. That's in about nineteen seconds. Then you start trying to take in breaths. Do you see what I'm saying?"

I swallowed hard. His eyes pinned me to the chair.

"In about 45 seconds, you'll start flexing inward. And then you'll hold that for a few more seconds, and then there's a loss of muscle control. It can happen in about two minutes. And then the last twitch is about four to five minutes in. It can happen fast, Ms. Easton. I don't think you understand how fast. We see it all the time."

"But you didn't see it in this case."

He laughed. The audacity of the fucker.

"Look," I said, removing the little sachet from my purse. "There's a single pearl in here. Don't you think that's strange?"

He laughed again. I clenched my jaw.

"You were seeing other people, too, weren't you? You run around with Victoria a lot, don't you?"

"I'm trying to tell you I don't think this was an accident or a suicide. I was with him all weekend. Hell, I was with him a lot. There was dust under the bed. But no dust on *this*."

"Oh, come on," he said, splaying his legs out again. "You think someone wearing pearls killed your boyfriend? That's a pretty good story. We can talk about this over dinner, huh? I'll take you to Galatoire's."

"Will you look into this some more if I do?"

"Is that a yes?" An alligator grin spread across his too-tan face.

"Maybe," I said, putting the sachet back in my bag. "I don't warm up easily."

"Oh, I know. I know about everything that happened to you. Your parents, your aunt, your brothers…"

"Shut up."

"You might not want to say that to an officer of the law, Miss."

I took a deep breath. This was going nowhere. I hesitated to tell him about what Ari told me. I'd have to think of a good opportunity to throw it in his face, to tell him what a shitty detective he was.

"I hear your aunt is getting out soon."

"What?"

He grinned again at what he was probably looking for: a crack in my emotions.

"Yeah," he said, bringing his hands down to his desk, forming a steeple with them. "I heard she has a new boyfriend, some pen pal. Those gossipy subs know everything."

"How the hell—"

"Prison's crowded. Good behavior. She's white."

"When is she getting out?"

"I heard a couple of weeks. Look, let me take you out. I promise to behave."

"Do you know the boyfriend?"

"Some guy named Christopher. Bartends over on Bourbon," he said. "He's a chatterbox. Talking about getting money from the tabloids. So, about Galatoire's…"

I stood up and grabbed my purse. "No." Scumbag, I thought as I punched the button on the elevator. What a waste of time.

I ached for the sun to go down, for the city to drape itself in black velvet so I could do the same and dance in its shadow.

I was fully committed to learning from Lady Dionne and Vic. I felt like my life was spiraling, and I needed to feel like I had some sort of importance.

I had seen Julia control something in her life when a lot of things were spiraling out of control for her. With that latex outfit and her queen-like stance, she cast a spell over Troy, making him pay attention. He shifted from a non-caring alcoholic to someone interested and willing, someone ready to do what she said. It had a profound impact on me when I began to realize what sort of situation she had found herself in: her sister, who she'd had a rival with for years, had died; she was in financial trouble, and she was using her daughter in a last-ditch effort to stash some money away for her family.

In some ways, I pitied her. Domination gave her some sort of control of her life. I wanted the same. Things spiraled out of control for me, too. I lost my parents. I had dealt with the awful story of my long-dead brothers, always trying to live up to their childhood glory, their perfectness. As a Domme, I could step into a power that gave no fucks about what other people thought of me. It was like living a past life as some sort of Queen, who lived as she pleased and had everyone do everything for her.

The storm outside pounded against the windows of the condo, mirroring the storm in my mind, forever raging and rumbling. Damn Julia for putting me in this position. And now what would happen when she was back into the free world? I listened to the rain beat against the window as I wrote the letter.

Dearest Julia,

I am sure you are ready to be released, but you will never be released from the prison of your mind. I will see to that.

Troy and I had a good time before he died. I'm sure you heard all about it. I can't wait to hear what you think, too. He loved me all along. He was only with you because you provided some sense of security for him, but he really loved me. How could he love you? You were mean and spiteful to the core, and your hatred showed in your face, too. And all the special things you did for him, I can do better, so well he was himself with me.

I see you have met a new, younger man. I'm

sure we'll cross paths one of these days. I'll be there to visit you soon, I hope. When I do, you'll be sure to tell me all about your adventures with Troy down in New Orleans, or I'll be sure to tell your new man all about you.

    Your niece,

    Marianne

If Julia hadn't moved in and ruined everything, I would never have had to burn down Azalea House. Now that she was getting out, she would be determined to make my life a living hell again.

I would show up to the prison where she was kept, dressed in something powerful, something that made people stare, so she could see my true beauty and poise. She would cower just like everyone else. I would make sure of that, one way or another. And I would differentiate myself from Vivienne once and for all. I wouldn't take orders or have anyone tell me what to do. Julia had managed her daughter's career, overriding her agent, telling her where she needed to be. Vivienne got most of her confidence from her mother and from other people's approval, but I would get it from myself. I didn't need Troy or Blake or anyone to tell me I was beautiful and capable. I knew I was.

Or did I? Every time Troy popped back up in my mind, I found myself yearning for him, my heart wrenching as I remembered the twisted way his body looked, dead and cold. I couldn't have done that to him. But Vivienne would have, just to keep him away from me, just to show her jealousy that he was paying attention to me and not her or her mother.

No, no! He had done that to himself. That had to be it. Just like the man by the hotel when I first arrived for Chloe's funeral. Just like all the other subs Vic told me about. It was an accident.

He said he was seeing me and no one else. Could I believe him? I wasn't being faithful to him, that much was true. Why would he bother to give me that same respect?

Oh, Troy, I'm so sorry it turned out this way, I thought. But I will see to it that things turn out the right way for once. I'll make Julia's life even more miserable. I'll become the writer you always said I could be. I'll be independent and break free from Blake forever. And I'll make Marcus love me again, too.

26

Vivienne continued to stalk me from the grave. She peered from around corners, watched me in my sleep, waiting to pounce upon me like a predator. Her voice followed me through anxious days and sleepless nights.

After another night of tossing and turning, I looked in the mirror to brush my remaining hair. It fell out in clumps. I had spent so much time growing it out after cutting it into a pixie cut in my teens, and it was falling out in sticky clumps now at the slightest touch. I sobbed, my sharp clavicles heaving in the reflection. I had lost even more weight without realizing it.

Marcus eventually came by for his beloved computer, and he let himself in without knocking. I listened to him packing. He did things with emphasis, as if trying to get my attention.

"Jesus," I muttered from my place at the mirror.

Marcus must have heard me, because he appeared behind me, his looming frame taking up the doorway. His eyes were dark behind his glasses.

"Marianne," he said, his tone thick with worry, "you need to get to a doctor."

"A doctor can't help me, Marcus. No place is safe. No *one* is safe. In fact, you should probably stay away from me. What if you're victimized by association?"

He studied me, unblinking, his brows knitted together.

"She's real, Marcus."

"She's in your head. You're giving her too much power. She's dead. But she's still taking up space in your brain, even years after her death. What you're haunted by is guilt. Guilt that you caused her death."

"What if I did?" I put my hands on the sink to steady myself. Weakness washed over me in a sudden gust.

"She wanted to die. That was her decision. Not yours. You didn't hang her. Just like you didn't hang *him*."

I put my head in my hands. Hanging. I still couldn't imagine Troy killing himself the same way. I still couldn't imagine him getting his rocks off by playing some twisted game, playing out some secret that he kept from me. He never would have kept that from me.

"Troy is not your problem, either. You feel like you should have been able to save him somehow." He sighed and looked at the floor. "I do believe that you can see her. Hear her. But I believe you can overcome that. We are all light and dark, good and bad, and we all make the best decisions for ourselves in that moment of time."

"What do you mean?" I asked, meeting his eyes in the mirror.

"I mean that just because you were seeing Troy and doing things you didn't think were right, it doesn't mean you were possessed. Don't beat yourself up for not being perfect." He turned away and I barely caught the rest of what he said: "God knows, I am not, either."

Marcus's words echoed in my mind as I drove out of the city and around through the backroads with a loose plan to visit Julia again. The drive always soothed me, punching the gas on the open, twisting swamp roads under the canopy of oak and cypress trees, the shoulder dangerously close, dropping off to deep ditches or black swamp waters. I enjoyed gunning the engine around the curves, making the ass end lose traction and slide. It became a game on left-hand corners to see how close I could come to sliding the rear end off the road, thinking about how my parents had lost control of their car. I enjoyed cheating death every time I got in the car, my brain fogged with exhaustion. There were times I drifted off and had to jerk the wheel back to center myself. But at least, I knew I wouldn't have to deal with Vivienne or the rest of my family, living or dead.

The sunsets on the way out of the swamp were often phenomenal, pink and purple set against flaming orange skies, pollutants cast from all the oil rigs off in the distance. Once out of the swamp and closer to the city, I began to feel as though it was calling me, beckoning me with its welcomeness, the kind I had always looked for in my family. I thought I had that with Marcus, but lately, it was beginning to feel like he was slipping away from me like everything else in my life.

I couldn't let Julia see me. Not like this.

I went back to the condo and stretched out on the bed, listening to the sounds of the Quarter. Donkeys' feet click-clacking on the pavement as they pulled touring carriages, calls from drunk people, and faint jazz music swirled around me in a comforting symphony, muffled by the window unit. There was a certain sense of peace here, knowing this place of dark delights was the place I felt most at home.

After some time, I did drift off. I dreamt of purple rope burns and bloated faces, of twin ghosts and water that swallowed me whole in a tsunami wave. When I opened my eyes underwater, it was full of dead bodies, my brothers, my parents, Vivienne, and Troy. They floated towards me until I screamed, fighting off phantom corpses and wrestling with the sheets.

I dragged myself out of bed and walked towards Cafe du Monde, hoping its strong chicory coffee would sear my throat and inject me with a heart-pounding dose of caffeine, but it did little to wake me up. I watched New Orleans transition from late night shenanigans to early morning calmness, hoping that witnessing this eclipse would transition some of that into my own life.

I could let Vivienne go. I could accept that this was who I was, that I was a person who had a need for control, that it would help me heal from my past. I could accept that I wasn't perfect, that some dark part of me longed to torment and squeeze the masculinity right out of a man. But I couldn't accept that something happened to Troy, that he kept something like that from me, or that he killed himself on purpose. The pearl I'd found, when I held it in my hand, it burned with a toxic femininity that seemed so familiar, it was like part of my blood. But it wasn't mine.

Two jazz musicians set up shop in front of the cafe, unloaded instruments and lit up a joint. The scent was green and powerful. A red sports car ran the stop light, bass thumping from inside blacked-out windows. A group of women stumbled by, laughing raucously and falling all over each other. They reeked of sweet-smelling vodka.

This place was my escape. It was a place I felt like an adult. It reminded me of Troy, of those first few encounters where he encouraged me. It felt so grown up and sophisticated, like what children always imagine happens past their bedtime. And I got to experience that early on, before a lot of my peers. In many ways, it made me different, made me march to the beat of my own drum. It was time I got to know myself more, this shadow side of myself that most people only got to catch a glimpse of when they came to a place like New Orleans. I got to live it, day to day. I had choices. I didn't have to marry Blake if I didn't want to. I could call off the marriage and buy the condo, or any condo if I wanted to. I could leave this place and go somewhere else, anywhere I wanted to, especially when Marcus turned eighteen.

It's like there were twins inside of me, struggling for control. The quiet nun and the whore, the Madonna and the Jezebel fighting to be in the limelight. I should just let Vivienne have the limelight! Who wanted it anyway? I couldn't exist as myself, as Marianne, because I was too terrified of myself, those parts of me that I thought I had to push aside. But it came out anyway. It came out just like Vivienne would, pushing and screaming and kicking her way out, angry at everything, ready to scream so loud so the world would hear her.

I could feel something taking over again, that awful thing that writhed like a worm inside me, always waiting for bad thoughts to form in my mind so that it could latch on and wiggle its way out. I gripped the edges of the table, my hands clenched so hard around it, the knuckles turned white.

"Hey, where y'at?" said one of the jazz musicians. I saw him out of my peripheral vision, approaching me. "You alright? Hey, I think she's on somethin'."

"Get away from me!" I didn't recognize the sound of my own voice. It sounded venomous, full of hate.

"Bro," his partner said. "I think you better back off."

The man hunched down, trying to meet my eyes.

"I said get away from me!" There was still a hint of my own voice left in the words that came out, but it was so far overshadowed by the black thing clawing its way out, I didn't recognize it.

The man backed off, his jaw slack. He said something to his partner I didn't understand—the rumbling in my ears sounded like a lion's roar. I held on to the edges of the table for dear life, like I was withstanding the worst of an earthquake. The table shook. My coffee spilled, then the cup tipped over and crashed to the ground.

"Girl, you better get out of here and quit trippin' before I call the police on you," a waiter said. I stood up and staggered out, but every step I took was countered by the black entity taking over, causing me to stagger like I was being pulled in several directions at once.

My skin burned. I clawed at it and screamed, then bolted towards the shade further away from the cafe. People either stared or averted their gazes as I shrieked uncontrollably and clawed at myself, hating my skin all of the sudden. When my hands flew up to my scalp and began tearing at the remaining hair, part of myself came back, and I punched the stucco wall, left right left right, until I could no more. The demon took over again and howled with laughter.

The pain pushed her back down and then I cried, really cried from the searing sensation that traveled up my arms. Looking at my hands caused the pain to swell: I had fractured both of them, beating them to bloody, pulpy masses.

27

Thankfully, Marcus came to the hospital and not Blake. At least I could tolerate him, and I was in too much pain to fight. I had passed out somewhere on Decatur like an addict or crazy person. Someone had enough pity to call an ambulance.

"Blake's very upset, though."

"I can imagine," I mumbled. I motioned for the glass of water that sat on the tray in front of me. I felt like I'd been hit by a truck. Marcus brought it to me, but held his body far away from me, like I was infected with something he didn't want to catch.

"You can't catch mental illness. Or demons. Whatever it is I have. At least, I hope not."

He looked at me, his eyes sparkling with tears. "I'm really sorry, Marianne."

"For what? *You* didn't do anything."

He blinked back tears. "Yes, I did."

I cocked my head to the side, the big sister in me making an appearance. "You didn't do anything wrong. This is my own problem. I don't know if I'm sick or if something is going on, like, with the other side, but I'm finally going to get help."

He opened his mouth like he was going to say something else. "What is it?"

He shook his head, brushed the tears out of his eyes, and forced a grin. "Nothing. I'm just glad you're okay. You shouldn't really go out and about by yourself for a little while. Your hands are really messed up. What are you going to do about writing?"

I would have to allow myself to heal, and I would have to force the demons out of my brain so that I could write again. Writing was the escape, not drugs or being a dominatrix or any of those things that weren't necessarily productive. I was wasting my life. And I had wasted even more of it believing in ghosts and letting them take over my life.

"Was I still…you know…when you got here?"

He stepped away, his eyes going dark. "I saw gray in your eyes, like storm clouds, full of fury. Destruction. Cold and angry. Like…"

"Like Vivienne's?"

He nodded, crossed his arms over his torso like he did when our conversations cut too deep lately. "There was no you in there. Your voice cracked like something was trying to tear its way out. You gnashed your teeth, tried to claw at me like she used to do."

Angry streaks etched my arms. I recalled the first summer when Vivienne moved into Azalea House with us, when she got angry with us and scratched me.

"I said your name," Marcus continued. "I think you heard me a few times. Your pupils…" His bottom lip trembled.

"What?"

"They kind of…quivered, like you were trying to look out through a window into the darkness to find me. It was terrifying." He hugged himself tighter, as if he were protecting himself from whatever thing dwelled inside me.

There was something else, too. He opened his mouth to speak a few more times.

"Marcus. Is there something you want to tell me?"

He lowered his head and stared at his feet.

My heart pounded. Did this have something to do with Troy?

"Don't be mad at me, Marianne."

Despite the pain, I clenched my hands, my nails digging into the bandages. "What? What did you do?"

He snapped his head up and stared me in the eyes. "Oh, come on. It's not like you really love Blake or anything. What did you think was going on?"

"Marcus," I said, not liking the shaking in my voice. "Tell me."

"We started seeing each other before Chloe died."

"What?"

"Marianne, calm down."

"So he was using me to get to you?" I scoffed. "Wonderful."

He met my eyes for a brief second, as if afraid Vivienne would come through again, wondering if she and I were one in the same.

"Get out!" I screamed. I cringed at my own voice, ashamed that I sounded shrill and demonic, like Vivienne did when she was angry.

I caught a brief glance of Marcus's face right before he left the room, and wished I hadn't. Pain, confusion, anxiety and pure, uncut fear. I had never seen him look like that, not even when our parents died.

They released me from the hospital. With no Blake or Marcus or Troy, I floundered to even get dressed. It took several days before I mustered up the courage to call Vic.

"Why didn't you call me before?" Her face was scrunched up in agitation.

"I'm not used to trusting people," I said, my hands a useless pile of bones in my lap. Vic stopped tossing groceries into the refrigerator and studied me.

"Me either," she said. "But we've done a lot of shit together so far, and you still haven't told me much about you." She shrugged, then let her hands fall to her sides with emphasis.

"You've really never heard of the Eastons?"

She cocked her head to the side. "No. I've never heard of the Eastons."

"There was this band, Spellbound Hearts…"

"I've heard of them. Synth."

I nodded. "My parents…"

She made a cutting gesture with her hand. "Wait a second. Your parents were in Spellbound Hearts?"

I just looked at her. I was used to this reaction.

She scoffed. "Wow. Okay. I think I get it now. But what did you think I would do? Tell everyone about you? Honey, I have famous clients. And I don't open my mouth about them."

There was something similar to Troy in the way she said it, like, you can trust me. And I could trust Troy. But everyone told me he was a predator, that he was using me.

"I'm your friend. I know what you're thinking. I mean, have you ever had a real friend? Like a close girl friend?"

I thought of Chloe, about playing on the Ouija Board with her, about her standing up for me at school, and then thought about how her head must have looked smashed into the steering wheel, the baby on her lap.

"She died."

Vic blinked. "No wonder you're closed off."

She sat down next to me and brushed the hair out of my eyes. "I'll help you here, okay? You did things for me too, you know. I never would have gotten out of that sex shop if it weren't for you. I'm making more money now than I ever did. Part of it was you pushing me to do it. You know, I didn't grow up with famous musician parents. I grew up in a trailer park that flooded three times a year. And now I never have to go back to a place like that."

I didn't know what else to say. "Thank you," was all I could come up with.

Six weeks. Six weeks of staying around that condo, relying on someone else to cook, clean, and do all the things I couldn't do with broken hands. Vic brought me a tape recorder to record my thoughts on the book. I spoke freely, well into the night. Sometimes, she listened.

Vic curled up beside me and looked at me through her lowered gaze.

"Wait a minute," I said, tensing. "I thought you were a dominant?"

Unless I was reading her the wrong way, she was using submissive posturing, and looking at me in a way that the subs in the clubs did. A smile played on her lips, and she put her head in my lap, her jewelry clinking like musical bells.

Her voice was low and throaty when she finally said, "I would love to play around some day when you're feeling better. I only do that with women."

"But what about everything I just told you? Don't you think I'm weak?"

She laughed. "Never. You're the strongest person I've met. And a true dominant. But you haven't stepped into your power yet. But with me, I could tell you what I need, and I could help you improve. I like doing it, that switching back and forth. It's called being a switch."

"Take your clothes off," I said, almost automatically.

She shed everything off her body, clothing so thin it was almost like water. She was dressed for this New Orleans heat wave. Her nipple piercings shone like beacons, and one sparkled at the shaved apex of her thighs.

"Undress me," I commanded. There was something different about my voice then, something stronger and confident, unlike the shrill, hysterical quality of Vivienne's voice coming through.

As I ran my hands over Vic's skin, I was fully present. Me, Marianne, Mistress M, and Vivienne, all rolled into one human being. I think we were always this way.

Yes. We really were; the parts of Vivienne I hated were also a part of me: narcissistic, dramatic, controlling. Now resurrected and roaring like a demon. I had freed myself from the restraints of guilt, and now I was with a person I really wanted to be with, responsible for my own actions.

I trained for this. I trained to control other people.

And that meant myself, too.

I saw Vivienne glance out through my mind's attic window. She smiled, sweet at first, and then her teeth grew into fangs. I locked the door to the attic. She could come out when she was ready to behave.

"Even without using your hands, you are dominating verbally, mentally," Vic said, downplaying a grin.

I thought of the first meeting in the adult shop, the way she paid me special attention, her eyes glowing with something mischievous. I was ready to be taken to some other place besides that dark attic of my mind.

As she slipped my clothes off, I felt loose and limp, ready to be pleasured in the way only a woman could offer. Not in a way a man took and took, greedy and parasitic. This would be all for me, my pleasure, my orgasm. Even when you were dominating a man, it often seemed like you were doing the things he wanted, not what you wanted. Spank me. Use me. Choke me. Do me. But this was only for me. As she ventured to the juncture of my thighs, I pushed into her, eager to be ravished, to be freed from pain.

Soon, her velvety mouth was on me, and I was helpless, wondering who was the one really in control here? She was the giver, I was taking. She told me she wanted it this way. Subservient. Willing to please. In those moments, I forgot about all my little mistakes, all the things I said and didn't say. Being perfect no longer mattered. We just were. No struggle for who was using whom. No relation by marriage. No age gap. No social difference at school like I'd had during my first experience with a woman. No pretending to be normal. There were no yellow lights of guilt or hesitancy. I could give myself to her, fully and completely.

She healed me, stayed with me like a friend and lover would do. This was nothing compared to Chloe. Chloe protected and looked out for me like I was a terrified little lamb, and I think I stayed that way because she enabled it. Vic ignored or didn't notice all the bad in me. There were no awkward silences with her. And I learned so much.

"Use your lack of words to create an intimidating air around you," she suggested when I told her about my past, struggling to talk. "The past is the past."

Me? Intimidating? I laughed, but I used it in the club, staying silent as a submissive babbled about his dirty thoughts, a nervous thread weaving through his voice. I could say so little and yet, much more with my eyes and a blank, inexpressive face.

28

"There's a famous heavy metal musician. He wants two girls," Vic said one night after I had finally written down all my notes from the tape recorder. Yet Vic still stayed with me, cooking and waiting on me. "He wants two really bossy girls, I mean."

"Who is he?"

"You know Paul Ansley?"

I blinked. I wasn't so much into heavy metal as I was gothic and industrial music, but didn't everyone know who Paul Ansley was? Ansley was in a band that had its roots in New Orleans. They were all over MTV's *Headbanger's Ball* back in my school days. Of course, I knew who he was. Even if you didn't listen to metal, even if you weren't from the area, you probably knew who Ansley was. He had a reputation for being rowdy, trashing hotel rooms, and for having something between his legs that was supposedly quite intimidating in size.

"You're kidding," I said. "He doesn't seem like the type."

"It's always the ones who don't seem like the type."

"My God. I heard he has a very large—"

"It's true. I've seen it. The pay for just touching and

commenting on it is quite good. You should come with me," she said, flashing me a quick evil grin over her shoulder.

I looked down at my hands, wondering what I'd do. Who would take over? Would my body yearn to scratch and hurt, take out my fury like a wild animal? Or would I just be Marianne, trying to find herself, observing and learning? My chest clenched thinking about Vivienne taking over. I shut that thought down and thought about the money instead. No. I had control. Vic would be with me. But still, the thoughts danced in my mind, chaotic moths, about the consequences of going ballistic on a beloved heavy metal god.

I agreed before my brain took over.

The night of, we got dressed as the beat of Nine Inch Nails' *The Fragile* CD thumped away in the next room, inspiring our dress and makeup.

I chose a black halter top with a plunging neckline and a matching skirt. Underneath, I wore thigh-high fishnet stockings and stilettos. A touch of class, a hint of corruption.

I found myself getting into it, pulling myself out through the makeup, emphasizing the parts of myself I had started to appreciate the most. Vic got me hair extensions. It looked like my mother's, chestnut waves, beguiling as it framed my face. With a little makeup around my eyes, the green was accentuated. I looked like a stark contrast to Vic, who embodied the goth look with black hair, dark eyes, makeup, piercings. My makeup made me look like a corrupted princess, while Vic kind of looked like a demonic prince.

I felt like myself, fully and completely. There was no hint of the dweller in my eyes. Vic threw an arm around me.

"Look at us," she said with a wicked smile, "ready to make money and rule the world."

I was ready. Tonight, I was going to empty my head of the past and focus on the present.

Vic drove us to the other side of the Quarter. I wanted to walk, but she said we would get too much attention in our heels and outfits. "Besides," she said, indicating our stilettos, "these are a bitch to walk in. And the hotel has a valet."

Nerves seared my insides as we walked into the lobby, out of place as zoo animals. Men ogled and women pushed their busts out as if challenged. In the elevator, a man and woman walked in behind us.

"How much do you charge?" he asked, his eyes popping. His companion slapped him.

"Too much for you," Vic said without missing a beat.

"You can get your own room," said the woman as they exited together. The man stopped and stared at her, dumbfounded, as the elevator doors closed. We rode up to the penthouse level.

My body felt as stiff as ever as we neared the room.

"Just follow my lead," Vic said. She knocked.

A man in a suit opened the door. "In here," he said. "Care for a drink?"

Champagne. Laughter in the other room.

We made our way in, drinks in hand, and entered a smoke-filled living area with the band and several women. All blonde, very similar looking.

"Well, hello there," Paul said, his voice baritone and rich, "glad you could make it."

I'd seen videos of him on MTV, interviews where he was standing next to people, and thought he'd be tall. But he was a mountain. When he stood and regarded me with dark, piercing eyes, I had to resist the urge to shrink. The blondes never let go of his body, clinging to him as if protecting him from us, trying to sneer us away.

"Ladies, go join the rest of the band," he said in his booming voice.

"But Paul," one of them said, sticking her chest out even more.

"I'm good," he said, still looking at me.

As difficult as it was, I didn't back down. I continued to lock eyes with him, never faltering, just like Lady Dionne taught me.

The blonde who spoke up made a point of bumping into my

shoulder as she left. I did not turn around to give her the time of day, but instead concentrated on what Vic was doing.

The room went quieter, the chatter far behind us. Vic pushed Paul down into his chair. She had not really told me much of anything, even though apparently she'd seen him before, only that he paid really well. Would we have to have sex with him? She said we didn't, but the thought still formed a tight knot in my stomach. It would mean that everything Blake accused me of would be true. It was everything he abhorred, right here in this hotel room.

"So, who's your friend?" Paul asked after Vic was situated on his knee. Even with her lanky height, he still made her look like a tiny goth fairy.

She ran her hands over his chest and said, "This is Mistress M, a friend of mine. She's a writer."

"Oh? What do you write?"

I blinked, anxiety clutching my chest. Should I conceal my identity? To hell with that, too. We were all here together. I could just as easily spill his secrets as he could mine.

"I'm a music biographer," I said.

"Seriously? What are you working on now?"

"A biography of Spellbound Hearts."

His eyes flickered with something. "I know who you are now."

Vic glanced back at me, her eyebrows raised, impressed. Then she shot me a quick, reassuring grin, a knowing look playing on her expression.

"We can talk about all that later, can't we?" Vic said. I joined her uneasily and copied her position on Paul's other knee. "Take your shirt off," Vic instructed.

He did, revealing a colorful array of tattoos. I had never seen anything like it before. I touched his chest, marveling. I was always told tattoos belonged to criminals and rock stars, something my parents worked hard to shield me from.

Vic pulled out a tiny case with a razor inside. She snapped on a glove. Thank God. Something I was familiar with. She handed me gloves and I put them on.

Paul's eyes went savage when I dragged the blade across his

skin, the blood signaling something primal. He sucked in a hissing breath between his teeth and bucked his hips.

"Slap me," he said through clenched teeth, his pupils so dilated his eyes looked demonic. I did without hesitation. He hitched down his jeans and the rest of his clothing and sat back in the rock god throne. Instead of being intimidated like I thought I'd be, I was fascinated, but tried not to show my inexperience. Still, I was sure it showed.

The rumors were true. I could not help but reach out and touch it. When I did, he groaned and bucked his hips again.

"Whoa, boy," Vic said, "don't get too overeager, else I'll have to cut deeper next time." She flashed the blade and turned it in a playful manner, the dim light catching metallic glints.

A flash of fear in Paul's eyes, then respect. "Yes, ma'am."

I touched him again. He put his hand around mine.

"Can I show you what I like?"

I nodded, and his hands guided mine, up and down and with varying pressure.

"Don't give him *too* much of what he wants," Vic said. "You'll spoil him."

I backed off and stopped when he groaned and stiffened.

"Jesus," he groaned. "You're torturing me." But through the agony, his smile was boyish and vulnerable. I couldn't help but laugh and revel in the torture I was giving him.

"Look at this," Vic said. "She's driving you crazy with just her hands. You wouldn't be able to handle anything else, would you?"

"No, ma'am," he said, and I laughed again with pure glee and amusement at this whole situation. Paul Ansley, the metal god, turned into a blushing schoolboy at just a touch. I backed off again and ran my hands up and down my own body to tease him.

"I bet you wish you could touch, don't you?"

And with that, without even touching him, he climaxed.

"You see?" Vic said with a conspiring glance. "Power can be subtle."

Momma had been so protective she never really explained the nuances of sex, so maybe part of me was doing this stuff because it seemed so tucked away and mysterious. We all showered together, the only time I ever let a man see me fully nude, and he paid us at the end of the evening. And though he never asked for sex, and we hadn't really done much, and I had done things on my own accord.

But was I still a whore? Society said yes. But Momma had a fling with Theo and never got anything out of it but pain and suffering, and Vivienne had expressed dismay at not getting paid for Joseph's lewd advances. But I did. I was whoring before I even knew what it meant.

"Wait a minute," Paul said as we were leaving. He touched me on the shoulder and motioned for me to step aside as Vic touched up her makeup. "There's some chick doing a biography of us, but she gets on my nerves."

My intuition flared. "The rude blonde who was here?"

"Ha! Yes, her. I'd rather work with someone I like. Someone I can trust. Interested?"

I couldn't help but gawk. "But you haven't read anything of mine."

"Oh, yes he has," Vic interjected.

Oh. She had planned this whole thing pretty well.

"If you're as good at writing erotica as you are at everything else, I think it'll work out really well."

I stood there and blinked like an idiot.

"You don't have to commit now. Let me give you my number. We wrapped up our tour, so we're here for the time being. Gonna start laying out new tracks pretty soon, though." He winked as he grabbed the hotel's pen and pad to jot down his number, then folded it neatly and gave it to me. "It was nice meeting you."

"You too."

Outside the hotel room, Vic squealed and grabbed my arm.

"You sneak," I said.

"Are you going to do it?"

"Why wouldn't I? It's a dream come true opportunity."

"You can do this first, then pitch the Spellbound Hearts thing. It'll help give you some buzz."

I threw my arms around her. "You are a friggin' genius. I don't even begin to know how to thank you."

A friend. A new book. And money in my pocket. On my terms.

I think the demon was always part of me, something I didn't want to let out. A part of me really was like Vivienne, gnashing teeth and screaming to let go of all my rage and hate. There were places I could be myself, expressing myself through writing or being out with Vic. I would have to accept that part of myself if I were to ever move forward. I would have to come to terms with that part of me, that bloodline. The Easton stare. I certainly had it. Cold, calculating. I could have killed Joseph or even Troy for being such predatory assholes. I could see myself do it, even feel their skin give as I pressed into their flesh, my nails like talons.

We left and stopped by the shop, four in the morning and dark as a tomb.

"Put one of these on," she said. The mask she handed me was leathery, buttery. It smelled new, ready to absorb me and become a part of me. Something black and sleek, emphasizing the eyes. Secretive, undercover, dark as a night creature in the woods.

I felt shadow Marianne ooze forth, sleek as a fox. Vic even looked completely different.

"We'll be recognized," I said.

"Not by the tourists. Come on."

Like thieves in the night, we slipped through the streets and into the thumping womb of some swinger's club over in the Warehouse District. Different yet again, like seasons it was, scantily-clad in the summers and fully draped in the winters, a new coat. It pulsed as if it was its own entity.

Watching new blood was entertaining. Always the voyeur, I moved from room to room, observing twisting bodies or bobbing heads. Tonight, everything was painted red and black, blood and bruise. It was as icy inside as it was out. I pulled my jacket tight and searched for Vic, who was covered in women. Let her be. We weren't committed, and I was happy to see her spaced out in ecstasy.

Riding the high of Paul, we stumbled about, blazed and drunk. The sun was already up, hot and bright over the Mississippi. As I walked in the condo, Vic leaning on me, I saw that I should have at least gotten some rest. A red 10 flashed on the answering machine.

29

"I'm going to be in trouble," I said, holding myself up, watching the blinking light flash like a metronome.

"For living the life you want? It's good to be bad sometimes, Marianne. You shut it away, it's like burning part of your soul in a fire."

The thing I liked about Vic was she accepted both sides of herself, the masculine and the feminine, the good and the bad.

"I guess you're right."

"You really want to be married to Blake? He doesn't understand you."

But I do, I expected her to say next.

As always, what about Marcus? He could sit there at Ivy Manor and rot with Blake for all I cared. I felt bad for thinking it. Marcus was clinging to anyone who gave him attention. And I had ignored him by fretting over myself, not getting to know this darker half and pushing it away, by getting too wound up with Troy.

A glutton for punishment, I pushed the button.

"Hey," Gabe Ledeau's brash, accented voice said, "I'm just reminding you about our date. Gimme a call."

Vic lit a cigarette and looked at me with half-slit eyes. "You're not dating Gabe, are you?"

"Marianne, I ought to come down there and bring you back right this minute," Blake said on the next recording. Vic mocked him in her best Blake voice as she paced around the kitchen, making coffee.

"This is inexcusable. You've left me in charge of your brother, and I didn't know that would happen next. Okay? So just come back. Otherwise, I'm coming there in the morning."

"Shit," I said.

"What is going on with you and all these men, girl?" Vic asked.

I met her questioning eyes at the knock on the door. She put her hand on her hip. "Want me to answer it?"

I shook my head.

I unchained the lock and Blake pushed in, opened his mouth, looked at Vic…

"This has been going on for some time, hasn't it?" I started before he could speak. "Since before Chloe died. That's why she ran off. You didn't want her to. She drove off all emotional because she caught you two."

He moved closer and tried to grab my shoulders. I stood my ground, brushed his hands off me. They felt cold, dead.

"I want to talk to you. Alone," he said, his voice thick with emotion.

"I don't want to be alone with you. I'm done. You groomed an underage boy, Blake. My own brother. I'm done."

"You want to leave me? I don't think so…"

I held up a hand. "Keep the damn house. I want to keep this place. And I want you to clear out for one week while I reason with Marcus."

He stalked away, slamming the door behind him.

"Holy hell," Vic said, "I never realized all this was *this* bad. I thought you were being dramatic. I could have helped you."

"You're already helping me. I'm fixing this." I held my head in my hand, my temples pounding. "Jesus."

"Take some coffee and go for a walk," Vic said. She always knew what I needed before I did.

The streets smelled like laundry detergent and backed up water, the concrete wet and shiny after a thorough street cleaning. Aside from a few residents hurrying along with newspapers tucked under their arms, walking their dogs, I was the only one out. I walked all the way to the Cathedral and sat down on a bench in front of it.

I sat there until people bustled around and the concrete dried.

Something familiar caught my eye.

Lily, walking on Chartres Street, her pace quick and efficient. She was alone, dressed in a navy shift and kitten heels. I stood up and walked towards her. How dare she visit this city again.

I watched as she walked into a jewelry store. Once she was inside, I went to the shop's window and peered inside. And then it all made sense.

I went back to get my car so I could drive to Lily's.

When I arrived, her Jaguar wasn't in the driveway, which meant I had beat her to her house. I parked on the street and waited for a few minutes, but restlessness had my heart hammering and my skin crawling. I got out and crept around her house, looking in windows, but there was nothing to see except moving boxes.

She really was moving.

I went back to the car, reclined the seat and took deep breaths, trying to calm myself. I had just drifted off when I heard a car pull into the driveway.

"Lily!" She stopped, stunned, her mouth gaping open at what she saw in me, smeared mascara, black clothing and a fully sated aura, something of witches.

"You," she sneered. "What are you doing here?"

"What were you doing at the jewelry shop, Lily?"

She rolled her eyes and sauntered to the door, ignoring me. I ran in front of her and blocked the door.

"None of your business," she snapped. "Get out of the way." She held her keys out like weapons. I shifted and let her go inside, but followed right behind her and jammed the door with my foot.

She threw her purse on the table and turned to glare at me. I reached into my bag and took out the pearl and slammed it on the table.

"If I knew you were having your pearls restrung, I would have given this to you sooner."

"What are you talking about?"

"You were at Troy's place when he died."

She took another step back. "Troy was a pervert. You should have stayed away from him. Now look at you. He was a predator."

Well, she was right about that.

"You walked in on him, didn't you?"

"He was looking at porn. I scrubbed everything clean for Julia's sake. She's been through enough."

"But you left something behind. One of your pearls. Why? Why'd your necklace break there?"

"Look, I put down a rabid dog for you." She descended deeper into the house, meandering around moving boxes.

"I'm not leaving until you tell me."

"Do you really want to know about your 'boyfriend?' I went to the house to reason with him. Julia is getting out of jail soon, and she wanted to see him. And I wasn't going to let her see him traipsing around town with his new trophy whore. But when I got there, no one answered and the door was open. And there he was, doing those perverted things to himself.

"When he slipped, the stool fell over, and he was grasping at the belt, holding on for dear life, with no pants, like the deviant that he was, reaching for me, begging me to help. He did break my pearls, desperate for his life. He would have sacrificed you, Julia, anything and anyone to save himself. Even deviants find God when they have no other choice.

"But God wasn't there for him that day. Satan was. And Satan kicked that stool far enough away for him not to get back on, and I watched the evil spirit drain from his body. The spirit that imprisoned my daughter. The spirit that infected my beautiful niece and doomed her. And now, all I have left from my beautiful family is what's left of my daughter, that deviant grandson… and you."

She walked back to her luxurious bathroom, looked into her Hollywood-style mirror, and began primping.

"You're distracting me. Is there anything else before I leave tomorrow?"

I didn't know what else to say. I stood there watching her, slack-jawed, the Marianne in the mirror a makeup-smeared, disheveled mess compared to Lily's elegant visage. She showed no signs of stress, no new wrinkles since Granddaddy had died, or even since witnessing what happened to Troy.

She acted like it was no big deal, like stepping on a spider. Maybe that's what he was, always pulling me into some sort of web of his making, training me to be a willing accomplice to his addiction.

"Leave town. I never want to see you again. And tell Julia to keep her mouth shut or I'll go to the police with this. I have a connection."

"My ass you do."

"I know you think they won't believe me. And maybe that's true. But lots of things run in the family, Lily. Maybe I'm willing to grow up to be just like my dear grandmother, willing to do whatever is necessary to eliminate a problem."

She straightened up and smoothed her dress. "I'd advise you, dear, to choose wisely from here on out. I could have set you up with someone notable, but well," she said, giving a fake laugh, "look at you now."

I said nothing, just crossed my arms over my chest. She shook her head.

A sense of relief twisted with something heavy in my heart. I wasn't responsible. Troy hadn't committed suicide. He was stupid enough to play with fire, and Lily walked in and finished him off like some bug.

She shook her head again. "You're just like your mother," she said, and walked into her bedroom. She went into her closet and began perusing the contents, not even glancing at me.

So what if I was like my mother? Janelle was good and bad, dark and light just like the rest of us.

Sensing I wouldn't get anything else out of her, I left with an imagined, ghostly image of Troy's pleading face burned into my brain.

30

A long week passed. I still had to deal with Marcus. What would it take to reason with him? I avoided sleep thinking about it, the sun filtering in through the blinds in eye-searing streaks. I'd have to go out there.

It hailed on the drive to Ivy Manor, the erratic weather shifting like my moods. I pulled off on the side of the road under a canopy of trees, waiting for it to pass, using the extra time to formulate what I wanted to say when I arrived.

No Blake when I arrived. Marcus answered the door, his worn features drawn into an irritable scorn.

"You live here," he said. "You don't have to knock." There were dark half-moons under his eyes.

"I thought it best, with everything going on." He turned to me and regarded me with sorrowful slits for eyes. "You've been crying," I said.

"You're a life ruiner, that's why."

"Look, you knew it was wrong to do this with Blake. That's why you didn't say a damn thing at Chloe's funeral."

"So? You've been entirely self-focused."

"Don't get angry, Marcus. The bottom line is that it's not right. You're still underage."

"Like you were with Troy?" He smirked slightly like he was satisfied with his jab.

I shook my head and looked down at the floor to avoid his vengeful eyes.

"That's why I want to protect you from this. Troy was a leech. So is Blake. They're the same."

He crossed his arms over his chest and looked away.

"Lily killed him," I said.

"What?"

"He was jerking off to porn and had a noose around his neck. He had a stool under him that I guess he would use to test his weight. Lily went in there to see why he wasn't accepting Julia's calls, and she literally caught him with his pants down. When he slipped from the stool, she just watched."

"How do you know all of this?"

"She told me."

He blinked. "So you didn't have anything to do it."

I balled my fists. "Of course I didn't."

"Well, I didn't know. You were acting crazy. Are you still…?"

"I don't know."

I did feel different. After going out with Vic and indulging, being myself around Paul, I really did feel like there was no Vivienne around us. Even Ivy Manor seemed free of her, just the bones left to stand the test of time like everything else buried around there.

"Well, Blake won't talk to me," Marcus said. "What are you going to do? Move back to New Orleans?"

"What do you want me to do?"

"You were supposed to look out for me here," he said, his voice quavering. "I thought you were going to…I don't know. Die or something."

"Marcus, I *was* dying." A pull at my core. She was trying to come out. To say something to Marcus again. I clutched my stomach and winced, pushing her away.

"What?"

"I never wanted you to follow in my footsteps like that," I said, pushing her down. I was not like Vivienne. I was not like Vivienne.

"Excuse the hell out of me! My life is my own, Marianne. Not everything has to do with you, you know."

I was myself. I was myself.

"You've achieved some sense of independence," I said, hoping to cool him down. "I just don't want either one of us to be used. He was using you and me both. Me to help him put up a front. You to retreat to. You understand that, don't you?"

He lifted one shoulder.

"Don't you want a more balanced relationship with someone?"

He was quiet a long time before he finally muttered, "I guess."

"I think we need some time apart," I said, trying to read him. He was stone-faced. "Then I think we need to get away from here. For good."

He didn't say anything. His eyes went glassy, cold.

That Easton Stare was back. I used to call it that when all the emotion drained from him.

"And I didn't mean for us to drift apart," I said. "I'm sorry."

He blinked several times but said nothing. He turned his body away from me.

"I can't make you come with me, Marcus. I can only promise you that I've accepted myself. Finally. The good and the bad."

"I'll come when I'm ready," he said over his shoulder.

It would have to do.

31

F orbidden Gardens became my playground.

I sauntered up to him in the club, my hips swaying to the beat. When he noticed me, his eyes devoured me.

He was mine.

How attractive. His jaw was sharp like Troy's, his eyes dark, a glint of mischief, a touch of naivety.

Young.

Too young for Julia.

Vic helped me find him. Christopher. He had a job in the French Quarter as a bartender. Julia liked those types.

I smiled.

He smiled back with an air of vulnerability.

Moments later, I coerced him into one of the club's private rooms. He was on his knees in seconds, kissing each carefully pedicured toe.

"Good boy," I said, just like Vic taught me.

I didn't have to choke him. There were other ways. I didn't have to lose control. Control could be had in many ways.

I dug my heel into his chest. His gaze traveled up from the spike heel to the newly shaped muscles that filled out the latex catsuit I wore. The smooth material felt like a comfortable caress against my skin, natural as the empowerment that swelled in my chest. I could feel the desire coursing through him, uncontrolled, involuntary, his power exiting his body and entering mine.

Three days later, I had him begging to be with me as I packed a suitcase.

"Please," he said. When I looked into his eyes, I saw that he meant it. "I promise, I'll make everything okay."

When I looked deep into his eyes, there was a fire there that raged for me. I had turned him into something soft and pliable. Weak.

He wanted to step into my world, to plumb the depths of my soul. I knew because I had seen that same look in Troy. And I was starting to see that same look in a lot of other men's eyes, too. I was becoming myself, all my own. I didn't need anyone.

No one person could make it all okay. I had to do that for myself.

Yet now he would pine for me and me only. I would be burrowed into his psyche forever, a tiny shard of glass, never forgotten. I would haunt him forever.

I smiled, bad Marianne relishing the spell I'd put on him. But this time, I didn't need to hear that it would be okay. I knew it would. I didn't need to hear that again from anyone.

And now he'd forget all about Julia. She'd get out of prison within a couple of days, ready to run this new boy into the ground, and would flail and fall, trying to control a man who was no longer there.

I rolled the suitcase out onto the street to wait for my cab. All around me, the revelry of Mardi Gras thrummed with people in masks and costumes, all pretending to be someone else. I turned at looked up at the condo. Marcus and Ari waved from the window as the cab pulled up.

The driver looked at me through the rear-view mirror. "Where you off to?"

"Airport."

"Not going to stay and enjoy the festivities, are ya?"

"Nah. Vacation."

"Oh? Where to?"

"Boston. I have a sister there."

"How nice," the cabbie said. "Goin' to see family for the holidays."

I didn't tell him I'd never met her. I didn't tell him it was my father's daughter from some quick one night stand he had, that my mother found out and built a relationship with her. I didn't tell him I would have never even known she existed if not for my mother, if not for my grandmother, if not for all the bad things people do and hide away from the world.

I closed my eyes as we drove through the best, then the worst parts of the city, no longer feeling trapped by the things I picked up from my parents.

Nothing felt forbidden to me.

ACKNOWLEDGMENTS

Thank you, J., for always accepting me the way I am. Love you, sugar.

A big thank you to my adoptive family, Jamie, James, PJ, and Bob. Big thanks to Norm for always having a kind, enthusiastic word and for believing in me.

Thank you to my editor, Michael Dolan, whose advice and unwavering belief in me helped shape this story. Thank you to Alex Nader, J., and Ian who read early drafts of this novel and provided valuable feedback.

Lastly, thank you to all of you who have embraced your shadow sides and aren't afraid of forbidden territory.

ABOUT THE AUTHOR

Clare Castleberry grew up in the swamps of Louisiana, which fueled her imagination for southern gothic stories, often with erotic, horrific, or crime-laden themes. *Forbidden Gardens* is the standalone follow up to *Azalea House*, released in November 2021 with Winding Road Stories.

You can find her online on Twitter @femmebionic or on Instagram at @femmebionic007.